Stagestruck

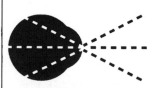

This Large Print Book carries the
Seal of Approval of N.A.V.H.

Stagestruck

A Jubilee Showboat Mystery

Cynthia Thomason

Thorndike Press • Waterville, Maine

Published in 2004 by arrangement with Tekno Books and Ed Gorman.

Set in 16 pt. Plantin by Myrna S. Raven.

Printed in the United States on permanent paper.

Library of Congress Cataloging-in-Publication Data

Thomason, Cynthia.
    Stagestruck : a Jubilee Showboat mystery / Cynthia Thomason.
        p. cm.
        ISBN 0-7862-6397-0 (lg. print : hc : alk. paper)
        1. Women theatrical producers and directors — Fiction.   2. Women detectives — Missouri — Fiction.
3. Mississippi River — Fiction.   4. Showboats — Fiction.   5. Large type books.   I. Title.
PS3570.H5925S73 2004
    813'.6—dc22   2004041218

For my husband, Walter, also a writer,
who has traveled with me on many
riverboats while together
we've shared the ride of our lives.

And a special thank-you to mystery writer
Nancy J. Cohen, who inspired me
to write this novel and encouraged me
to the end.

As the Founder/CEO of NAVH, the only national health agency solely devoted to those who, although not totally blind, have an eye disease which could lead to serious visual impairment, I am pleased to recognize Thorndike Press★ as one of the leading publishers in the large print field.

Founded in 1954 in San Francisco to prepare large print textbooks for partially seeing children, NAVH became the pioneer and standard setting agency in the preparation of large type.

Today, those publishers who meet our standards carry the prestigious "Seal of Approval" indicating high quality large print. We are delighted that Thorndike Press is one of the publishers whose titles meet these standards. We are also pleased to recognize the significant contribution Thorndike Press is making in this important and growing field.

Lorraine H. Marchi, L.H.D.
Founder/CEO
NAVH

★ Thorndike Press encompasses the following imprints: Thorndike, Wheeler, Walker and Large Pr int Press.

Chapter One

Apple Creek, Ohio, 1898

"Oh, for Heaven's sakes!" Gwen Barlow choked back a mild oath, plucked a tightly curled strand of pale auburn hair off her flushed cheek, and shot a piercing glance around the perfectly organized row of books. Robbie Simpson ought to know better than to bellow her name in a hushed library. How many times did she have to tell her new assistant to whisper, and that nothing short of a fire or flood was urgent enough to upset the quiet dignity of a place of meditation and learning?

She spied the lanky teenage boy craning his neck and jumping up and down to see over the narrow bookshelves. "Miss Barlow!" he hooted through an opening in the tomes.

Before he had a chance to embarrass her further and jeopardize his already precarious employment, Gwen strode down the aisle on silent rubber-soled shoes and grabbed him by the back of his collar. It proved to be an unwise move, however, as

Robbie's shouts mutated to squeals of alarm. "Lordy, Miss Barlow, you scared me to death."

Gwen released him and watched as he ran a finger around his collar to set it to rights again. "You'll be frightened enough when you join the ranks of the jobless, Robbie," she said. "It's time you stopped confusing a library with a baseball field. Now what's so important that you have to upset everyone in the building? Did someone refuse to pay a nickel fine?"

Hardly repentant, Robbie's eyes sparkled with the excitement of unshared news. "Nothing like that, Miss Barlow," he said. "It's Margie Lundgren, your next-door neighbor. She just came bursting in the front door to find you. Your mother wants you home right now."

"Now? In the middle of the day?"

"That's what she said, ma'am."

"Is Mama hurt or ill?"

"No. I asked Margie that very question. She said it was a matter of utmost importance however. She's still here. I can ask her what it's all about."

Robbie whirled around to question the messenger, but Gwen stopped him with a firm grip on his wrist. His eagerness to help was obviously overshadowed by his

8

desire to get to the bottom of what might turn out to be a community scandal. Like everyone else in the small town of Apple Creek, Ohio, Robbie enjoyed the notoriety that came with scooping a big story and spreading it around before anyone else had gotten wind of it.

"Never mind," Gwen said. "I'll talk to Margie myself." She pointed to a wheeled cart loaded with books at the end of the row. "You may continue stacking where I left off."

His shoulders drooping in defeat, Robbie sighed, "Yes, ma'am."

Gwen headed toward the front of the library. Of course, she didn't wish for a true emergency to befall any member of her family, but she was becoming slightly impatient with her mother's too frequent calls of distress. Lillian Barlow was behaving very much like the boy who cried wolf. Since the untimely death of Lillian's brother ten days ago, she'd been turning even the most insignificant of life's problems into complicated dilemmas that supposedly could not be solved without her daughter's help. Her reaction was understandable, considering her grief, but these daily emergencies were beginning to wear on Gwen's nerves.

Margie Lundgren, her wild straight hair in the disarray one expects of a ten-year-old on a Saturday afternoon, stood by the front door of the library. When she saw Gwen, she removed her fingers from her mouth, relinquishing the chewing of her nails for more pressing concerns.

"What is it, Margie?" Gwen asked, instinctively keeping her own voice at a low pitch.

"I don't know, Miss Barlow. Your mother sent me straight to get you." She crooked her finger, indicating Gwen should lean closer. "You have a visitor, though. A fat man who arrived in a fancy carriage."

"Hmmm . . ." Gwen considered the unflattering description. The only truly fat man in all of Apple Creek was the Presbyterian minister, and he wheeled about town in an old open buggy pulled by a notoriously stubborn mule that often stopped in the middle of the street and refused to transport its weighty passenger another yard.

Seeing no other option, Gwen decided this situation did indeed call for her personal investigation. "Thank you, Margie," she said. "Please tell Mama I'll be there right away."

The child raced from the library and

Gwen went to inform the head librarian that she needed to leave for a short time. How she wished her mother had a telephone, but Lillian staunchly refused to have one of the "newfangled things" in her house. "Those nosy operators . . . it's just a way for people to know more of your business," she'd said. So while Gwen could contact many of the citizens of Apple Creek by ringing the telephone operator right from the office of the Hopewell College Library, she couldn't reach her own mother.

The matronly head librarian patted Gwen's arm. "Yes, Gwendolyn, of course you may go. And please give my regards to Lillian. I hope it's nothing serious."

"I'm sure it isn't," Gwen said, securing her narrow-brimmed straw boater under her chin with its grosgrain ribbon. "I'll be back soon."

She left the building and fastened her pocketbook to her back with the strap she'd made for just that purpose. Then she crossed to an ancient elm tree in the library yard. Leaning against the venerable tree was Gwen's shiny, steel gray Monarch Woman's Bicycle with its sturdy pneumatic tires and wicker basket attached to the handlebars. Raising her skirt to the tops of her boots, mindful to reveal nothing of her stockings, Gwen mounted the wide saddle seat and pedaled toward home.

Once free of the stately quadrangle of ivy-covered buildings which constituted Hopewell College, it was only a five-block ride to Gwen's neat, two-story bungalow on Red Maple Lane, a pleasant street lined with the trees that bore its name. When she slowed to make her turn onto Red Maple, Gwen saw her brother, Preston, running toward her from Center Street. She braked, lowered one foot to the bricks, and waited.

He skidded to a stop beside her. "She sent for you, too?" he inquired between gasps of air.

"Yes. Do you know what this is about?"

Preston shook his head. A mop of sand-colored hair fell over his brow with its usual untended abandon. "I only know that she isn't sick or anything. But Billy Lundgren said it was an emergency. And since I don't see any smoke coming from the direction of our house, I can only guess at the reason."

"I don't know the problem either," Gwen admitted. "Mama hasn't been herself since Uncle Eli died so suddenly."

"If you ask me, she's been *too much* like

herself. It's like she's Mother, only steam-powered. I'll tell you this, Gwennie, it better darned well be important. Mr. Buchanan wasn't happy when he had to finish sweeping the loading dock behind the hardware store. Said one more interruption and he'll fire me. As bad as that job is, I'll be scooping make-a-wish pennies out of the town fountain without it."

Picturing the scowling face of Apple Creek's hard goods store owner, Gwen readily believed he'd follow through with his threat. Gripping the handlebars, she pushed off from the street. "Let's go, Preston. The sooner we see what's troubling Mama, the sooner we'll both be able to save our jobs."

Gwen noticed the gleaming black carriage from a block away. She didn't know of anyone in Apple Creek who had such a fine conveyance, and she was certain such a vehicle wasn't available to rent from the local livery. And this one came equipped with a uniformed driver who at the moment napped against the squabs of an exterior bench seat. A small sign on the passenger door identified the carriage as belonging to a livery in Dayton, Ohio. Its passenger had traveled ten miles to meet with Lillian Barlow. Strange indeed.

Resting her bicycle against the white fence surrounding the small, tidy Barlow property, Gwen proceeded up the brick sidewalk and three steps that led to the bungalow's front porch. Preston followed closely behind. The glass-paneled front door was open to admit the warm breeze of a perfectly splendid spring afternoon. Through the screen door, Gwen heard her mother's voice. It positively chirped with good humor.

"More tea, Mr. Cavanaugh?"

A slightly hoarse but pleasant enough voice responded. "Don't mind if I do, Mrs. Barlow."

The screen door banged behind Preston as he bounded into the foyer on Gwen's heels. Together, brother and sister crossed to the family parlor and stopped at the entry. The scene they witnessed would have been more aptly described as an afternoon get-together than a dire emergency.

Lillian Barlow had covered her flour-dusted everyday dress with her best Sunday apron, the bleached and starched one trimmed with delicate eyelet lace. This fine garment had obviously been hastily donned in deference to her visitor's lofty importance. Lillian's startled gaze was fixed on her children standing like statues a few feet away, and her best china teapot was poised in mid air over a treasured cup and saucer currently in the pudgy hand of a stout man in a business suit.

A motherly smile spread across her face. "Hello, dears," she said, then added in the tone disappointed mothers have, "Really, Preston, must you slam the door? It's quite rude."

Preston sucked in a sharp breath, and Gwen sensed his effort to maintain his composure. "Sorry, Mother," he said. "Next time you declare an emergency and call me home from work, I'll be sure to mind my manners."

Lillian turned her attention to the teapot and finished pouring. "I know you will, dear."

Gwen and Preston came all the way into the room. "Mama, what is this about?" Gwen asked.

Lillian set the teapot on her gleaming marble top parlor table. "Mr. Cavanaugh, this is my daughter, Gwendolyn, and my son, Preston."

The cup and saucer rattling in his hand, Mr. Cavanaugh raised his portly frame from Lillian's best fringed brocade chair and shook hands with both Barlow children. "A pleasure to meet you," he said, and settled comfortably once more.

Lillian threaded her hands at her waist and looked from Gwen to Preston. "Mr. Cavanaugh is an attorney, dears."

"An attorney!" Preston exclaimed. "Mother, what have you done?"

"Why nothing, nothing at all. Mr. Cavanaugh isn't even from around here. He's from St. Louis, not far from Hickory Bend, Missouri, the town Uncle Eli moved to before he . . . well, anyway, the most outrageous thing has happened. Mystifying really. Truly more unbelievable than mystifying. It's quite a shock . . ."

Gwen's foot began to tap against the cabbage rose rug that covered the center of the parlor floor. Her foot always warned her when her patience was being tested to its limits. "Mother?"

Mr. Cavanaugh set his teacup on the table and leaned forward. "Would you like me to explain the situation to your children, Mrs. Barlow?"

Lillian bestowed a conciliatory nod. "Yes, perhaps that would be best."

"I wish someone would explain," Gwen said.

The attorney twisted the waxed end of

his moustache before placing his hands on his knees. "I represented Eli Willoughby, your mother's brother," he began. "In the last year of his life, Mr. Willoughby made some interesting, and if I may say so, daring financial decisions . . ."

"Oh, my yes. Quite daring," Lillian repeated.

Gwen was not at all surprised that her mother couldn't keep her silence during Mr. Cavanaugh's explanation. Lillian Barlow lived to embellish a story.

"Remember, children, when I went to see Eli last fall? He was very excited about a business venture. He wouldn't give me the details, said he wanted it to be a surprise, but oh, my, he was like a young lad again." Lillian's eyes sparkled with a fond remembrance.

The attorney cleared his throat with a pointed stare at Lillian. "As I was saying, Mr. Willoughby risked his significant savings on a venture I would have advised against had I been his counsel at the time. But it seems Eli was audacious to the end."

"He always loved to amaze people," Lillian said.

Another pointed look from the attorney. "Yes, Eli marched to his own drummer. Of course, to his credit, he didn't know he would become the victim of a most curious accident and die before his investment could come to any sort of fruition . . ."

Lillian heaved a great sigh and shook her head. "Poor Eli, God rest his soul. Children, Mr. Cavanaugh has been kind enough to explain some of the particulars of Eli's death. I still can't believe it. Bludgeoned by a heavy piece of equipment falling on his head."

"Yes, poor Eli," Cavanaugh echoed and focused his attention on Gwen and Preston. "I had serious questions about the incident when it happened, but the constable in Hickory Bend investigated and declared it was an unfortunate accident. Anyway, to continue with the will . . . Eli ordered the thing made, brand new, from the bottom up. Spared no expense, demanded the latest in theatrical technology and architectural design. Not my taste of course, but having just seen the thing before coming here to tell Mrs. Barlow, I must admit, it is impressive in its ostentation."

Lillian pressed her hands to her cheeks. "Yes, indeed. My dear Eli had a flair for the fantastic."

Gwen's jaw dropped in dismay. What in the world were these two talking about?

She'd known, of course, that Eli had died in a freak accident, but what was all this talk about theatrical technology? A quick glance at Preston convinced her that her brother was no less baffled than she. "Mr. Cavanaugh, please, what are you saying? Did my uncle purchase a theater before he died?"

The attorney chuckled at some secret levity. "Nothing as substantial as that, Miss Barlow. No, not a theater per se. And since he was never married and had no children, it seems that your mother is the sole beneficiary of Eli's rather imprudent middle-aged recklessness."

Lillian rushed to take her children's hands in each of hers. If it were possible to witness skyrockets in someone's eyes, Gwen saw them now in her mother's gray orbs. "Isn't it thrilling?" Lillian asked.

"I don't know, Mama," Gwen said. "I still don't know what we're talking about."

"Allow me to conclude, Mrs. Barlow," Cavanaugh said. "Miss Barlow, Mr. Barlow, your uncle spent his last dime building a . . ."

Lillian whirled on him. "No! Let me tell." Turning back to her perplexed children, she clasped her hands under her chin and announced, "Eli left me a floating palace. A showboat! My dears, we're going into show business!"

For the next few minutes, Gwen felt as if she were on that showboat, rocking and tipping with the waves of a turbulent river. Voices ebbed and flowed around her, but she hardly heard the words. Still she surmised that Lillian's inheritance had a name. It was called *Eli's Jubilee Palace*. Ironically, jubilation was the last emotion Gwen experienced at the moment.

When Cavanaugh rose to leave, Lillian thanked him profusely for diverting his travel plans to include a personal stop in Apple Creek. "This has been such an exciting day," she said as she walked the attorney to the door. "Of course, this news doesn't compensate for dear Eli's passing, but knowing he remembered me in his will helps to assuage my grief."

The attorney tipped his wool bowler in parting. "I'm certain you'll be up to the challenge of your inheritance, Mrs. Barlow. If there's anything I can do to help you, don't hesitate to contact me in St. Louis."

Gwen and Preston watched and waited from the parlor door for Mr. Cavanaugh to depart. When his carriage had moved down Red Maple Lane, Lillian faced her children. "Well, now," she said breathlessly, "what do you think of all this?"

Preston threw his hands in the air. "I think it's insane, Mother! What do you know about running a showboat?"

Lillian's lips parted, allowing her to draw in a gasp of disbelief at her son's insensitive outburst. She sniffed loudly and drew herself into her most rigid posture. "Why, Preston, of course I don't know much myself, but I assumed my children would help me. I'm sure that among the three of us, we can manage . . ."

". . . manage to make utter fools of ourselves!" Preston finished for her.

Tears welled in Lillian's eyes, and Gwen crossed the foyer and took her hand. She shot her brother a scathing look. "Mama, what Preston is trying to say, quite badly I might add, is that operating a showboat would be an extremely risky proposition for us." She swept her arm around the cheerful entryway of their neat little bungalow, her gaze resting on first one, then another of the pleasant handmade knickknacks on the walls and furniture. "Besides, Mama, this is our home."

Lillian pulled her hand free and waved it around as if she were swatting a fly. "Oh pish tosh, Gwendolyn. It's a pile of wood and glass, that's all. We'll rent it out."

Preston, who'd never before shown an inclination toward familial nesting, squawked with surprise. "Mother, Dad built this house for us."

"I'm well aware of that, Preston, but Leonard intended for it to be a house, not a prison."

Gwen held up her hand to stop the flow of words threatening to burst from Preston's lips. This was going to turn into a mammoth argument if someone didn't do something. Besides, the yellow cuckoo on the wall had just thrust open the doors of its colorful chalet and chirped three times. "Preston and I need to get back to work, Mama," she said. "Let's not make any decisions now. We can talk later and figure this all out rationally."

Lillian stepped clear of the doorway to let her children pass. "Fine," she said. "But I'm not sure I like the word 'rationally' any longer. I prefer 'imaginatively.' Say what you will about Eli. He may be dead as a winter marigold now, but when he was alive, he knew how to live!"

Gwen walked to the fence to retrieve her bicycle. She waved goodbye to Preston, hoping to avoid further discussion on this matter before she'd had a chance to sort it out. But he grasped the handlebars and prevented her from leaving.

"She's gone bats, you know that don't you, Gwennie?" he said. "The old girl's finally gone 'round the bend."

"Don't be so dramatic, Preston," she responded. "You sound like an actor in a dime-ticket melodrama." She giggled despite the seriousness of the moment. "Now that I think about showboats and such, perhaps your reaction is fitting."

"Oh really? And now that *I* think about it, I'm quite certain the undertaker reported that the accident that killed Uncle Eli happened on a boat."

This grim reminder erased all trace of humor from Gwen's demeanor. "Yes, as a matter of fact, he did."

"No doubt the very boat Mother just inherited. For all we know, dear Uncle Eli, his brains oozing from the gash in his head, will roam the passageways of his floating palace for eternity."

Inwardly grimacing at this tidbit of morbid irony, Gwen still scoffed at her brother's prediction. "Now who's bats, Preston?" When he didn't respond, she gifted him with a faint smile of encouragement. "It'll be all right. Mama will come around. Maybe she'll even decide to sell the thing and we'll never have to leave Apple Creek."

But, deep down, Gwen had her doubts.

It wasn't going well. Lillian refused to be persuaded by logic and common sense. Once Gwen put the supper dishes away, she joined her mother and brother in the parlor where, for the moment at least, peace reigned. She sat opposite her mother and poured a cup of tea from the everyday, crockery pot. "Mama," she began, "you have to see this from a reasonable standpoint. Mr. Cavanaugh said that Uncle Eli invested his last dime in this showboat. He didn't leave you any capital with which to operate it. And, frankly, Mama, we don't have any money of our own."

Lillian's face tightened like an overripe peach, and she raised her chin obstinately. "I have a little," she said. "And Gwen, you have a little. And Preston, you have . . ."

A silence fell over the room during which Preston's eyes widened in anticipation.

Lillian managed a faint smile. "And Preston, you have . . . personality. So that makes up for a lack of actual dollars."

"Why, thank you, Mother, for that vote of confidence." Sarcasm dripped from

24

every word, but Preston couldn't entirely hide a little grin at the truth of Lillian's statement.

"As a matter of fact, Preston," Lillian continued, "you should be especially interested in this venture."

His eyebrows raised in question.

"Here you are, nineteen years old, and totally without prospects. A future of doing odd jobs for a tyrant like Buchanan is not what I'd call particularly rewarding." Lillian looked down at her teacup and swirled the contents idly. "Really, dear, sometimes I don't know how you have the enthusiasm to get up in the morning."

Preston grimaced. Perhaps Lillian had gone too far. "It's the smell of breakfast cooking that works for me, Mother. I'm always afraid you're burning the house down instead of the bacon. But since you mentioned my future, I should tell you that I don't intend to be a dollar-a-day chap forever."

Oh dear, Gwen thought. He'd opened the floodgates now and Lillian was sure to take full advantage.

"That's the spirit, dear!" Lillian exclaimed. "And this is the perfect opportunity for you to show off your many talents. There's no telling what heights you could reach by taking advantage of Eli's generosity."

Satisfied apparently that she'd scored a point with Preston, Lillian turned her persuasive powers on Gwen. "And you, Gwendolyn, you're hardly a sight better off than your brother."

"What? Mama, I have a perfectly respectable job which I enjoy, and which . . ."

"Oh, pish tosh! Lolling around a bunch of musty old books all day? What kind of a life is that for an attractive young woman, who's not getting any younger, by the way."

Gwen kept her indignation to herself, though it was difficult. There would have been no point in defending her position now. Lillian was not to be silenced.

Her voice rose a notch in excitement, and wisps of springy gray hair quivered around her pink cheeks. "Your life could use a change, too, dear, if you want to know the truth. You spend your leisure hours wheeling around on that death machine or attending the occasional concert with Harold Latimer. Really, Gwendolyn, Harold Latimer!"

"What's wrong with Harold?" Gwen asked, though she knew the answer.

"He's older than you by ten years at

least, and by more than that in spirit. But I'll admit he's all that's available in Apple Creek, at least in terms of fresh goods. You're twenty-eight years old, Gwendolyn, older than nearly all of the eligible men in Apple Creek. If you ever hope to marry, you'll have to settle for a widower, someone else's used property. Take my advice, dear, and get out while you still have the looks to be in the race."

Gwen cringed at the blatant analysis of her prospects, though she tried to hide it with a disinterested shrug. But she didn't feel at all disinterested. Sadly, there was a lot of truth to what her mother had just said. Gwen was comfortable with her life in Apple Creek, but she certainly wasn't inspired by it. Or excited by it. Or really even satisfied with it, if she honestly analyzed her feelings. But still, to give up security and respectability for a madcap scheme rooted in an eccentric middle-aged man's fantasies — it was unthinkable. Or was it?

Her mother's voice suddenly sparkled with confidence. "Gwendolyn, what are you thinking?"

Oh, no, Mama, you can't win this easily. "I was thinking, Mama, that we don't know the first thing about operating a boat or managing theatrical productions. Surely you don't think my knowledge of books, Preston's personality, and your determination will see us through."

"I certainly do. I have all the confidence in the world that my intelligent daughter can run a showboat. But since I know you don't believe it, I'll tell you what Mr. Cavanaugh told me. Before he died, Eli hired a partial crew, including a small troupe of actors. I'm sure these people will be able to handle things while we supervise. And as for managing the plays and such, well, Gwendolyn, you've been to the Apple Creek Players several times with Latimer. You've seen productions from the front of the curtain. How different can it be from the back?"

As if there hadn't been volumes written on just this question!

But Lillian, a trouper herself, plunged ahead. "I've heard that show people can be delightful. And think of the stimulation to our own lives for us to be around creative individuals. To mingle in the footlights with handsome leading men and beautiful ingénues."

Gwen stole a glance at her brother. A look of innocent wickedness flashed in

Preston's eyes, while a devilish grin curled his lips.

Mama had seen it too, for the answering smile on her own face was one of triumph. That last argument had reeled Preston in like an Apple Creek bluegill drawn to a night crawler.

"I've been thinking, Gwennie," he said. "Perhaps we should give this a try."

"Should we, Preston? But I wonder. Have you been thinking with your head or some other body part?"

"Gwendolyn Barlow," Lillian snapped. "For shame! The boy is entitled to his opinion."

It was obvious now. They were going to Hickory Bend, Missouri, on the banks of the Mississippi. Three heretofore staid Midwesterners who lived routinely quiet lives of industry and comfortable apathy on the edge of a cornfield were actually going to operate a floating palace in the sinful center of America. Lillian had said the possibilities were endless, but at this moment, Gwen could only think of potential disasters in those terms.

Yet, how was she to quell the tremors of excitement that right now fluttered in her stomach? With common sense, that's how. Someone had to think of this family's future. "Mama," she began, "if I agree to do this . . ."

Lillian's pale eyes twinkled with victory. "Yes, dear?"

"You promise not to sell the house. You'll only rent it."

"Of course."

"And if we fail at this endeavor, you will admit it, and we'll come home?"

"Naturally."

Gwen sank back in her chair and rubbed her forehead. If she knew her mother, and at times she wondered if she ever would, then Lillian would soon traipse to the attic to retrieve the family's traveling cases.

Chapter Two

Six days after learning of Eli Willoughby's strange and dubiously generous bequest to his sister, Gwen, Preston, and Lillian Barlow boarded a westbound Ohio Central express train bound for the Mississippi River. In that time, Gwen had found a suitable replacement for her position at the Hopewell College Library. A professor's middle-aged wife would be the new, and hopefully temporary, assistant librarian. Gwen prayed the woman wouldn't prove to be overly competent or satisfied with her employment. If the Barlows returned to Apple Creek with their theatrical tails between their legs, a conclusion Gwen anticipated, she counted on getting her old job back.

Lillian rented the Barlow bungalow to Apple Creek's most recent newlyweds, Wendell and Juanita James. Wendell assured Gwen that he would keep the lawn mowed and the shrubs tended, and Juanita promised to prune the roses along the fence. All Lillian asked of the young couple was that they deposit their rent payments to the Apple Creek Bank on time and that they not burn the place down. Preston had walked out of Buchanan's Hard Goods Store without giving so much as a day's notice.

Two camelback trunks and four large valises contained the Barlows' possessions bound for Hickory Bend, Missouri. These items traveled in the baggage car with Gwen's Monarch bicycle for which she'd paid the exorbitant sum of one hundred dollars two months previously, and which she wasn't about to leave behind.

After an eighteen-hour train ride, the Barlows arrived, dusty and weary, at Quincy, Illinois, located southeast across the Mississippi River from Hickory Bend. They hired a wagon to transport them to the ferry which crossed the river from Quincy to LaGrange, Missouri. Once they'd rested a night in a LaGrange hotel, the Barlows again rented a wagon to take them ten miles north to their final destination.

In the middle of an April afternoon which seemed determined to fulfill its prophecy to bring as many May flowers as possible with unrelenting rain, the Barlows finally saw a wooden placard by the side of the road which announced their arrival in Hickory Bend. Their hired driver asked where they'd like to go.

Tipping her umbrella enough to see the man's face, Gwen was tempted to say, "Apple Creek, Ohio," but she refrained. Wiping a stream of rain water from her face, she said, "The riverbank, where we're most likely to locate a boat called the *Jubilee Palace*."

The driver, who was accustomed to the route from LaGrange to Hickory Bend, looked over his shoulder at his passengers and responded with a hearty belly laugh. "Oh, you won't have any trouble locating the *Jubilee Palace*, ma'am," he said between fits of laughter. "Folks around here call it *'Eli's Folly.'* Even in a rip-roaring little town like Hickory Bend, the *Jubilee* stands out like a whore at choir practice."

"Mercy! Watch your mouth, young man," Lillian scolded. "There are ladies present."

Gwen felt her face redden both from shock at the driver's language and from his unflattering description of their inheritance. Preston, however, hooted with glee. "I'm beginning to appreciate the *Jubilee Palace* more all the time."

A shiver of apprehension snaked down Gwen's spine. Her anxiety increased when the driver's description of Hickory Bend as

33

"rip-roaring" proved to be accurate. A smattering of legitimate businesses populated the one main street. Gwen noticed a general store, a dentist's office and barber shop combined, a print shop, and a constable's office. These buildings were utilitarian in design, and well kempt.

Their commendable attributes were dwarfed, however, by an unequal number of drinking establishments and gambling halls. Tinny melodies and bright lights came from open doorways and windows. The businesses seemed to be enjoying a large and boisterous clientele despite the daylight hour and nasty weather. Hickory Bend was indeed a colorful and energetic community apparently populated with people from all walks of life and, until recently, one enigmatic Eli Willoughby.

"How long had Uncle Eli lived here?" Gwen asked her mother.

"Let's see . . ." Lillian calculated on her fingers, not an easy task since she also held an umbrella. "Five months, maybe six," she said. "He was still in St. Louis when I visited him last fall. I would imagine he moved here after he decided to build the *Jubilee*. The St. Louis harbor might have been too crowded for Eli's boat."

Gwen leaned forward to capture the

driver's attention. "Do you know how long the *Jubilee Palace* has been here?"

The driver ran a hand over his dripping hair and flicked his wrist, sending a spray of water flying. Gwen dodged the droplets as best she could.

"Let's see," he said. "About three weeks, as I recall. I heard that the poor guy who built it died right after the boat got here. Don't that beat anything? The poor fella pays all that money to build the foolish thing and then ends up in the wrong place at the wrong time. You know, don't you, that he was sent to the hereafter when a piece of his own theater clobbered him on the head. A mighty peculiar circumstance if you ask me."

This was the first Gwen had heard this particular information about the accident that had claimed her uncle's life. She started to ask the driver for details, but Lillian interrupted.

"I'd hardly call that a sympathetic testimonial to the man's misfortune," Lillian said. "I'll have you know that the man you're referring to is . . . or *was* . . . my brother, and his demise is a terrible tragedy. I like to think of the *Jubilee Palace* as Eli Willoughby's legacy."

The driver's mouth hitched up in a grin.

"Didn't intend no disrespect to your kin, ma'am," he said. "But darned if it wasn't a hell of a way to meet his Maker." Tugging gently on the reins, the driver steered the wagon around an easy curve at the end of Main Street. He rested an elbow on his knee and pointed to a spot in the near distance where sloping, muddy land met brown, churning river. "As for the *Jubilee* being Mr. Willoughby's legacy, well, I guess you'll have to decide that for yourselves. There she sits, whether she's legacy material or not."

Gwen peered through a rippling veil of rain at a gigantic, three-story red and white likeness of the most garish wedding cake anyone could imagine. However, instead of the bride and groom on top, there was a whimsical hexagon glass enclosure from whose ceiling hung a tremendous brass bell. And behind that, sitting lower than the fanciful glass cupola, were two long, low box-like structures with windows and doors and enough gingerbread trim to have graced the finest bakery window at Christmastime.

Matching wood trim ran the length of both lower stories of the *Jubilee Palace* from the top to the bottom of both promenades. Gwen had seen Battenburg lace that wasn't as intricately woven as the decorative balconies of Uncle Eli's legacy. The siding and elaborate Victorian railings were painted a white so stark Gwen could just imagine their stunning brilliance on a sunny day. Numerous doors and long rectangular window frames graced each level and, painted fiery red, lent an air of brazen confidence to the entire vessel.

Porches extended from each end of the showboat with gangways connecting both to land. At the front, the area Gwen would now have to refer to as the bow, wide double doors with stained glass panels could be opened to allow admittance of a large number of people. Inset in the leaded glass and glittering in what may well have been twenty-four carat gold, was the name, *Eli's Jubilee Palace*. Since the boat was similarly identified by a four-foot-high wooden banner along the top of the second story, Gwen considered the golden letters to be the costly extravagance of a man whose mind must have taken a wrong turn somewhere along the road of his midlife.

As the wagon pulled alongside the *Jubilee Palace*, Lillian Barlow expressed her delight in a series of tremulous "Oh my"s, to which Preston added a third syllable, making his reaction an awed, "Oh, my God."

Gwen, realizing the necessity for cool logic in an illogical situation, addressed the driver. "You will help us unload our parcels to the bow to prevent further water damage, won't you?"

"I'll lend a hand for an extra four bits," he said, "but from the looks of your welcoming party, I doubt you'll be needing me."

To Gwen's surprise, several onlookers had ventured from the interior of the *Jubilee Palace* to stand under the overhang of the forward porch. The varied congregation consisted of four men and two ladies. As Gwen watched, a tall, muscular Negro man and two Negro women came through the double doors and stood behind the others.

"Excuse me," Gwen called to the assemblage on the main deck. "I'm Gwendolyn Barlow." She gestured to her family seated beside her. "This is my brother, Preston, and my mother, Lillian Barlow, sister to the late Eli Willoughby." The expressions on the faces of the gawkers changed by degrees from curious to apprehensive. "We've come to tend to the *Jubilee*," Gwen said as explanation.

A tall, stout, middle-aged gentleman in a formal black alpaca coat stepped forward. With dramatic flair, he swept a strand of abundant white hair from his forehead. "What is it exactly that you mean by 'tend to,' madam?" he asked. A strong British accent made the question sound more like a judicial inquisition than a simple query.

Gwen stood in the wagon, steadying herself by gripping the back of the driver's bench. She raised her umbrella to make her face clearly visible. "What I mean is that we have recently been informed that quite unexpectedly my mother has inherited this showboat. We've come all the way from Ohio to manage it."

The man pinched his nose above his wire-rimmed eyeglasses. Though he appeared distraught, he said nothing.

"Is there anyone here who is in charge?" Gwen asked.

The man's eyes widened slightly. "It appears that your mother is, madam, if we are to believe your pronouncement."

The hairs on Gwen's neck bristled. She hated impertinence, and this man's tone certainly suggested it. "Indeed you should believe it, sir, for it is true."

A gruff-looking fellow, shorter than his arrogantly cultured companion, edged around the small crowd to the gangway. "Don't pay him any mind, miss," he said. "Sir Clyde's nothing but a blow-hard. We all figure he didn't have to pay passage on a steamer to get here. He just hovered above deck all the way across the Atlantic on the hot air from his continual jab-bering."

This man tugged on the waistband of ill-fitting trousers and, after a scorching look at Sir Clyde's smug face, waddled duck-like down the gangway. He spat a stream of brown liquid on the ground and held his hand up to Gwen. "Dickey Squires is the name, ma'am. Hired by Mr. Willoughby to push this bucket up the river." He jerked his thumb toward a smaller vessel moored directly behind the *Jubilee*. "That's my steamer, the *Dixie Damsel*."

Gwen accepted his hand and allowed hers to be pumped like a bellows. "I'm pleased to make your acquaintance, Mr. Squires."

"I'm the one that's pleased to see you. It's about time we got this tub underway. If I sit around here any longer eating Peaches's cooking and listening to the same old stories from this lot of blarney spinners, I'll lose what's left of my waist-line and my mind."

He called over his shoulder to the group who still hadn't moved from the porch. "Phineas, get over here and unload Miss Barlow's luggage."

The crowd parted to let the black man through. He strode to the wagon, hoisted a trunk onto each shoulder, and effortlessly carried them to the deck. Then he returned for the valises. When, on his third trip, he reached for Gwen's bicycle, she started to warn him to be careful of her most prized possession. She didn't have to. He reverently raised the Monarch from the wagon, held it with one giant hand, and impulsively spun the rear tire. "A beauty, miss," he said.

"Thank you, Mr. . . . ?"

"Phineas Johnson," he said. "You just call me Phineas." A few seconds later the Monarch bicycle was safely on the main deck of the *Jubilee Palace*. And the Barlow family dismissed their driver and proceeded to join it.

It was eventually decided by all those whose self importance deemed them worthy of a vote that the Barlows' belongings would be transferred to two cabins. The largest one, which boasted a full-sized bed, was located on the third level behind the glass-enclosed pilot house that had first caught Gwen's attention. This cabin had been the accommodations of Eli Willoughby. The other, a cabin at the stern of the second floor of the boat with two narrow bunked beds, was deemed suitable for the remaining pair of Barlows.

"You take this one," Gwen said to her mother when they stood upon the plush red carpeting in the center of the elaborate master cabin.

Lillian walked to the window overlooking the Mississippi, gazed at the river below, and gasped with alarm. "Oh, I couldn't, Gwendolyn. You take it for yourself. I shouldn't sleep a wink this far from solid ground."

Gwen eyed her mother suspiciously. "Now is hardly the time for you to express a predilection toward solid ground, Mama," she said. However, she accepted Lillian's offer with good grace. How could anyone refuse such a magnanimous gift of spacious accommodations decorated with embossed red and gold wall coverings, a four-poster bed, two gleaming mahogany bureaus, and a cast iron kerosene heater to keep it all cozy? Not that such garish appointments were Gwen's taste, of course, but she could definitely make do.

Preston plopped down on the feather mattress and scowled. "But Mother, why should Gwennie be given the best cabin? If she digs in here, that means you and I will have to bunk together. Hardly appropriate you must admit."

"Oh, pish tosh, Preston. You could stand stark naked in the noon sun and I'd not waste a glance. You haven't added a thing to your body I haven't cleaned or powdered a thousand times in the past."

A rare blush crept up Preston's cheeks and made Gwen chuckle. "Mother!" he croaked. "How can you speak of such things? A man's privacy is paramount."

Lillian placed her fists on her hips and stared at her son. "And just what might you be thinking of doing in your privacy that isn't fit for your mother's eyes?"

Gwen knew. She'd seen the way Preston had looked at the dainty, petite blond girl who greeted them with downcast eyes and a charming pink tint on the crest of her fair cheeks. Marianne Dresden she'd called herself, and explained that she was the newest member of the *Jubilee Palace*'s troupe of actors, hired by Eli Willoughby just days before his death. Preston's puppy-dog eyes had left no doubt as to what he was thinking of the beautiful

Marianne. No succulent sausage link could have tempted a canine more than the lovely ingénue tempted Preston.

He jumped up from the bed, practically knocking Lillian on her ample backside. "Nothing! I wasn't thinking of doing anything. I just don't fancy sharing a room with my mother, that's all."

Lillian waggled a finger at her son. "Don't think for a moment that it's the lemon in my tea, either."

Laughing, Gwen stepped between them. "Stop it, both of you, or I'll ask you to leave my room so I can have peace and quiet."

Preston glared at her before a sly grin curled his lips. "Awfully smug, aren't we, Sis?" he said. "I think I actually prefer bunking with Mother than sleeping with the ghost of dear Uncle Eli."

"Never mind trying to scare me, Preston. I don't believe in ghosts." Gwen ran her hand over the surface of a bureau and blew the dust off the tips of her fingers. "Anyway, once I take a polishing cloth to this place, there'll be no hint of ghosts, and I'll be cozy as a winter's fireside."

"Or cold as an empty scuttle with Uncle's spirit hovering about," he countered.

"Remember, the old boy bought the pro-
verbial farm right here on this . . ."

A look from Gwen halted Preston's
morbid comment mid-sentence. "Okay,
never mind that," he said. "Mother and I
will leave you to your unpacking." Preston
grabbed his mother's elbow and ushered
her to the door. "Come along, bunk-mate.
If you're a good girl, I'll let you have the
upper." Ignoring Lillian's squawks of protest, Preston nudged her out the door.
"You know, Gwennie," he said over his
shoulder, "I think I'm going to like this
showboat business."

"I think you already do, Preston."

Once her brother and mother had left,
Gwen set about the task of unpacking her
trunk. As she worked, her curious gaze
wandered over the furnishings of the cabin
— Eli's cabin. Her uncle had slept in the
wide, soft bed. Though the bureau drawers
had been emptied, some of his personal effects still remained about the room — a
gold watch fob, collar stays, a tin of moustache wax.

"What did happen to you, Uncle Eli?"
Gwen asked the otherwise vacant room
and then shuddered when she realized she
almost expected an answer. She slammed
the lid on her empty trunk. "Darn you,

Preston, for putting foolish notions in my head."

To clear her mind of spirits and mysterious deaths, she turned her attention to the people of the *Jubilee Palace*. So far they appeared a reserved lot, far different from the creative, personable actors Lillian had predicted they would be. Apart from a few perfunctory greetings, and the discussion of the Barlows' accommodations, not one of the troupe hired by Gwen's uncle expressed genuine pleasure at the Barlows' arrival.

Marianne Dresden was an amiable, if quiet, girl, however, and Dickey Squires was likeable enough, but she wasn't at all certain about the others. The second female in the acting troupe, raven-haired Anabel Whitedove, was aloof, uncommunicative, and therefore rather mystifying. Sir Clyde Peacock, obviously the most experienced actor, was haughty to a fault, and Jason DeVane, the leading man, had yet to utter one word. A young man introduced as Travis Veazey merely scowled his opinion of the new arrivals behind a face that definitely had an aversion to soap and barber shops.

Gwen had liked the *Jubilee*'s hired help right off — handyman Phineas Johnson, as well as his plump, good natured wife, Peaches, who cooked the meals on the *Jubilee Palace*. Their young daughter, Danita, quiet and reserved, had yet to make a distinct impression, but she had kind, doe-like eyes the color of coffee beans, and they seemed to reach into Gwen's own soul.

Catching her reflection in the mirror over her bureau, Gwen decided her own hazel eyes held a message in their depths every bit as compelling as Danita's. It was one of anticipation and curiosity combined. She tucked a rain-dampened strand of strawberry blond hair into the loose knot at her crown and smiled. "It will be an interesting few days, Gwendolyn," she said, and felt strangely bolstered by the challenge.

Chapter Three

Finally, late in the afternoon of their arrival, the three Barlows found something upon which they could all agree. The *Jubilee Palace* theater, occupying a generous two stories of space, was magnificent. Eli had spared no expense when selecting the most opulent appointments.

Three levels of seating faced the elaborate, velvet-draped stage. Alternating red and gold Victorian parlor chairs occupied the first thirty rows of seats. Behind them, thirty rows of benches provided seating for a more modest cost. Most impressive were the four box-seat compartments along both side walls. Each one was flanked with Grecian columns and festooned with a velvet garland.

At floor level below the raised stage, there was an orchestra pit, though earlier in the day, Gwen had been given to understand by Dickey Squires that the *Jubilee* musical section consisted of only eight members, each only marginally qualified to call himself a musician. "It'll depend where they're needed most," Dickey had said. "Either they'll toot their horns or do walk-ons in the play. Mr. Willoughby hired people with versatility."

"And what is your other talent besides running the *Dixie Damsel,* Mr. Squires?" Gwen had asked him.

"Pray you don't have to see it, Miss Barlow," he'd said. "My special skill is throwing out the miscreants."

Gwen had turned away from the boasting Mr. Squires so he couldn't see her smile. A less threatening bodyguard she'd never seen, but the old adage was often true — one can't always tell a book by its cover.

The entire theater was shaped similarly to a trapezoid for sound projection, wider at the back, and narrowing to the performance area. The stage itself was the epitome of modern technology with electric footlights rimming the acting platform, and more lights mounted from overhead guide wires. There was both an inner stage curtain and an outer one, so one could be closed and scenery changed while the play continued in front.

Despite the general opulence of the stage, one feature stood out above all others. This was a thirty-six-inch-square portrait of Eli Willoughby framed in gilded mahogany which occupied the center of the arched proscenium. From any seat in the theater, the audience could see the stern face of the *Jubilee Palace* creator.

Preston sat in one of the parlor chairs and looked up at his uncle. "Really, Gwennie," he said so Lillian couldn't hear, "is this sour looking chap truly the fellow of whom Mother boasts, 'when he was alive, he really knew how to live'?"

Gwen found it hard to believe also. She hadn't known her uncle well . . . in fact had only seen him a half dozen times in her life. As a child, she had thought him a spooky sort. As a teenager, she'd decided he was merely aloof and bewildering. Now as she studied his portrait, she decided he was all of these things, plus his stern visage might have made him a perfect villain in a gothic novel.

Squinting eyes peered at her from beneath scraggly brows. Heavily greased hair of no determinate color lay parted on top of a prominent forehead. Uncle Eli boasted a long, jutting nose and entirely too much facial hair. His mouth was hardly visible under an abundant moustache, which swept downward to meet a wiry gray beard flowing to his shirt-front like Spanish moss. This unseemly face wasn't even saved by the ears, which were extraordinarily wide for Eli's elongated face.

"I know what you mean, Preston," Gwen said. "I'm afraid that if our Uncle Eli had attempted to send an anecdote to a newspaper, it would have ended up as a piece on the obituary page. He seems that humorless."

Preston wiggled his nose in distaste. "Humorless? The man is positively ghoulish if you ask me."

"Ah, there he is . . . dear Eli." Lillian's voice silenced her children. "As handsome as I remember him."

Gwen watched her mother walk down the aisle toward them, her gaze fixed reverently on the portrait. "He certainly is a presence on this boat still," Gwen admitted.

Lillian brushed a tear from under her eye. "Cut off in the prime of his life. Such a shame." She pivoted once around, taking in the lush details of her inheritance before resting her gaze once again on her brother's portrait. "Yet how fortunate for us to benefit from the tragedy."

"It was in this very theater that he died, you know."

Preston jumped to his feet, and all three Barlows turned toward the sound of the

51

unexpected, oddly timid voice. Marianne Dresden stood next to the last row of benches, her delicate hands folded over the ivory sash of a sky blue organdy dress. Her silky blond hair, gathered at her crown and left to fall in loose curls over her shoulders, created a halo effect in the waning sunlight of a dreary day.

Preston muttered a few unintelligible syllables at the vision in the back of the theater. The most that could be expected from him under the circumstances, Gwen decided. Marianne's words had nearly startled her speechless as well.

"Do you know something about Eli Willoughby's death, Marianne?" Gwen asked. "I had heard that he died in the theater, but I don't have any details." Somehow it seemed impossible to Gwen that a man should meet his untimely fate in the very room whose opulent splendor he created. If Uncle Eli died in the *Jubilee Palace* theater, it should have been make-believe, Act Three of a well-scripted tragedy perhaps.

Marianne came slowly toward them, her face a placid contradiction to the trembling flow of her words. "Yes, he died on the stage, there, in back." Her finger shook when she pointed beyond the second curtain. "It was horrible. It was just after one o'clock. I was awakened by the noise, the whine of the pulley, the crash of the back-drop, Mr. Willoughby's scream." She dropped her hand and lowered her head. "I shall never forget it as long as I live."

Preston was at her side in an instant. "Oh, my dear Miss Dresden. Do sit down." He led her to a chair and gently lowered her into it.

Gwen tilted her head to the side to better see any evidence of grief on Marianne Dresden's porcelain-like features. Suspicion battled with sympathy for Gwen's attention. Really, Preston, she thought, we must remember that the girl *is* an actress.

Lillian marched to the stage and stood at the bottom step. "Can you talk about it?" she asked Marianne. "Can you show us where it happened precisely? Can you tell us the particulars, dear?"

Placing her hands on the chair in front of her, Marianne rose. "Oh, yes, ma'am, I can tell you exactly where it happened. I entered the theater myself just minutes afterwards. I had brought a lantern since I didn't know how to control the electric lights. I will always recall Mr. Willoughby's face when the light from my lantern illuminated his features . . ."

Marianne proceeded up the stairs. The Barlows followed her. She went to the upstage area and looked up at the intricate web of pulleys and ropes which controlled the raising and lowering of backdrops.

"It was this one," she said, pointing to the rear scenery drop. "The one painted with trees and mountains. It's supposed to be an Ozark landscape, the one in Act Three of *Belle of the Ozarks*, the play we'd been rehearsing." She paused and glanced briefly at each member of her rapt audience. "I play Belle, you know."

"Yes, go on," Gwen said.

"Something slipped, they said. An unfortunate accident. Mr. Willoughby just happened to be standing under the backdrop when a pulley malfunctioned and the whole thing plummeted. Each scene drop is operated by a system of counterweights, you see, so the canvas will drop quickly and smoothly." She looked down, presumably at the spot where Uncle Eli had once lain. "It worked even better than it was designed. It dropped fast . . . deadly fast."

Lillian sighed. "Oh, my, what a terrible thing. Poor Eli."

Appearing to choke back tears, Marianne crossed the stage, ran back down the steps and up the center aisle. She

54

turned to the Barlows before departing the theater by the main entrance. "And there was never a kinder, more generous man . . ." she said, and this time Gwen sensed genuine grief.

"So what do you think, Preston?" Gwen asked forty-five minutes later as she and her brother walked down the outside passageway to the dining room at the stern of the *Jubilee Palace*. Lillian had gone earlier to meddle, or as she put it, "assist" Peaches in dinner preparations.

Preston sighed. "I think she's an angel. I think I would sell my soul to play opposite her in a scene. I think I want to kiss those pouting lips . . ."

Gwen administered a jab to his ribs. "Not about Miss Dresden, you idiot. About Uncle Eli's death."

"Oh." A frown indicated he was not a bit happy about the true nature of the conversation. "What's to think, Gwennie? He lived. He died. *Finis.*"

Gwen stopped walking and grabbed Preston's elbow. "I don't think it's that simple at all. Something our wagon driver said has come back to haunt me . . ."

Preston grinned at her. "I knew you had haunting on your mind."

"Not that kind of haunting. No, he mentioned how Uncle Eli ended up in the wrong place at the wrong time, and called it peculiar. It seems so to me as well. What was Uncle Eli doing on the stage at that late hour? And why were the lights off as Marianne indicated? And how did a freak accident like a falling backdrop occur when he had paid a fortune for the latest in theatrical technology? Doesn't that seem strange to you?"

"Of course it's strange, Gwennie. Why do you think they call them 'freak accidents'? Believe me, I've imagined more freakish ways than that to do away with Mr. Buchanan over the last year."

Gwen tightened her grip on Preston's arm. "That's just it, Preston. You said 'do away with.' Don't you think it's possible?"

Preston gently extricated his arm from Gwen's grip. "Now hold on. I'm not about to turn my good fortune into a macabre scene from one of your gothic novels." He sniffed the air. "Besides, whatever that clever black woman has cooked up smells awfully tempting. More tempting than standing here listening to you recount some hare-brained theory."

Preston scurried off toward the dining room. Gwen continued her slow pace as two thoughts occupied her mind. One was how Marianne Dresden's pretty face had so quickly turned Preston's skepticism about the showboat into his "good fortune." The other was that he was probably right. She really had no basis for her irrational thoughts, or for thinking that Uncle Eli had any enemies. And Peaches's meal did smell inviting.

The dining hall of the *Jubilee Palace* functioned as its kitchen as well. A huge cast iron and porcelain stove with six top burners occupied a good portion of one wall. Next to it was an equally impressive double door oak ice box. Along an adjacent wall stood a mammoth pantry which Gwen thought capable of storing supplies for a small army. It nearly dwarfed the deep sink beside it, with its red water pump and wooden drain board loaded with graniteware bowls and platters. Iron pots and skillets hung from the ceiling on shiny brass hooks. For someone skilled in the art of food preparation, and this certainly didn't describe Gwen, the *Jubilee*'s kitchen had to be a dream come true.

The eating area, however, might have been more suited to a monastery. There were two long, wood-planked tables, each surrounded by eight serviceable, but plain, ladderback chairs. A smaller table with six chairs occupied an area nearest the stove — an enviable position in the winter, but certainly the most unpleasant setting during the hot summer months, the time when showboats generally plied the inland rivers.

Gwen immediately recognized a hierarchy for the inhabitants of the *Jubilee Palace*. Eight rather scruffily dressed men sat around one table. Gwen assumed these must be the versatile band members Dickey Squires had spoken of. Consuming their meal with gusto, these men barely spared a glance in Gwen's direction.

Seated around the other table for eight, the one closest to a bank of windows, were the supposed elite of the *Jubilee* family — the four principal actors, and the showboat's management, which once was comprised solely of Eli Willoughby. Now, two chairs were occupied by Preston and Lillian Barlow, with a third chair waiting for Gwen.

Before taking the vacant seat next to Preston, Gwen issued a general greeting to everyone in the room, including Phineas, Peaches, Danita, Travis Veazey, and Mr. Squires, who sat at the table nearest the stove. Preston handed Gwen a giant platter of roasted potatoes, beans, and pork cutlets fragrant with mysterious spices. While he held the heavy plate for his sister, Preston grumbled under his breath. "A bit of bad luck, eh, Gwennie? And all because you made me listen to your theory about Uncle Eli."

Scooping portions of food onto her plate, Gwen gave Preston a puzzled look. "What are you talking about?"

He nodded toward the man next to him, the lead actor named Jason DeVane who was seated between Preston and Marianne Dresden. "But for a few seconds I would have had that seat," Preston muttered.

Preston was fretting about Marianne again. Gwen should have known. She leaned forward to catch a glimpse of the object of her brother's fascination. It hardly seemed like sitting next to the ingénue was such an enviable position. The young woman sat as quiet as a mouse, an open paper-bound book occupying her attention while she daintily picked at her meal. "What's she doing, Preston?" Gwen asked.

"That's her script," he said. "I saw the title on the front. *Belle of the Ozarks.* Marianne must be extremely dedicated to her craft. She even studies her part during meals."

Commendable? Gwen supposed so. But what explained the pall of silence that hung over the rest of the diners? The atmosphere in the *Jubilee*'s dining room was more conducive to a wake than a family style meal. Only Lillian did her part to liven the crowd. Eating with her usual good appetite, she commented often on the flavor and preparation of the food. Peaches beamed.

Sensing that the presence of the Barlows might be the reason for the lack of communication, Gwen decided to try and prod her somber companions into something resembling amiability. After all, she and her family were the newcomers, and as such, needed to earn the trust of the rest of the *Jubilee* group. And it didn't help that the Barlows held positions of authority over the established regime. The others must be worried about their futures with Eli gone.

Gwen took a sip of amber liquid which she determined was apple juice. "I know I speak for the rest of my family when I say that we would be most grateful to learn as much as we can about the workings of the *Jubilee Palace*," she said. "Goodness knows we can use all the help we can get, and the more information you can provide about the boat, the better our chances for a successful endeavor." She looked at her mother and brother for support. "Isn't that right?"

"Absolutely," Preston said.

Lillian, whose mouth was full, nodded enthusiastically.

A few of the eight musicians glanced up from their food, paused for a moment as if analyzing the importance of Gwen's request for assistance, and returned to their meals. The actors all looked at Sir Clyde and waited, indicating that if he wasn't their literal commander, he was at least their figurative one.

Finally the senior actor removed his spectacles and aimed them at Gwen. "Your request to learn as much as possible about the *Jubilee Palace* is well taken," he said. "But if we are to tutor you in your quest for knowledge, are we to assume we may also make suggestions as to the improvement of our lots, and that you will strive to alleviate the problems?"

Problems? They wanted to tell her their problems? Gwen pictured a swirling eddy of complaints issuing from a sort of Pandora's Box and mentally cringed. In fact she even squirmed under Sir Clyde's scrutiny, and she definitely hated squirming. "We will do what we can," she said.

The floodgates opened, and Gwen soon realized that Uncle Eli's family on the *Jubilee Palace* had serious problems and concerns beyond their temporary loss of leadership. It was enough to make the new leader wonder once again why she'd ever gotten herself into this mess.

Jason DeVane, whose extraordinary good looks were beyond the attributes of most mortal men, was the first to speak. He tugged at the narrow ruffles at the ends of his shirtsleeves, flashed a disconcerting grin that if it weren't beset with troubles would have found a permanent home in any girl's heart, and said, "First of all, Miss Barlow, we are broke. None of us has been paid in over a month now."

His blunt announcement was met with a general nod of agreement from all three tables. One of the band members raised his fork and mumbled, "Can't play an instrument just for the promise of a good meal."

"No, no, of course you can't," Gwen agreed. "This matter must be looked into immediately. I haven't had a chance to peruse Uncle Eli's books yet, but when I do . . ."

Sir Clyde cleared his throat. "When you

do, Miss Barlow, you will not find so much as a shilling. There is no money in the Willoughby coffers. The last weeks of his life, starting even before the *Jubilee Palace* came to Hickory Bend, your uncle kept us on marionette strings with the promise of wages. Not one American red cent appeared in our hands, however."

It was inconceivable. The actors hadn't received wages in a month? "Then why have you stayed?" Gwen asked.

"Mr. Cavanaugh persuaded us to. He said new owners were coming to assume management of the *Jubilee Palace*. Under the circumstances, the boat being the jewel that she is, we thought it advantageous to wait and see what happened. Before that we stayed because we believed in Willoughby when he assembled this troupe of actors two months ago. I hope you'll not disappoint us."

Gwen thought of the modest savings her family had brought to Hickory Bend. She doubted there was enough money to pay back wages, and certainly none would be left over to continue the *Jubilee*'s operation. She folded her napkin and set it beside her plate. Suddenly Peaches's cooking had become less palatable.

"Gwendolyn . . ."

Gwen stared at her mother.

"I insist that we immediately arrange to pay . . ."

Gwen held up her hand. She definitely could not let her irrationally generous mother make promises the Barlows couldn't keep. "We'll see, Mama," she said before turning her attention once more to Sir Clyde. "Do you know what my uncle intended to do about this problem, Sir Clyde?"

"He intended to set this boat afloat, Miss Barlow. We're actors. We are ready to act. We *need* to act. Our souls are starving just as our stomachs soon will."

Gwen glanced at the platter still overflowing with food. "What do you mean, your stomachs will starve?"

Sir Clyde motioned to Peaches. "Mrs. Johnson. Why don't you open the doors to the larder?"

Peaches ambled to the massive pantry. "I'm sorry, Miss Barlow," she said and opened the double doors. The shelves were bare except for a few bags of flour, some sugar and potatoes, and a small assortment of condiments. "The ice box is almost as empty," she added.

Gwen couldn't believe her eyes. "But this meal," she said. "Pork and fresh beans . . ."

"All won this morning in the boxing ring by Phineas," Peaches responded, pride evident in her voice despite the dire situation.

"And I scared up a few pounds of beef the day before that," said a member of the band.

"And I got us that mutton after playing the squeeze box at the wedding of the butcher's daughter," another said.

Lillian clapped her hands together and beamed. "You're all so clever," she said. "Bravo!"

Gwen sighed. "Mama, please . . ."

Suddenly the coral-cheeked and corseted Miss Anabel Whitedove stood up and looked around at her companions before settling her lavender shadowed gaze on Gwen. Miss Whitedove's exotic yet stern countenance certainly commanded attention. She took one long, dramatic breath which straightened her spine, made sure everyone was listening, and said, "Of course things wouldn't have gotten this bad if Mr. Willoughby hadn't hired more mouths to feed." Her eyes flashed a challenge to a reticent Marianne Dresden who hiccoughed into her napkin.

"Anabel, sit down!" Sir Clyde bellowed.

Gwen looked at Peaches who still firmly grasped the handle of the pantry door as though she considered herself guardian of what was left of the *Jubilee's* meager supplies. "Is it really so bad, Peaches?" Gwen asked.

" 'fraid so. They won't give us no more credit at Davenport's General Store. Fact is, Mr. Davenport says we got to pay up our debt 'fore we can leave Hickory Bend."

"And the printer," Jason DeVane added. "Willoughby owed him a fortune, even after his wheeling and dealing. Kruger came by again yesterday trying to get blood from a turnip." Jason sighed. "At least I paid for our licenses up north with cash, not credit."

Gwen lowered her head to avoid the piercing gazes of the *Jubilee* troupe. She needed to think. While it was true that Mr. Cavanaugh had said that Uncle Eli spent his life savings on the *Jubilee Palace*, he certainly hadn't indicated that the showboat suffered from this magnitude of financial difficulty.

It didn't take long for Gwen to realize that there would be no miracle cure for the *Jubilee's* problems. Logically, there was only one thing to be done. She would have to make arrangements to begin paying the *Jubilee's* debts, and if there was money left over, procure enough supplies to refill the pantry. Her goal was to get the showboat moving. The only way to compensate the actors was to attract audiences and start making money.

She raised her head to find that all eyes were still upon her, anxious and expectant. She stood and folded her hands at her waist. "I must ask your indulgence for a while longer," she said, and immediately regretted her five feet six inches of height. She would have much preferred to be the size of Tom Thumb to skitter off to a dark corner somewhere.

"I intend to turn the *Jubilee Palace* into a profit-making venture," she said, surprised at the confidence in her voice. "But I can't do it without your cooperation. The only step we can take now is forward." She looked down the table at Jason DeVane. "Mr. DeVane, you said that the licenses for our first stops up river have been acquired?"

"They have. At Mr. Willoughby's request, I went myself and paid the expenses."

"Good." She turned her attention to all the actors, concentrating on each one individually before proceeding to the next. "And you all know your parts and are ready to perform?"

Sir Clyde eyed her over his glasses. "We are all professionals here, Miss Barlow."

Anabel Whitedove took a long swallow of her drink, which was much darker in color than Gwen's own. Wine no doubt. She set her glass down with a thump. "Speak for yourself, Clyde," she said. "My leading role was taken away and given to another as you'll recall." Another scathing glance at Marianne Dresden left no doubt as to who was the recipient of this generous bequest. "I haven't had time to learn my new part yet."

Sir Clyde pounded a fist on the table. "Balderdash, Anabel. You've had nothing but time!"

Gwen raised her hands, a placating gesture. "Please, let's not argue among ourselves. I'm sure Anabel will learn her new lines quickly." The less than agreeable expression on the actress's face prompted Gwen to add, "You wouldn't want to be responsible for holding us back, would you, Miss Whitedove?"

Fluttering a hand over the bodice of her dress, Anabel said, "Heaven forbid."

Gwen ignored the sarcasm in Anabel's tone. "Good. Then we're agreed. We'll leave as soon as possible, tomorrow even."

Sir Clyde stood up. "I'm afraid not, Miss Barlow."

"Why not? What's wrong now?"

"Haven't you noticed the lack of one rather significant necessity?"

Gwen racked her brain. They had actors, musicians, a cook, and a handyman. They had licenses, and Travis Veazey, the errand boy. They had Dickey Squires and his *Dixie Damsel* steamer waiting to push them upstream. What in the world did they need? "I'm sorry, Sir Clyde, but I haven't the foggiest notion what you're talking about."

"A captain, Miss Barlow. Someone to keep us from grounding on the first sand bar or ripping a hole in our hull at the first jutting log. It seems that your illustrious uncle, in his infinite wisdom, fired our captain the day before the unfortunate accident in the theater."

Gwen's heart sank, and her spicy pork cutlets threatened a revolt.

"Other than that small detail," Sir Clyde said with an exaggerated wave of his hand and an impertinent snort, "we're off to achieve fame and fortune."

"That's not the only thing holding you folks to Hickory Bend," came a gruff voice from the dining room's entry.

Everyone turned to stare at the unexpected arrival.

"Ah, Constable O'Toole," Sir Clyde said. "Won't you join our jovial repast?"

"Not hungry," said the official, who looked as if he hadn't missed many meals in his life. "But thanks just the same. I just stopped by to tell you folks that you're not going anywhere."

Gwen stepped forward, struggling to maintain her composure in light of this new potential complication. "How do you do, Constable. I'm Gwen Barlow. My mother is the new owner of the *Jubilee Palace*."

"Then I guess it's you ladies I should be talking to. I'm going to have to hold the *Jubilee Palace* right here in Hickory Bend for a while."

"Why for Heaven's sakes?"

"I didn't have reason to think it at first, but now I do. Now I believe that Eli Willoughby was murdered."

Chapter Four

None too gently, Gwen thrust the last hairpin into the topknot she'd carelessly fashioned at her crown. After a fitful night's sleep, meticulous grooming was not a priority. Constable O'Toole's announcement had kept her up half the night.

Her theory that Uncle Eli had been murdered had been given credence. She should have felt vindicated for her suspicions, but the gruesome knowledge only brought intense discomfort, bordering on outright fear. Never before prone to wildly imaginative speculation, Gwen had actually locked her cabin door and thrust a straight-back chair under the handle. Still she'd flinched at every odd sound during the long night, and there are many strange noises when one isn't accustomed to sleeping on water.

This morning Gwen was more disheartened than afraid. Complaints from the *Jubilee* actors last night and Constable O'Toole's proclamation that the *Jubilee* must remain in Hickory Bend, only added to the showboat's financial woes. And she now believed that, contrary to Marianne

71

Dresden's tearful praise of her uncle, Eli Willoughby did indeed have enemies.

A knock on Gwen's door made her jump. Obviously she was still frightened after all. This whole murder possibility made a person's skin feel too tight. "Who is it?" she called.

"It's me, Gwennie. I've brought coffee."

"Oh, Preston. Just a moment." She removed the chair and placed it next to the cabin's desk. She didn't want Preston teasing her about her insecurity. "All right," she said. "Come in."

He opened the door. Bright sunlight streamed in behind him, though Gwen's clock said it was only seven thirty. It promised to be a nice day.

Preston handed her a steaming mug. "I've called it coffee," he said, "though it's strong enough that a gallon of it would be enough to fire up Dickey's *Dixie Damsel*. Peaches told me it's Louisiana chicory. Our Apple Creek brew pales by comparison."

It smelled wonderful to Gwen. She blew on the contents and took a sip. "It's delicious." Then she looked at her brother over the rim of the mug. "I'm surprised to see you up so early."

"Not by choice, believe me. But you

know Mama. Has to have her hand in every skillet. I think she and Peaches raced to the kitchen this morning to see who would light the coals."

Preston sat in the chair Gwen had just set by the desk. "Well, go ahead and say it, Gwennie. You've a right to."

"Say what?"

"That I have egg on my face."

She smiled and swiped her index finger along Preston's perfectly clean chin. "Maybe just a wee bit there."

"Who would have thought it," he said. "Uncle Eli murdered! I saw you talking to the constable when I left to walk Marianne back to her room. And then you disappeared and Sir Clyde said you'd excused yourself for the night."

"I was tired, Preston, especially after talking to that disagreeable Mr. O'Toole."

"I understand, but did the old boy give you any reason why he'd suddenly come to this conclusion?"

"He said he'd always thought Uncle Eli's death a bit suspect, but it was a visit from one of the members of the *Jubilee Palace* late yesterday afternoon that convinced him to investigate further."

"Did he say who this visitor was?"

"No, he didn't. But I think I know who it

was, and I believe you do, too."

"Marianne?"

"She was awfully upset when she left the theater after telling us about Uncle Eli's death."

"And quiet during dinner."

"That's right. And of all of us in the dining room, she seemed least surprised by the constable's arrival. In fact, now that I think about it, I remember Marianne becoming even more interested in her script when O'Toole entered the room. It was almost as if she were avoiding any contact with him."

Preston shook his head. "Poor Marianne. To think she's been living with this suspicion all this time. She must have been frightened for her life to keep silent about it. We know she was extremely fond of our uncle."

Gwen took another sip of coffee. "She seemed to be, yes. Of course that might have something to do with the fact that Eli hired her for the lead actress role."

"Perhaps. Still, it was our coming here that gave her the courage to go to the authorities. I think she trusts us, Gwennie."

"Right now, Preston, I should think that trust is in short supply all around the *Jubilee Palace*."

"Yoo hoo! Anyone in there?"

"Ah, it's my roommate." Preston hurried to open the door. "Good morning, Mother," he said as Lillian floated inside trailing the scent of cooked bacon.

"I thought you didn't like the third floor of the *Jubilee*, Mama," Gwen said.

"I don't, but curiosity is a great inducer to overcoming one's fears. Peaches said Preston left the dining room with coffee for his sister. The thought that you two were meeting without me was too much to bear. Do you have secrets, dears?"

"No secrets, Mama," Gwen said. "We've been discussing the constable's visit last evening."

"Dreadful. Poor Eli. And more problems for these lovely showboat people. We have to do something for them, Gwendolyn. This murder business will delay our leaving and make matters even worse."

"I know, Mama, and last night at dinner I wondered how things *could* get any worse. Especially when I learned that Uncle Eli had fired the *Jubilee* captain, leaving us marooned here. But they *have* gotten worse. I told the constable that I would come to his office today. I plan to impress upon him the importance of the *Jubilee* heading up river." Gwen crossed her arms over her chest to ward off an involuntary shiver. "Though why we would even consider sailing with the possibility of a killer on board . . ."

Lillian squealed. "Gwendolyn, you don't think that someone on the *Jubilee Palace* . . ."

"I don't know, Mama. But we have to consider it."

Lillian collapsed on the bed. "I refuse to think such a thing. Why, these people must have held Eli in the utmost regard. He built this fabulous boat, gave them jobs . . ."

". . . left them with a mountain of unpaid bills, held their pay for weeks," Preston added.

"Which reminds me," Gwen said. "Even if I do persuade the constable to let us leave, we still don't have a captain."

Once again a knock on the door interrupted Gwen's thoughts. In a voice edged with mounting anxiety, she called, "Come in."

The door opened, and a man Gwen hadn't seen before popped his head inside. A devilishly handsome man, she couldn't help noticing. "Is this where I might find the Barlows?" he inquired.

"I'm Gwendolyn Barlow," Gwen said. "This is my mother, Lillian, and my brother, Preston. How can we help you?"

The man's large frame, clothed in a gleaming white shirt and quite form-fitting trousers, filled the narrow doorway until he ducked his head and entered the room. He was no less impressive up close. "I hope *I* can help *you*," he said. "The name's Carson Stockwell, Captain Stockwell. I understand you need an experienced captain for the *Jubilee Palace*."

A shiver of another kind ribboned its way down Gwen's spine . . . a shiver of admiration for the workings of Fate. It did indeed act in mysterious ways. Fearful of appearing too anxious and losing whatever command she might hold over Captain Stockwell, Gwen narrowed her eyes and stared at him. "We might be looking for someone to fill this position," she said. "I will need to know your qualifications of course."

"Of course," he said. "But that's only a formality. I'm definitely your man."

Once it occurred to Gwen that job interviews are best conducted in a less informal environment than a lady's bedchamber, she suggested that Carson Stockwell proceed to the dining room and she would meet him there. He quite willingly accommodated her. When he left, Lillian positively glowed with good humor.

"How fortuitous, Gwendolyn," she said. "Why the man practically fell out of the sky and into your lap."

"Nothing is as simple as it first appears, Mama."

"Pish tosh. The man is undoubtedly a wonderful captain."

Gwen merely shook her head at her mother's hasty and untested evaluation. "Would you care to join me in the interview?" she asked.

"No. I trust you to make the right decision. Besides, I want to make new curtains for my quarters. Preston, walk me to the general store so I can buy fabric."

"Absolutely not, Mother. Men do not accompany women on such errands. Besides, I'm going with Gwennie."

Lillian sighed. "Suit yourself. I'll take Peaches." She flounced out with the air of confidence, or whatever it was, that always defined her.

"No ruffles, Mother!" Preston called after her.

Several minutes after her mother had left, Gwen walked with Preston to the dining room. They had just descended the third floor steps when Preston said, "I haven't had the chance, Gwennie, but there was something I wanted to talk to you about this morning."

"All right. What is it?"

A sparkle of excitement lit the backs of Preston's nut brown eyes. A definite energy radiated from him that Gwen hadn't seen in a long time. He cleared his throat and began. "Last night when I walked Marianne to her room, I asked her if she would lend me her script for the night."

"Oh? She seemed like she would be reluctant to part with it."

"She is. But still she let me have it. I read the play until the wee hours. Did you know it was written by Uncle Eli?"

Was there no end to Eli's talents? Gwen wondered. "No, I didn't."

"It's one of those melodrama things, meant to be overacted, I fear, but even so, it's quite good."

"That's a relief. I'm happy to know you approve. Perhaps once we get the *Jubilee* on her way, we might actually please the audiences."

"We will. I'm sure of it."

Since they were approaching the dining room, Gwen assumed Preston had concluded his conversation. Not so. He stopped her outside the kitchen entrance and pulled several sheets of paper from the back pocket of his denim pants. "I took the liberty of adding another character," he said. "Nothing too weighty. Certainly not anything that would upstage the characters that are currently written into the play."

"Another character?" Gwen was beginning to read between the lines of her brother's dialogue. "And this new role," she said, "would it be for a male?"

"Yes, as a matter of fact. Very minor though, as I said. A few lines only. He's a rather interesting young chap. Sterling qualities. Adds a new dimension that I believe improves the overall script."

"But Preston . . ." Gwen hoped to end this conversation before it raced to the inevitable conclusion. "We only have four actors in our troupe and the occasional musician filling in for bit parts. How many actors are called for in the play as Uncle Eli originally wrote it?"

"Four. But I know once you read what I've written, you'll agree that my addition of a fifth character will only improve our production."

"Hmmm . . . I see where this is leading, Preston, and really you can't be seriously thinking . . ."

"But I am, Gwennie! I'm a natural for this part. I've always wanted to be an actor . . ."

". . . or a fire fighter or a clown, or a . . ."

"Don't tease, Gwennie." He fluttered the papers in her face. "Just read it, please. I'll leave a copy of the script in your room, along with my addition. Don't say no until you've at least looked at it."

And to think Gwen had actually entertained the notion that Preston had brought her coffee out of the goodness of his heart. She should have known better. "You can leave them, but I'm not promising anything, Preston. I'll read it, but right now I have a captain to interview."

She'd turned her back to him, but still heard him utter the word, "Splendid!" with total jubilation. As she often did in her relationship with her brother, she felt as if she were eating her breakfast right out of the palm of Preston's hand.

Gwen entered the dining room perplexed about the recent past and her uncertain future. *How did this happen?* she wondered. *How did I become producer, financier, problem solver, investigator, and personnel manager all at once?* "These are entirely too many job titles for a simple librarian," she muttered under her breath.

★ ★ ★

Carson Stockwell was nothing if not charming. Within minutes Gwen decided that if the engaging captain lacked the navigational skills to guide the *Jubilee Palace*, he might very well be able to coax the boat out of trouble with flowery phrases.

But, at the same time, he did possess the skills she assumed were required of a competent captain. At least he had ready answers to her questions. He'd been piloting on the Mississippi and adjacent rivers since he was twenty years old. In those fourteen years, he claimed to have encountered every perilous turn, dangerous channel, and treacherous snag of Midwest river.

Certainly his experience was etched on his remarkable physical features. Under his clean and pressed cambric shirt, Captain Stockwell's arms swelled respectably below broad shoulders, indicating he must have towed a line or two or poled his way out of many a jam. A fine webbing of lines at the corners of his eyes proved he was no stranger to sunlight. And contrary to masculine fashion of the day, Carson Stockwell was beardless and wore no moustache. There was nothing to interrupt the flawless combination of swarthiness and sun-warmed vigor in his skin tone.

His appearance was not perfection however. His nose was too broad, his ears, under a neatly trimmed patch of cinnamon colored hair, were a bit too small.

But his eyes were most remarkable of all. A woman would not likely forget them once she'd allowed herself an imaginary journey through their jade windows. And, too, a cocky assurance in their deep glimmer positively dared a person to challenge his claims of mastering the river. But should one trust the swaggering brashness of such a man? Gwen had her doubts.

Near the end of the interview, Captain Stockwell heaved a great, satisfied sigh, pushed his chair away from the table where he'd been sitting across from Gwen, and stretched his long legs out in front of him. It was the first she realized that during her questioning of his abilities he had managed to consume a large portion of scrambled eggs and biscuits without ever pausing so much as a syllable in his answers.

"No one can fill a man's belly as satisfactorily as your Peaches, Miss Barlow," he said. "It's no secret that I'd like to captain this boat, and one of the main reasons is the steady diet of your cook's many talents."

"You've sampled Peaches's cooking be-fore this, Mr. Stockwell?" Gwen asked.

"Yep. I've visited this boat several times since she arrived over three weeks ago." He grinned like a little boy who'd successfully accomplished a prank on his teacher. "And always I managed to arrive at mealtime."

"You must have known my uncle, Eli Willoughby, then."

"I knew him, yes," Stockwell said. "But not well."

Was it Gwen's imagination or did a hint of shadow dull the spark of confidence in the captain's eyes? If so, it vanished as quickly as it had appeared. But it was enough for Gwen to wonder if perhaps this was not Carson Stockwell's first interview for captain of the *Jubilee Palace*. The possi-bility increased her unease. "Did my uncle interview you for this position himself, Mr. Stockwell?"

He crossed his arms over his chest. His lips pulled down at the corners. "Yes. He chose Solomon Wade over me for the job. It was an unfortunate mistake."

Strange indeed. If Eli had hired Wade as captain, then why did he fire him the day before the accident in the theater? That is what Sir Clyde said at dinner, and now that occurrence was even more puzzling.

The best way to solve a puzzle was to openly seek its solution. And Gwen did just that. "Mr. Stockwell, I must ask this question. Do you know why my uncle fired Mr. Wade before the *Jubilee* could leave Hickory Bend?"

The captain's straight brown eyebrows knitted together. "I do."

She waited and when no more information was forthcoming she said, "And? Will you tell me?"

"It's not my story to tell, Miss Barlow. One thing you will learn about me. I keep confidences."

"An admirable quality, Mr. Stockwell. But in this circumstance I believe a full revelation is justified. The success of the *Jubilee Palace* may be in the balance. I need to know what has happened in the past so that I may avoid mistakes in the future. Surely you understand that."

"I understand, of course, but I'm not at liberty to tell the story of Solomon Wade." He paused and passed his finger along his lower lip several times. "I can tell you this much, Miss Barlow. If you want to know why Solomon Wade was fired, ask Phineas Johnson."

"Phineas?" Gwen struggled to find a plausible explanation for how the affable

Negro man could be involved in Eli's decision to fire his captain. None came to mind.

Stockwell stood up and pushed his chair under the table. "Is our interview concluded?"

His voice startled her. "What? Oh, yes. I did neglect to tell you, Mr. Stockwell, that the *Jubilee*'s financial situation is not especially sound at the moment."

He smiled. "I've heard rumors."

"I won't be able to pay you the sum you asked until we begin selling tickets to performances. But then, of course, I will pay you in arrears."

"Acceptable, Miss Barlow."

"I'm going into town today to try and settle some business with the constable. After that I will make my decision about your employ. Where can I reach you?"

"I'll reach you. This evening around sundown?"

"Fine."

Carson Stockwell strode from the dining room with the same confidence he had displayed during his interview. After a moment Gwen stepped outside onto the first floor promenade of the *Jubilee Palace*. Leaning on the decorative railing, she watched Stockwell head up the rocky bank toward Main Street. Instinctively she knew he would be a competent captain. He had his secrets though. Like why hadn't Eli hired him? And why wasn't he willing to explain why Solomon Wade was fired? A code of ethics perhaps? If so, that was admirable.

While she pondered these questions, Gwen saw her mother and Peaches approach from town. Apparently Lillian had been successful in recruiting Peaches to accompany her to the general store. Lillian had on her wide-brimmed straw hat, and Peaches wore a colorful bandanna around her head. They made a pleasing picture, these two robust, plump women in simple dress — like a muted pastoral painting of country life. Baskets swung from both women's arms. Lillian's was overflowing with fabric. Peaches's had fresh vegetables. When Lillian spotted her daughter on deck, she waved gaily. "Yoo hoo, Gwendolyn. I'm back!"

As soon as the two women came on board, Peaches asked if Mr. Stockwell had enjoyed his breakfast. Obviously rewarded by Gwen's answer, she smiled and headed for the kitchen.

"Where did Peaches get the money for those vegetables, Mama?" Gwen asked.

"She bartered, dear. Clever woman. The *Jubilee Palace* has one less skillet, but as Peaches says, Eli bought too many to begin with. And once we leave Hickory Bend, she says we'll find fields along the way and perhaps she and I can 'borrow' a few staples from the farmers."

"Hmmm . . ." Gwen envisioned visiting her mother in a jail cell after she was arrested for pilfering crops. But Gwen had enough problems without worrying about ones that may come in the future. "Mama," she said, "Mr. Stockwell said the strangest thing."

"Really, dear? What's that?"

"Well, you remember Sir Clyde saying that Uncle Eli fired his captain the day before the accident?"

"Yes, I do remember. Dreadful man, that Solomon Wade."

Lillian knew his name? Gwen had only learned it this morning. And how had Lillian drawn the conclusion that Wade was 'dreadful?' Gwen stared at her mother. "Do you know something about this, Mama? Because Mr. Stockwell wouldn't tell me the circumstances surrounding the firing. He told me to ask Phineas."

"Oh, I wouldn't do that, dear. He's still

quite out of sorts over the whole occurrence."

"What occurrence, Mama? What did Solomon Wade do to Phineas Johnson? And how do you know what it was?"

Lillian raised her eyebrows and *tsked* as if the answer to Gwen's question were obvious. "Peaches told me, of course. When she doesn't resent my interference in the kitchen, she's actually quite fond of me." Lillian smiled. "I really have quite a sympathetic ear."

Gwen waited, her toe tapping an impatient beat against the floor boards. "Well? What did Solomon do to Phineas? Do I have to drag it out of you?"

"It's not a very pleasant topic of conversation, Gwendolyn."

"Mother!"

Lillian waggled a finger, imploring Gwen to bend closer. Then she whispered, "That horrible man, Solomon Wade, tried to . . . well, he attempted to . . . *have his way* with Peaches's and Phineas's daughter, Danita."

Gwen could practically feel the heat of Lillian's flushed face. It blended well with the steady rise of her own internal thermometer. "He tried to rape her?"

"Really, Gwendolyn, such phrasing!"

"But that's terrible! That sweet girl."

"Oh, yes," Lillian agreed. "And if Uncle Eli hadn't fired Mr. Wade, Peaches thinks Phineas would have killed the evil man."

How quickly the fires of injustice could turn to a chill of alarm. Solomon Wade now figured into this complex tapestry. The ex-captain of the *Jubilee* certainly had reason to fear Phineas Johnson. But it appeared he also had reason to hate Eli Willoughby.

Chapter Five

As soon as Lillian left to make curtains for her room, Gwen immediately went to find Travis Veazey. She needed the deckhand to run an important errand. After searching the backstage area and the dining room, Gwen finally discovered him on the front porch behind the colorfully painted and stenciled *Jubilee* ticket booth.

Unaware of Gwen's presence, Travis stood facing the river, both elbows propped on the boat's railing. A cane fishing pole dangled from his hand, its thin twine threaded through a faded red float bobbing listlessly in the murky ripples of the Mississippi.

Gwen stepped close to him and accidentally scraped the toe of her shoe against a bucket by Travis's feet. The bucket skidded a few inches across the polished floor. Water sloshed against the sides and lapped over onto her leather boots. She jumped back, but not before glimpsing a strangely hideous creature with long glistening whiskers staring up at her with glassy eyes from the bucket. The thing flopped about in an effort to escape its galvanized prison by leaping free and finding the river. Unfortunately it was a feat doomed to failure.

"Hey, watch it!" Travis hollered.

"Sorry," Gwen said, though she was mostly uncertain as to why an apology was necessary. She looked around for a rag with which she could wipe her shoes. When she couldn't find one, she used the palm of her hand. "Is that a catfish?" she asked.

He looked at her like she'd descended from the moon where, as everyone knew, the topography was dry and dusty and devoid of fish of any kind. "Yeah," he said, and returned his attention to his cane pole.

Gwen risked another glance at the angry beast in the bucket and frowned. "I hope Peaches didn't send you out here to catch our dinner."

"Nope. But she said if I caught a cat, she'd fix it for my lunch. Since I only got one, I ain't sharin'."

Gwen stepped away from the bucket. "More's the pity."

Obviously immune to her sarcasm, Travis muttered, "Do you want something?"

"Yes, as a matter of fact, I want you to

run an errand for me."

He flicked the cane pole into the air and watched the bobber settle a little further downstream. "Oh yeah? What?"

"I want you to go into town to the constable's office. If he's there, ask him if I may call on him within the next hour."

Travis shook his head. "Can't do it now. I'm fishing."

Gwen had never encountered outright insubordination in a job hierarchy situation. Even considering his poor judgment at times, Robbie Simpson at the Hopewell College Library had been respectful and obedient to her demands. She felt the hairs on her neck bristle.

"Excuse me, Travis . . ." She waited for him to slowly turn away from the river and face her.

His jaw slacked open with impatience as he flipped dirty strands of what might have been light brown hair from his eyes. "What?"

Her toe started its tap of temper control against the floorboards. "Is it or is it not your duty on the *Jubilee Palace* to run errands?"

" 'spose it is."

"Then that is precisely what you shall do. And you shall do it when asked. Otherwise I don't see any reason to keep you in the employ of the showboat any longer."

Travis stared at her for a most uncomfortable period of time, as though he were actually debating his options. Finally, he raised the cane pole from the water and settled it against the railing. The hook dangled in the air, a wad of sodden bread still attached. "Don't get your bloomers in a knot, Miss Barlow."

"Travis, how dare you . . ."

"Relax. I'm going. Gotta take care of my fish first, though."

Despite the tirade sitting on the tip of her tongue, Gwen clamped her mouth shut. At least that was a reasonable demand. Gwen didn't fancy having the catfish sitting on deck with the warm sun climbing higher each minute. She backed away as Travis reached into the bucket and grasped the fish under its gills. She hoped he would throw the wriggling creature into the river, but, of course, he didn't. Instead, he drew his arm over his head and, summoning all his might, flung the fish onto the deck of the *Jubilee*. It landed with a splat and, after a final thrashing of its tail fin, lay still.

Travis dumped the contents of the bucket into the river and drew an odd-looking, serrated knife from his back pocket. He held it by its carved handle, which was the color of winter grass and resembled, oddly enough, the tip of a buck's horn. He tested the sharpness of the blade with the pad of his thumb.

Gwen shuddered at the thought of bacteria on the dirty blade and prayed it hadn't broken the skin. "What is that knife used for?" she asked, more than a little wary of the answer.

Travis held the knife so Gwen could see its details. "Scaling and cutting filets," he said.

That explained the silvery bits hardened on the blade. Fish scales.

"It's the best fish knife you'll ever see," Travis told her. "And damned if it isn't still sharp as a razor. Handle's made from the antler of a stag." He picked up the pole and the fish. "After I take this stuff to Peaches, I'll go into town."

"Thank you," Gwen said. "I'll be waiting to hear what the constable says." Watching Travis walk away with a lackadaisical slouch to his posture, Gwen added under her breath, "What an unpleasant young man."

Anticipating a positive response from Constable O'Toole, she headed to her quarters to prepare for the trip to his office. She decided she would investigate Travis Veazey at the earliest opportunity. Why had Uncle Eli hired such a sullen, belligerent fellow? And where had he come from that his training in personal hygiene had been so obviously overlooked?

When she walked in her room, thoughts of Travis immediately fled from her mind. On her bed was a copy of *Belle of the Ozarks*. Next to it was the sheaf of papers her brother had shown her earlier — his addition to the script. In all the excitement of interviewing Carson Stockwell, learning of Phineas's resentment against Solomon Wade and her uncle's reaction, and her recent encounter with Travis, she'd forgotten about her promise to read it.

"Oh, dear, Preston," she muttered to herself, "you couldn't have picked a more inopportune time for me to attend to this matter." She picked up the script and fanned through the pages. "I'll need at least two hours to grasp even the most shallow interpretation of this play." Tossing it back on the bed, she took her straw boater from a hook on the wall and tied it around her head. "But I haven't a spare moment now."

She left her room and descended the

stairs at the stern of the *Jubilee Palace* which led to the porch where she had secured her bicycle. Just the thought of pedaling into town lifted Gwen's spirits. How she'd missed the freedom she experienced during every encounter with her beloved Monarch.

On the second level of the showboat she paused a moment to consider the occupants behind the several doors that opened onto the landing from this part of the vessel. These were the rooms of the *Jubilee* actors and musicians. She'd learned from Phineas Johnson that the eight band members shared two rooms, Sir Clyde and Jason DeVane shared one, and Anabel Whitedove and Marianne Dresden each had her own tiny quarters.

Just as well, Gwen thought, imagining the friction if the two women had been forced to share sleeping arrangements. Miss Whitedove's resentment of Marianne had been made quite clear the night before. No evidence of discord was evident at this early hour, however. All the doors were closed, the occupants either in town or still sleeping.

When Gwen reached the porch at the stern of the *Jubilee*, she inhaled a strong aroma of tobacco. It was not an unpleasant smell. In fact, it reminded her of cherries and the tobacco blend her father had often used. Satisfied that the Monarch bicycle was where she'd left it the day before, Gwen looked around the porch to determine the identity of the smoker. She gasped with surprise when she realized the person drawing on the stem of a plain birchbark pipe was none other than Anabel Whitedove, who was seated in a chair facing the river.

Reacting to the unexpected disturbance, Anabel whirled about and glared at Gwen. Reading material, immediately recognizable as a copy of *Belle of the Ozarks*, dropped from her hand and into her lap. Strands of loose raven hair blew around Anabel's face which was now free of tints and powder and etched with telltale creases of age. It was a different, but not unpleasant, change from the actress's appearance at dinner. The pipe hung limp from her hand.

"I . . . I'm sorry to disturb you," Gwen said.

Anabel clutched the lapels of an old bathrobe whose color had grown nondescript with time and many washings. "No one ever comes out on this porch," she said almost as an accusation. "It can't even be nine o'clock yet."

"It is just barely past that hour," Gwen said. "I came to retrieve my bicycle for a trip into town."

Anabel slid her chair away from the railing and stared at the Monarch leaning against the back wall of the boat. "Oh, that silly looking thing," she said. "Belongs in a circus, not on a showboat. Defies gravity and tempts fate if you ask me."

Gwen smiled. "I'd be glad to teach you to ride," she said.

"Not on your life," Anabel snapped. "I'm satisfied to let the doctor mend *your* bones, not mine."

Bridging an uncomfortable silence, Gwen said, "I didn't see you at breakfast this morning."

Anabel snorted through her nose, a most unladylike sound. "And you aren't likely to either, though Peaches stubbornly keeps the food warm for hours, just in case I change my mind." She pointed to an empty mug by her feet. "Coffee is all I can stomach before noon." She grabbed the unruly mass of her hair and twisted it over one shoulder. "You'll learn that about show people, Miss Barlow. We don't need energy in the mornings. We need sleep."

"I'll remember. And please, call me Gwen."

Though she didn't offer the same informality in return, Miss Whitedove's eyebrows arched slightly, perhaps a sign of surprise at Gwen's token of friendship. She nodded. "All right, Gwen."

Knowing Travis would be a few minutes longer completing his errand, Gwen moved to stand at the railing beside Anabel's chair. At the moment she decided that getting to know this elusive member of the *Jubilee* family could be just as important as her appointment with the constable. "Your name is quite unusual, Miss Whitedove," she said. "Can you tell me its origin?"

Anabel's eyes narrowed. "Are you making fun now, *Miss Barlow?*"

"Certainly not. Why would you think that?"

"Because it's no secret. Everyone knows. In fact, Eli used my heritage as a pitch, an oddity to draw in crowds. It worked in the little joints he set me up in when we were in New Orleans." She passed her hand across the Mississippi horizon as if painting an imaginary sign. "See beautiful Anabel Whitedove, full-blooded Cherokee Indian, last of a dying breed . . ." A sneer

100

twisted her mouth when she added, "Only one thin dime." She dropped her hand and looked at Gwen. "He even had Manfred Kruger, the printer here in Hickory Bend, do up posters with those very words."

"I see," Gwen answered placidly, though inside her heart was racing. She'd never met an Indian, and she was fascinated to know more.

"It's a lie, of course," Anabel said. "I'm only one-quarter Cherokee. My grandmother is full-blooded. And we're not dying at all . . . not any more at least. There are hundreds of us living perfectly comfortable lives in North Carolina." She grimaced before taking a drag on the pipe. "Unfortunately I was never too satisfied with comfortable."

Gwen tried not to show her disappointment that Anabel's exotic heritage was really just a sideshow gimmick. "So how did you meet Eli Willoughby?" she asked.

Anabel looked away, but not before Gwen heard that same disdainful snort. "I met him at a saloon in New Orleans. He fancied me . . . or rather my singing. Promised me an acting career. That was eight years ago." She laughed, but it was a bitter sound. "Don't it beat all, Gwen? The minute he keeps his promise, or sort of keeps it anyway, he up and dies on me."

Hardly a sympathetic reaction to the loss of an eight-year companion, Gwen thought.

"But you're still an actress, Miss Whitedove." Gwen pointed to the script on Anabel's lap. "And I see you're learning your part."

Anabel's cool violet gaze seemed to be lit with backfires when it settled on Gwen's face. "Yeah. My *new* script. I was supposed to be Belle. The part was written for me, and Eli promised I'd get to do it. He said he was looking for an older woman to play Belle's aunt." Anabel rolled up her script and tapped it against her palm. A deceptive calm settled over her, accompanied by the rhythmic beat of the paper. Sort of like the gentle swish of leaves before a cyclone. "So what does Eli do? Hires that pasty Marianne and tells me she's going to play Belle. I either play the aunt or it's nothing."

So that explained Anabel's resentment of Marianne. As well as a resentment of Eli. "I didn't know," Gwen said.

"I forgave Eli an awful lot in the last eight years. But I vowed the day he brought Marianne Dresden to the *Jubilee*, that I'd never forgive him that."

Anabel twisted the script with both hands until it was nearly as thin as a poker. She looked over the water once more, saying nothing until Gwen was convinced she had forgotten her presence. She hadn't.

She sucked on the stem of the pipe and blew a long stream of cherry scented smoke into the air. Then, her voice hardly above a whisper, she said, "You'd best get along on your bicycle, Gwen. Go away and leave me so I can learn this part and, like you said last night, 'not hold us back.' "

The *Jubilee Palace* was situated next to a sloping, rocky embankment which just the day before had been slick with mud and practically untraversable. Amazed at the difference a dry night and sunny morning could make, Gwen effortlessly walked her Monarch around a few shallow ruts and up the incline until she was on level ground.

She pointed the bicycle north where, a few hundred yards away, a shady copse of shagbark hickory trees invited her to take a closer inspection. Knowing the showboat would never be out of sight, and she wouldn't miss seeing Travis Veazey return from his errand, she headed in that direction. The sun was warm on her face, yet the breeze from the river was cool and re-freshing. A perfect day for a ride. De-lighted to be perched on the comfortable saddle again, Gwen pedaled mightily for a time and then coasted along the narrow path bordered by wild strawberries and Queen Anne's Lace. She stretched her legs out from the sides of the bicycle and re-sisted the urge to let out a whoop of sheer joy. She would have to be much more iso-lated than the outskirts of a populated town to actually whoop.

When she reached the grove of trees, she stopped, straddled the bicycle and let her gaze meander along with the lazy flow of the Mississippi. Her thoughts, however, were not as carefree as the river. They wandered stubbornly back to Anabel Whitedove.

Gwen now knew for certain that Anabel harbored a great deal of resentment and anger, and the object of her ill will seemed to be as much Eli Willoughby as it was Marianne Dresden. There was a coarse-ness about Anabel, a hardness of heart that all but masked her pleasing, exotic attrib-utes — and made her appear a most formi-dable enemy. Still, assuming that Constable O'Toole was right in his as-sumption about Eli's fate, could Anabel have been enemy enough to execute Eli's demise?

"No, I won't believe it," Gwen said, knowing full well it was an untested loyalty to the *Jubilee* family, people she scarcely knew, that made her say this. Naturally she was reluctant to believe that any one on the showboat could have murdered her uncle. Yet he was indeed quite dead. That fact was indisputable, and the list of possible assailants was growing longer with each passing hour.

Shielding her eyes and peering into the distance toward town, Gwen saw Travis. His slow, loping gate was easily recognizable. Who else strode with such a devil-take-it attitude? She pushed off from the ground and headed back to meet him, leaving her amateur investigating for later.

"He said he'd see you," Travis called before Gwen had even slowed down her bicycle. Without waiting, the youth took a sharp right turn toward the showboat. "Hope they're still biting," he mumbled.

Gwen stopped long enough to call to Travis's back. "Thank you so much, Travis."

He managed a disinterested wave and kept walking. "Yeah."

A few minutes later, Gwen rode down

the center of Main Street. Surprisingly, in the early hour, the town of Hickory Bend seemed not much different from Apple Creek. The gambling establishments were closed and shuttered. A few saloons had already opened for the day, something the village council of Apple Creek would never have allowed before noon. Gwen glanced in the windows and saw patrons at the bars.

The rest of Main Street could have been any town with modest businesses doing respectably well. As she passed Davenport's General Store, Gwen decided she would stop on her way back to the *Jubilee* and purchase a basket lunch. It was a way to begin making amends with the proprietor for her uncle's debts.

She noted the location of the post office, thinking she might write a letter to Harold Latimer. He had indicated during their last meeting in Apple Creek that he would participate in a correspondence, provided she initiated it of course. She also noted the building belonging to Manfred Kruger, the town printer. Since Uncle Eli owed that man money too, Gwen supposed she ought to pay Mr. Kruger a visit as well.

As she progressed through town, she noticed that one factor distinguished Hickory

Bend from Apple Creek. Several shop-keepers and customers had ventured onto the sheltered porches protecting business entrances and simply stood there watching her ride by. In Apple Creek no one stared at a woman on a bicycle as if she might suddenly sprout wings and fly — at least not anymore. Gwen smiled to herself. She would have to educate the women of the Mississippi, just as she had educated those of Apple Creek, about the benefits of cycling to both mind and body.

The constable's office was the last building on Main Street before the town boundary gave way to the hard-packed shady road whose winding path Gwen and her family had taken from LaGrange just the day before. She stopped, leaned her bicycle against a hitching post, and entered the office.

Constable O'Toole's chair squeaked on its hinges when the big man looked up from paperwork and rocked backwards. He patted his hand over his midsection and gave Gwen a halfhearted grin. "Well, well, Miss Barlow. Been expecting you since that no-account Veazey boy blew in here a while ago."

O'Toole motioned for her to sit in a straight-backed chair across the desk from his. He reached for a pencil threaded through his thick gray hair and tapped it on the desk. "Why old man Willoughby hired that shanty boat trash Veazey, I'll never know. Built that damned boat like it was fit for royalty, then hired a nineteen-year-old dock rat to work on it." Laughter sputtered from O'Toole's thick lips. "Surprised that ragbag hasn't robbed you of your brass fittings."

Resentment, black and strong as Peaches's coffee, bubbled in Gwen's stomach. True, she also had her doubts about Travis Veazey, but that didn't give the constable a right to voice his venomous opinion against a member of the *Jubilee* family. She made a mental note to investigate the term "shanty boat," knowing it would provide a clue to Travis's background.

She sat in the chair O'Toole offered, but remained straight as a fence post, her hands folded in her lap. She kept her straw boater tied under her chin, a sign to the constable that this wasn't a social call. "Has Travis committed a crime, Mr. O'Toole?" she asked, still bristling about his opinion of the young man.

The constable narrowed one eye at her. "Not yet. Or not that I know of. But you're not here to talk about him, are you, ma'am?"

"No." *Get right to the point, Gwen.* "I'm here to plead for your compassion and sense of reason with regard to the *Jubilee Palace.*"

Obviously enjoying his upper hand in this situation, O'Toole steepled his fingers and peered at Gwen over them. "And just how might I show this compassion, Miss Barlow?"

Gwen never minced words when a direct approach was best. "By letting the *Jubilee* leave," she said. "Constable, the showboat is experiencing a slight cash problem at the moment. It seems my uncle, while no doubt well intentioned, irresponsibly left several debts . . ."

"Willoughby was flat busted, Miss Barlow."

Apparently the constable didn't mince words either. And was somewhat lacking in that needed compassion. "Well . . ."

"Half the population of Hickory Bend has been waiting for you folks to get here so you could settle up his bills."

Gwen leaned forward, thinking she'd take advantage of the constable's state-ment. "I would very much like to do that, Mr. O'Toole, but even you must admit that if the showboat is not making any money, then the debts cannot be repaid."

"I don't admit that at all. You folks could pay them."

"We certainly cannot," Gwen stated emphatically.

His eyes widened under bushy gray brows. "You mean you don't have any money?"

"You needn't sound so disappointed, Constable. But no, we don't."

"That's not going to make Davenport and Kruger too happy. They lost the most, dealing with Willoughby."

"I know that. I'm perfectly willing to do anything within reason to settle my uncle's affairs, but I won't be able to do that if we're forced to remain in Hickory Bend. We've already paid for our licenses up north."

Sensing that she hadn't convinced the constable of the seriousness of their plight, Gwen softened her attitude, sacrificing her own sometimes too rigid logic for a more helpless, superficially female tactic, one which she'd heard men responded to. "Please, Mr. O'Toole, let us leave. I give you my word that I will send regular payments to the businesses that have suffered due to my uncle's negligence. I want to restore his good name . . ."

" 'Course you do," O'Toole said with a smirk. "He was your kin after all. Bet you hate to think that somebody mighta murdered him."

"Yes, I hate to think of it. In fact, I'm not at all convinced someone did."

Gwen didn't consider this last statement to be an outright lie. While she did lean toward the belief that her uncle was murdered, she still entertained a modicum of doubt in the matter. And she hoped she could use this doubt to persuade the constable to let the *Jubilee* leave Hickory Bend. "Was there a post mortem performed, Mr. O'Toole?" she asked.

" 'Course there was. And it showed that Willoughby's head was bashed in by a heavy piece of scenery. But a post mortem can't tell you who dropped it on him."

"Or, indeed, if someone *did* drop it."

O'Toole's fist came down hard on his desk top. "Well, I'm convinced that someone did, Miss Barlow. Your own people told me how that rigging was as tight as a fat lady's corset. That means to me that somebody messed with it. Fact is, I might even consider you a suspect because of that monstrosity of an inheritance Willoughby left you. But I figure if you did do the deed, you're being punished enough having to deal with the passel of problems your generous uncle left behind."

Gwen smiled sweetly, though inside her blood boiled. She recognized a counter tactic when she saw it and resented the implied threat. "Of course you considered the fact that I wasn't even in the same state as my uncle when he passed away . . ."

His lips curled at the corners in a tight grin. "Not that I know of." He spread his fingers and began to enumerate on one hand. "Let's look at the facts, Miss Barlow. Your uncle had a pile of enemies, some in town, some even in that cozy little social club of actors on the *Jubilee*. Motive — that's the key to investigating any murder, and I can think of a whole list of people who had a motive to knock off Willoughby. I was willing to believe the accident theory for a while, but not after one of your own set me to thinking again. Why was Willoughby in the theater, in the dark? Why did he just happen to be standing under a piece of equipment that had the capacity to turn his brains to curdled milk? And why did that fancy rigging of his just all the sudden drop like an anvil from the ceiling?"

Gwen winced at O'Toole's description,

but had to admit he posed all good questions. Ones Gwen had thought of herself. Eli Willoughby probably had been murdered. Still, Gwen hated to think that a member of the *Jubilee* troupe . . .

"Constable," she said, "I assume you interviewed the people on the showboat and noted their whereabouts at the time of my uncle's death."

"I didn't get this job yesterday, Miss Barlow. Of course I interviewed each and every one of them . . . the same bunch that's still there living off the fat of Hickory Bend charity."

Charity? Ingenuity was more like it. Gwen mentally added another reason not to like the constable. "And?"

"Seeing as it was the middle of the night, your happy little family were all tucked in their warm little beds. That's what they told me anyway, and I had no reason to dispute their stories . . . at least at the time I didn't. The only one out roaming around that night was Eli himself."

"And the killer, if your theory is correct," Gwen hastened to point out. "Do you know why Uncle Eli was up at that hour?"

"He'd just come in from a poker game at Hattie McBride's place."

Gwen sat forward, placing her elbows on the constable's desk. How interesting. Depending on the outcome, a poker game might provide other motives. "Did you question the players?"

O'Toole shot her a smug grin. "Naturally. Your uncle, who was drunk as a skunk that night, by the way, lost his shirt, like he usually did. Ain't anybody who won money in a poker game gonna murder the loser. No, ma'am, we gotta look to someone else as the murderer. Plain and simple.

"After yesterday's visit from one of the *Jubilee* tribe, I started thinking again. I wondered at the time why ropes could have come loose from a pulley. Now that I hear someone on your showboat believes Willoughby was murdered, I figure the culprit who done him in arranged for a knot to slip. Or he tampered with a counterweight. It's all there staring us in the face. We just have to figure it out."

Gwen now knew she wouldn't win her argument. The *Jubilee Palace* wasn't going anywhere, and she would have to cooperate with the constable. "Indeed, sir," she said. "And the sooner the better, since there's nothing I can do to change your mind about the *Jubilee* leaving."

"Nope. There isn't. But I will promise you this. I'm making your uncle's death a top priority. And you can help."

"How can I do that?"

"By keeping those pretty little ears open. Just listen, Miss Barlow, to the scuttlebutt around that boat."

As if she wasn't already! But she did intend to check O'Toole's findings to discover for herself just exactly where each inhabitant of the *Jubilee* was at the time of the murder.

"Keep your eyes open, too," the constable added. "Watch what's going on around you. You come tell me any little ol' thing that seems strange to you and we'll track it down. Might save your own life in the process." He stood up, dismissing her. "Have a nice day now, ma'am, and we'll talk soon."

Gwen stopped at the office door and turned back to O'Toole. "I'd like you to remember one thing, Constable," she said.

"What's that, Miss Barlow?"

"Just because a person has enemies doesn't mean he'll be murdered. I would think you'd know that as well as anyone."

Her confidence restored, Gwen left the office and retrieved her bicycle. She'd failed in her mission, but oddly she didn't feel discouraged. Deep down she knew the constable was right. Uncle Eli had been the victim of foul play. And they simply had to figure it out.

Chapter Six

Before returning to the *Jubilee Palace*, Gwen remembered her promise to make amends with the people who were owed money by Uncle Eli. And at the same time she hoped to learn more about who her uncle's true enemies might be.

She went first to a one-story, clapboard building next to the much larger Hickory Bend Hotel. The smaller building was stained a pleasing gold color, like the shade of an autumn maple leaf. A sign swinging from the porch ceiling, as well as script in both front windows, identified the establishment as *Manfred Kruger's Printing Service*. Gwen parked her bicycle outside and stepped through the entrance of the printing office.

The interior was tidy and neat, surprising for a printing company. Giant wheels and levers operated machines that clicked and hummed as they spit out sheets of paper. Supplies were stacked on shelves and identified with clear, precise handwriting on the cartons. The pungent, oily aroma of ink pervaded the room but was not overwhelming since the windows were open. A few pieces of shredded or crumpled paper littered the floor, but there were no telltale smudges of black on the walls or wainscoting which one might expect in such an establishment.

A tall, broad-shaped man with a balding pate and short, trim chin beard approached Gwen. The front of his shirt and trousers was covered by a long white apron which had obviously been through many launderings. Faded gray splotches were ingrained in the comfortably worn canvas fabric.

"May I help you?" he asked in a clipped, precise German accent. "I am Manfred Kruger."

"Yes, thank you." Gwen offered her hand. "My name is Gwendolyn Barlow. My family and I have recently . . ."

The welcoming smile that the man had affected for a new customer slid downward to become a frown, and he stuck both his hands in his apron pockets. "I know who you are. A relative of Willoughby's. And as such, you can only do business here if you pay cash."

Gwen supposed she should understand the man's attitude. Still, to be a stranger in town and to be treated with such obvious

118

disrespect rankled. She dropped her hand to her side. "I assure you, Mr. Kruger, that I have no intention of further increasing my family's debt to you. As a matter of fact, I stopped by today to discuss this matter."

Skepticism veiled his eyes, but it was preferable to the outright scorn that had been there a moment before. "Oh, really?" he said.

"I would like a complete accounting of what my uncle owes your company for your services. As soon as I'm able, I will begin paying back the debt."

Kruger removed his hands from his pockets and planted them on his wide hips. "That's easy enough, Miss Barlow. Eli Willoughby owed me one hundred and twelve dollars!"

A small fortune! Gwen was just beginning to contemplate the magnitude of the debt when movement from the back of the shop caught her eye. A buxom young girl with full, rounded hips skirted the machinery and came toward her in a rustling swell of turquoise satin and white ruffles. Artistically fashioned finger curls in rich, golden blond framed a moon-shaped face that was split with a wide grin. A similarity in build to Manfred Kruger clearly indicated that this ebullient girl was a relative.

She snatched Gwen's hand before Gwen even offered it. "Miss Barlow!" she cried, pumping furiously. "I've been dying to meet you."

Dumbstruck, Gwen looked up into startling blue eyes. The young woman was a good three inches taller than she.

Mr. Kruger snorted his opinion of this meeting, and the girl waggled a finger at him in warning. "I'll have none of your grumpiness, Papa. I won't have you spoil my meeting with Miss Barlow. Leave us alone so we can get acquainted. I've been wanting to meet her since she came to town, and I won't let you scare her off like you do all my friends."

Friends? Had they gone from a handshake to this intimacy?

Kruger glared at his daughter, disapproval darkening his gray eyes. "Have your little chat, Hildegard. It'll come to no more than the last one did. And you, Miss Barlow, mind that figure I've given you. We'll see if *your* word's any better than your uncle's."

Intending to utter some phrase of sincerity to convince Kruger of her good intentions, Gwen ended up muttering a few syllables at his back. He stormed off, apparently washing his hands of both females. Then, without warning, she was forcibly pulled toward a small sitting area enclosed within a three-foot wood fence. Once inside the swinging entrance gate, Hildegard commanded, "Sit, Miss Barlow," while backing Gwen into a padded oak chair.

Hildegard sat across from Gwen, blue eyes glittering and large white teeth gleaming. "I do so adore the theater," she gushed. "I have many talents in that area, and you must let me tell you about them. I can act wonderfully well, but that's not all. I can paint scenery, and procure props, and, why, probably even direct! I can work the lights. I'm familiar with electrical currents because of working here in the shop. But what I most want to do is act . . ."

Gwen's head buzzed with the seemingly endless listing of Hildegard's talents. At the first indication that the girl might actually take a breath, Gwen held up her hand. "Am I to assume, Miss Kruger, that you are seeking employment?"

Hildegard clutched her two hands over her ample bosom and cried, "You're so intuitive, Miss Barlow." The long finger curls quivered around her face. "Yes! Absolutely. Mr. Willoughby wanted to hire me as soon as we met."

"He did?" Conscious of the high-pitched tone of her voice, Gwen spoke more sedately. "He did. Really?"

"Why, yes. He even asked Papa for permission. The two of them talked the whole thing through."

A gruff snort came from the other side of the office, indicating Mr. Kruger was listening to every word. "And it cost me a pretty penny too," he said. "Your bill should be twice what it is, Miss Barlow. But that conniving uncle of yours promised Hildegard a part in his play, so I lowered my customary rate."

Mr. Kruger's face, pink with anger, was visible through an open shelf of ink bottles just beyond the sitting area. Gwen felt her own cheeks flush with color. So this was why the printer was so angry and bitter. She already suspected the end of this tale.

"Reneged on the deal, too," Kruger added as confirmation. "Broke my little Hildy's heart, and left me holding the bill for printing materials provided at half their value."

Hildegard placed soft, plump hands on Gwen's cheeks and pulled Gwen's attention back to what really mattered . . . her. "Never mind him, Miss Barlow," she said.

"Papa could rant on for hours. Besides, that's all in the past. Mr. Willoughby's dead, after all. You and I don't have to pay attention to all that old history. Now about a position on the *Jubilee Palace* . . . goodness knows, I adore that boat. Some people say it's outrageous to a fault, but not me. I would do anything . . ."

The tinkling of the front doorbell broke Hildegard's concentration for a moment. It was followed by an oath from her father. "Isn't this a fine day?" he snapped. "Here's another one."

Hildegard bounded up and scurried out of the sitting room leaving Gwen to stare at the flounce of her skirt. "Buddy!" she called. "How wonderful. Your sister's here, too."

Buddy? Gwen turned slowly in her chair. Who in the world was Buddy? Surely not Preston . . .

But there he was, standing in the doorway, shifting his weight from one foot to the other. Guilt was evident in the impish brown eyes that settled fleetingly on his sister. "Hi, Gwennie. Didn't know you would be here."

"Nor I you, Preston."

Hildegard picked up a long, narrow box and gave it to Preston. "Here, Buddy. I told you we could have them done in a couple of hours. Just like you ordered. Calling cards with your name printed across the top. *Buddy Barlow, Actor and Showboat Entrepreneur.*" She pulled a rectangular card from the box and held it up for his approval. "Doesn't it look grand?"

Had the entire world gone mad? Or just the unfortunate folks breathing Hickory Bend air? Gwen continued to stare at her brother as she stood up and walked slowly toward him.

Mr. Kruger joined the group and held out his hand. "That'll be three dollars, Barlow," he said. "No credit."

Preston fished in his pocket and thrust three bills at the printer. "Right. I remember."

Hildegard looked from one to the other of the Barlows. "Now, let's get back to me. Miss Barlow, Buddy said you and he would most definitely be interested in talking to me about a position of importance on the *Jubilee* . . ."

"Oh, Buddy said that, did he?" Gwen took Preston's arm and turned him around. After a well-placed jab to his spine, he was out the door. "I haven't time now, Hildegard," Gwen said. "My brother and I have something to settle."

A pout tugged unpleasantly on Hildegard's lips. "Oh, pooh. Well, I guess if you have to go . . ." Then brightening again, she added, "I'll come see you on the showboat. Soon. Tomorrow morning!"

Rising on her toes, Gwen pressed her mouth to Preston's ear and said through clenched teeth, "Thanks for getting me into this mess, *Buddy!*"

"I can explain . . ."

They walked toward Gwen's bicycle as Manfred Kruger called out a warning. "Don't forget that figure, Miss Barlow. One hundred and twelve dollars!"

"Hold on, Gwennie!"

Preston's hollering only induced Gwen to pedal faster. She didn't intend to stop in the middle of Main Street and air her complaints in front of the citizens of Hickory Bend. And she knew once she started giving Preston a piece of her mind, her temper would blow like a geyser. She passed Davenport's General Store without a thought to stopping. Trying to smooth Mr. Kruger's ruffled feathers was enough for one day.

Even though she didn't look back, Gwen sensed Preston was running like the dickens to keep up with her. "That's fine with me," she announced to the wind in her face. "Let him run and holler till his lungs burst!"

Once at the *Jubilee*, Gwen raced over the gangway and coasted all the way down the promenade to the stern deck. While she secured the Monarch to a porch rail, she looked for Anabel Whitedove. Good. The actress had left. There was no one in this area of the *Jubilee* but her . . . and soon Preston.

He skidded around the corner, nearly colliding with her. "For Pete's sake, Gwen, you didn't have to make me run all the way back."

"I didn't make you run anywhere," she said. "And I couldn't care less if you ever came back."

He managed a stricken expression — purely pretense of course. Maybe he was an actor after all. "Why? Just because I bought some calling cards? I figured it was a good way to get back in with the printer."

"Hogwash! You did it for yourself. What do you think you're doing changing your name and introducing yourself as an actor . . . not to mention 'entrepreneur of the *Jubilee Palace*'?"

His facial features mutated from stricken to sheepish. "Well, I did write that addition to the script. And I figured after you read it . . . and what's so wrong with calling myself an entrepreneur? I plan to live up to that title."

"By doing what? Hiring gushing, scatterbrained girls in exchange for a favor? Uncle Eli already tried that!"

Preston clutched the box of calling cards close to his chest. "I had to do something. Mr. Kruger about bit my head off when I stepped into that printing office and introduced myself. When Hildegard found out who I was, she talked her father into taking my special order . . . after I sort of promised her we'd think about a place for her on the *Jubilee*. I only said *think*, Gwennie. I said the final decision was yours."

For a moment Gwen could only shake her head in dismay. "And I'm supposed to be grateful for that? Frankly, Preston, I think our *entrepreneur* ought to take care of it."

His face brightened at the prospect of issuing his first executive order. "Really? Because I'd probably hire her and be done with it. I bet her father would cancel that printing bill. I don't think anything else will because Hildegard hated Uncle Eli almost as much as her father did."

Gwen threw her hands up in frustration.

"I was kidding, *Buddy!*" But all at once the calling cards and Preston's future acting career faded to insignificance. "What did you say? Hildegard truly hated him?"

Relieved that the topic of conversation had switched from his crimes to someone else's, Preston set down the box of cards and settled into the chair Anabel had vacated. "You bet. I guess when Eli refused to hire her as an actress after promising to, it really popped her cork."

Good heavens. Did anyone in Hickory Bend actually like Eli Willoughby? Besides Marianne Dresden, that is. Gwen had many reasons to doubt it. She walked away from Preston and headed for the back entrance to the kitchen.

"Where are you going?" he asked.

"To get something to eat. I'm starving. And I have a headache."

He jumped up from the chair. "I'll go with you."

"No you won't. I'm taking whatever I can find that's edible up to my room. And if you dare come near there, I'll throw you overboard."

Gwen had never been fond of fish, and the smell of frying catfish in the *Jubilee* kitchen only exacerbated her headache.

Travis Veazey, his hair hanging down in his eyes, stood next to the huge stove. He had a large platter in his hand. With a spatula, Peaches scooped several breaded filets from a sizzling skillet onto Travis's plate.

Without so much as a mumble of thanks, Veazey dug into the golden fried fish with the gusto of a person who hadn't seen food in days.

"You git, now you got your lunch," Peaches said. "And don't come back in this kitchen till you've at least washed those hands!"

Travis looked at the hand holding his fork and shrugged. Obviously his eye found nothing objectionable at all. Nevertheless he shuffled toward the back entrance. When he saw Gwen he stopped in his tracks and glared at her. "I ain't doing no more errands now, lady," he said. "So if you got a pile of 'em stored up, you find somebody else to do your bidding. It's lunchtime for ol' Veazey."

Wondering again why her uncle had hired this disagreeable fellow, Gwen stepped out of the way to let him pass. "I have no intention of disturbing your lunch, Travis. But with an attitude like yours, I might very well disturb your next paycheck!"

Breaking into a strong stride, Travis breezed by her. "Hah!" he called over his shoulder. "That'll be a fine day!"

Gwen couldn't prevent a shudder of distaste.

Peaches wiped her hands on her apron and chuckled. "Don't pay him no mind, Miss Barlow. Travis is like that with everybody. It's like he's got a slingshot aimed at the world, and folks better stay out of his way."

Gwen went to the larder and began to scrounge for something to eat. She settled for a wedge of cheese and the remainder of this morning's biscuits and set them on a table. "I don't understand him at all," she said. "I should think Travis would be grateful to my uncle for hiring him. From everything I can see, the boy doesn't deserve a job or a salary." *Even one that has been withheld for a time,* she thought to herself.

Peaches ambled over to the table and watched Gwen wrap her food in a checkered napkin. "That's not really the way it is," she said.

Gwen picked up her package and looked at Peaches. "What do you mean?"

"What I mean is, Travis don't exactly get a salary. Don't get me wrong. I don't much

130

admire the boy. He's disrespectful and contrary, but he's got more reason than most around here to complain. He never got one penny from Mr. Willoughby."

Gwen was incredulous. "He's never been paid?"

"Nope. Mr. Willoughby didn't exactly hire him. He got him on trade."

Disbelief was slowly building to outrage. Trading human beings? "What are you saying, Peaches?"

"Travis was part of a shanty boat family that drew up alongside the *Jubilee* just after Mr. Willoughby got here."

There was that term again. Shanty boat. Apparently its connotation was as disagreeable as Gwen had thought.

"Them people was starving. There was a half dozen kids, not to mention a couple of old coon dogs, all of 'em living in a little one-room cabin on a log raft. The pappy asked Mr. Willoughby for a handout. A lot of folks along the river don't mind giving to the poor shanties, but I guess Mr. Willoughby thought different."

"He wouldn't give them anything?"

"Oh, he eventually did. Gave 'em a basket of potatoes and a side of bacon, some other things as I recall. But he made darned certain he got something in return."

131

The tightening knot in Gwen's stomach told her what that something was. Apparently her uncle equated a boy's life with a sack of potatoes and some bacon. "Uncle Eli bartered for Travis." It was more a statement than a question.

Peaches chuckled at the expression on Gwen's face. "Don't look so put out, Miss Barlow. Travis done all right in this deal. He's got a place to sleep and three meals a day, and no young 'uns nipping at his heels day and night. Compared to where that chile come from, he's living like royalty."

"But still, he receives no pay for his work, as difficult as it may be to get any out of him." Gwen shook her head. "That amounts to slavery, Peaches, and is strictly outlawed in this country."

Peaches drew herself up straight as a broom handle. "Respectfully, Miss Barlow," she said in a voice edged with defiance, "it ain't nothing like that. Phineas and me — we lived those slave times, and Travis is a whole lot better off than we were."

Gwen patted the woman's hand. "I'm sorry, Peaches. I didn't mean . . ."

Peaches waved away Gwen's apology. " 'Course not, honey. I knows that. Just don't worry about dat boy. Like you said yourself, he don't deserve no pay anyhow. And I guarantee he wouldn't go back to that shanty family of his if he had a chance."

"No, probably not."

Peaches poured milk into a crockery mug and handed it to Gwen. "You go on and have your meal, Miss Barlow. We'll all put up with Travis Veazey like we been doing for weeks now. Can't very well toss him out with the catfish bones, now can we?"

Gwen carried her lunch from the kitchen. Behind her, Peaches's mellow chuckling followed her to the stairs.

Gwen hadn't realized how hungry she was. She layered cheese slices between halves of the biscuits and consumed three of the sandwiches and the entire mug of milk in minutes. Feeling pleasantly lazy, she settled back against her pillows and closed her eyes, thinking a short nap would refresh her for the duties that lay ahead. Unfortunately her mind would not cooperate. Her thoughts kept going back to the events of the day.

She'd learned interesting details about several people this morning. Constable O'Toole, while an ill-mannered, unsympathetic individual, would probably do his best to uncover the truth about Uncle Eli's death. And he certainly hadn't been the one to murder him. Then there was Hildegard Kruger. She was a silly chatterbox of a girl who would probably grate on Gwen's nerves endlessly until she found a way into the acting troupe of the *Jubilee*, but no matter how strongly she resented Eli for breaking his word to her, surely she wouldn't have murdered the man who could most help her accomplish her goals.

But Anabel Whitedove, Travis Veazey, and Manfred Kruger — their relationships with Eli were a different, more sinister, story. These people did not try to hide their dislike of Eli. But would the printer kill Eli over a hundred-dollar debt and a broken promise? Would Anabel resort to murder to avenge her pride and feelings of rejection? Would Travis do away with Eli over being traded away from his shanty boat family for Eli's offer of potatoes and bacon?

After a few minutes, Gwen gave up the idea of trying to sleep. She sat up in bed and reached for the script which lay beside her on the coverlet. "I might as well get started on this," she said and opened the cover to the first page.

Belle of the Ozarks was, Gwen supposed, a typical melodrama, but in her opinion it was probably better than most. The opening scene depicted Belle, grieving over the death of her father, welcoming her kindly aunt at the train station in a small Arkansas town. Belle bemoaned the fact that her father left her responsible for a small hotel and the many debts he had incurred over the years to keep the place running.

"Hmmm . . ." Gwen chewed on the tip of her fingernail. "A man dies leaving a mountain of debts for someone else to take care of. Now I can believe this was written by Uncle Eli!"

Belle's kind Aunt Winnifred, who would now be played by Anabel Whitedove, has come to the town to help her niece run the hotel. Unfortunately, help is all Winnifred can offer since she has no money to add to the hotel's coffers. Enter Mr. Benedict Crenshaw, the town's menacing, boorish, British banker, and mortgage holder of the hotel's deed.

"Perfect casting for Sir Clyde," Gwen said.

Of course, Mr. Crenshaw would consider postponing the overdue mortgage payment for another month if sweet Belle would consider him a serious suitor. Never mind that he's thirty years her elder, and a low-down snake. His lascivious advances to Belle in broad daylight would surely bring hisses and boos from the showboat audience. Just as the actions of Belle's defender, the town's handsome sheriff, would elicit cheers. This was a perfect role for handsome Jason DeVane.

"Not bad," Gwen said, coming at last to the unbound pages of script that had been added by her brother. "This is hardly worthy of a British stage, but I should think it would do nicely for a showboat audience. I understand that hooting and hollering is all part of the entertainment."

She picked up the first page written in Preston's bold script. "Now let's see where you put yourself in this little saga of good and evil, *Buddy* Barlow," she said.

She read a few lines of dialogue depicting the first meeting at the hotel between Roderick Manley, Buddy's character, and Belle, and laughed out loud. "Preston, really! An umbrella salesman come to save the day and help pay Belle's debts?"

Though she had a difficult time visualizing a parasol-peddling hero, Gwen had to admit that Roderick was a likeable chap. His chivalrous promises to Belle and moral uprightness were sure to bring strong reactions from an excitable showboat crowd. After reading a bit more, Gwen closed the script and set it beside her. "Okay, Buddy, you can do it," she said, imagining his face when she told him. "But remember, Jason DeVane gets the girl in the end. No upstaging allowed."

Gwen left the bed and crossed to the small desk under a window. She sat down and gazed out at the river three stories below. "So, Uncle Eli," she said, "what would you think of your nephew tampering with your play?"

Becoming even more reflective, she added, "In fact, I wonder what you would think of everything that has happened in the last two days. Are you happy that your troupe is still together, at least for now? We are trying, Uncle — Mama, Preston, and I. We're trying to keep your legacy afloat — despite the obstacles you left behind! Like how do we sail without a captain?"

Gwen thought of her second interview with Carson Stockwell scheduled for later that night. She would hire the captain. She'd already decided to trust her instincts. He seemed competent. And he was certainly confident. And most of all, he was willing to work despite the *Jubi-*

lee's financial woes.

"And another thing, Uncle," she said. "I'm especially trying to discover who did you in. I almost wish you *were* a ghost and could talk to me through the spirit world. I have so much to ask you. Like who met you in the theater that night and bashed your head in? And why didn't you hire Carson Stockwell when you had a chance? And why . . ."

She stopped, deciding the logical thing to do would be to write down her questions and possible answers. She opened each drawer of Eli Willoughby's desk, searching for paper and pen. When she opened the bottom drawer, she removed a layer of miscellaneous items and found a small, leather-bound notebook at the back. She pulled it out, thinking to find blank pages upon which she could write. What she discovered instead made her heart race as she repeated the words written across the top of the first page. *The Journal of Eli Willoughby.*

With trembling fingers, she thumbed through the pages, settling on one near the back to read first. "Today I interviewed Carson Stockwell," it said.

Gwen drew in a sharp breath as she focused on her uncle's script. Here at last was one mystery about to unfold. The entry was short and lacked details, a pattern she was to discover about all of Eli's writing, but it definitely revealed her uncle's opinion of the man she had decided to hire to guide the *Jubilee Palace*.

Carson Stockwell is bad luck on a river boat — the worst kind of trouble. I'll make it my business to tell every honest boat owner on the Mississippi to stay away from a captain who's followed by fire! Stockwell is a torch, the scourge of the river!

Gwen clapped her hand over her mouth to stop a gasp of alarm. A torch? Did Carson Stockwell set fire to the boats he captained? An even larger implication slammed into Gwen's conscious thought. Did Uncle Eli really tell everyone on the river not to hire Stockwell? If so, then the captain had his own reason to hate Eli Willoughby.

Taking the journal back to her bed, Gwen plumped the bed pillows against the headboard and settled back to read more. They were all mentioned in Eli's journal: Anabel, Travis, Marianne, the crew, and the people of Hickory Bend. Even the short-lived ex-captain of the *Jubilee*, Solomon Wade. While there were no more startling revelations, Gwen sensed she was reading about a cast of characters in a drama about her uncle's last days. And one of them played the lead role in his death.

Chapter Seven

"Supper's ready, Gwennie!"

This enthusiastic announcement was followed by three loud raps on Gwen's door.

Her eyes flew wide open and she sat up with a start. Eli Willoughby's open journal tumbled from her chest to the mattress. She mumbled a series of confused syllables as she attempted to acclimate to her surroundings. "I must have fallen asleep," she said, though she didn't remember doing so. The last thing she recalled was reading page after page of her uncle's cryptic entries in the journal. But pink-tinged rays of a setting sun, and the clock on her bureau confirmed that an hour had passed since she'd last noticed the details of her environment. "Preston, is that you?" she called, her voice husky with sleep.

"Who else? Peaches sent me to get you for supper. Can I come in?"

Gwen sat on the side of the bed and planted her feet on the floor. She felt more alert when grounded. Her blouse was mussed and pulled loose from the waistband of her skirt. A quick inspection of her hair with the flat of her hand indicated that her topknot had come undone. "No, Preston, you can't," she called back. "Give me a minute to tidy my appearance, and I'll come out. Or go to the dining room and I'll meet you there."

"I'll wait here," he said. "But do hurry. I'm famished."

For what I wonder . . . hopefully not catfish. Gwen padded to her wardrobe for a fresh blouse and then proceeded to the small private lavatory, her favorite feature of Uncle Eli's plush quarters. She splashed cold water on her face, pinched her cheeks to restore color and changed blouses. Then she pulled the remaining three pins from her hair and tied the unruly curls at her nape with a brown ribbon. Frowning at her make-do preparations, she lowered the flame on the gas light in the lavatory, slid her feet into impractical slippers, and went to meet her brother.

Preston turned from the third floor promenade railing when she came out. "Sleeping in the middle of the day, Gwennie?" he said with an accusing grin. "That's what I like about this new venture of ours. The gentle slap of the river against the sides of the showboat, the cool breezes — it's designed to make a body forget the cares of the world."

She leveled a stern glare on him. "Speak for yourself, *Buddy*. I've found more cares here than I ever had in Apple Creek. And if I fell asleep in the middle of the day, it's because I'm exhausted with worrying."

He shrugged and walked toward the stairs. "Right. This murder business can be trying. Why don't you tell me what progress you've made today as we go down to the dining room."

Gwen was dying to talk about the journal and pleased that Preston was showing concern. Even though each contribution Eli made was short and lacked detail, she had learned some interesting tidbits about the *Jubilee* family. "Preston, I found something this afternoon," she said. "It seems our uncle kept a journal. I discovered it in his desk drawer."

Preston stopped and looked at her, his eyes wide. "Really? Did it give you any clues about his murder?"

Unfortunately it hadn't, at least not in a definitive way. But it had confirmed what Gwen had already suspected. "Not in so many words," she said, "but it was quite revealing nevertheless."

Preston resumed walking along the promenade, and Gwen fell in step beside him. "Like how?" he asked.

"Well, for instance, Peaches told me that Travis Veazey . . ."

Preston affected a shiver. "Horrible fella, that one. Like something dragged up from the river bottom."

"Don't be crude, Preston. Anyway, Peaches said he came off a shanty boat, that our uncle actually traded him away from his family for some food staples."

"The family got the best of the deal."

A scathing look was wasted since Preston was staring straight ahead. "Uncle Eli's journal corroborates the story. Plus he wrote that he intended to train Travis to eventually work backstage. If Travis proved worthy, then Eli would pay him a salary. At the time of the journal entry, over three weeks ago, Travis hadn't earned so much as a penny."

Preston nodded. "So you think Veazey bumped off Uncle because he felt he was due a stagehand's wages?"

"No, of course not. At least I doubt it. But it's an example of how people must have felt about Uncle Eli." Gwen shook her head. "I'm sorry to say it, Preston, but our uncle didn't have many friends. If anything, his actions earned him a long list of enemies."

They went down the stairs to the second level. Preston waggled his eyebrows and grinned. "So, Sherlock, tell me more."

"Eli was contemplating firing Anabel Whitedove because of her attitude toward his newest discovery, budding star Marianne Dresden. When he threatened Anabel, it seems she retaliated with undisclosed threats of her own." Gwen sighed and leaned close to Preston's ear. "I'm not certain of this, but I think those threats may have had something to do with a questionable relationship that might have existed between our uncle and Anabel. I think that relationship was more than strictly business."

Preston stopped on the second floor landing and stared at his sister. A hoot of laughter followed his open appraisal of her staid features. "That's what I like about you, Gwennie, your purity of soul. Everyone knows Eli and Anabel had been bed partners for years."

A damnable flush of heat crept into Gwen's cheeks. "Everyone knows?"

"Yep."

Gwen figured she was about to be the recipient of more teasing from her brother, but suddenly Preston's eyes rounded. "He didn't mention having the same relationship with Marianne, did he?"

"No."

"Well, bless his lecherous old soul for that at least." Preston started down the last flight of stairs. "So who else could have hated our dearly departed?"

They were approaching the dining room, and Gwen knew they might be overheard. She quickly summed up the list. "Solomon Wade. Uncle Eli hired him to captain the *Jubilee*, and then fired him the next day."

"Oh, yes, the nasty little incident with Danita Johnson," Preston said.

Of course Preston would know that, too. He bunked with the *Jubilee*'s leading gossip — their mother. "Then there's Manfred Kruger, the printer," Gwen continued. "Uncle Eli made a deal with him to put darling Hildegard on the stage in exchange for reduced printing fees, and then he backed out of the deal. And Carson Stockwell. Eli admitted in the journal that he attempted to ruin the captain's reputation."

"Sounds like Uncle Eli wouldn't win any popularity contests," Preston quipped.

"No. And I have a hunch his list of enemies is even longer. Our uncle had a habit of making promises and not keeping them. And I would say he had a heart of lead."

Preston's features turned thoughtful. "These are all reasons for wishing him dead, Gwennie, but who among this list would most benefit from his death?"

Gwen had her hand on the dining room door, but Preston's question stopped her from opening it. "Of course!" she exclaimed. "Sometimes you amaze me, Preston. I must examine the motives with that very question in mind."

Preston looped his thumbs in his pants pockets and smiled with satisfaction. "Happy to help, Sister, but doesn't one good turn deserve another?"

"What do you mean?"

"I mean you've monopolized this whole conversation and kept me from bringing up what's really important."

For a moment Gwen couldn't imagine what he was talking about. What could be more important than their uncle's murder?

"*Belle of the Ozarks,*" he prompted. "Did you read it or spend all your waking hours poring over Eli's journal?"

Preston's features exhibited all the expectancy of a puppy waiting for a treat. Gwen wouldn't have been surprised if he'd actually started panting with excitement. "I read it," she said, being sure to keep all emotion from her voice.

"And? Don't keep me in suspense. What did you think?"

She yanked open the door to the dining room. "I think I will ask the other actors if they mind your being added to the play. If they don't, then I have no objection."

A huge grin monopolized his face. "They won't mind," he said. "They all love me."

"Sure they do. Anyway, *Buddy*, I hate to see all that money for new business cards go to waste!"

Dinner was delicious, thanks to Dickey Squires's ingenuity. The tugboat captain had spent the day pushing a livestock barge up river to Warsaw. For his efforts he received a modest pay plus a dozen plump, plucked hens, half of which Peaches sectioned and deep fried for dinner. Phineas and Danita spent the day cleaning out a woman's barn on the outskirts of town, for which they'd been given fifty cents, an apple cobbler, and two dozen ears of corn.

Everyone, even the sullen Anabel Whitedove and prim Marianne Dresden, rewarded the clever trio with robust thank you's and hearty appetites. Lillian remarked again on the generous natures of her showboat family. And Gwen had to agree.

For the second night in a row, an unofficial meeting began as soon as the dinner plates were cleared. Gwen briefly explained Preston's addition to the script and gave her own reserved, yet complimentary opinion of his efforts.

Preston beamed with pride.

Gwen then assured the other actors that Preston's first venture into show business would be quite minimal, and until the *Jubilee* began making a profit, he would receive no pay.

Preston frowned at this unexpected bit of news.

In addition, Gwen said, her brother would in no way diminish any other actor's role, and even though his character was basically heroic, he would not get the girl in the end. That honor would still go to Jason DeVane's character.

Preston gritted his teeth.

In a unanimous vote, it was decided that Preston, or rather, Buddy Barlow, could join the acting troupe. Sir Clyde pointed out, however, that the veteran actors didn't have much faith in such a young upstart. Anabel Whitedove agreed to the decision, though not without a grumble or two. "Everyone else gets to join the *Jubilee* troupe, why not this wet-behind-the-ears relative of that no-good Eli?" she said.

And Lillian clapped her hands together and exclaimed, "My son the actor," as if Preston had just saved the world from all catastrophic diseases.

Jason DeVane added, "All right. It's settled. Now if we could only get to perform!"

Gwen scanned the disheartened faces around the dining room tables. "I'm working on that," she said. "I went to see the constable today. He has promised to make the investigation into Eli Willoughby's mysterious death his primary concern. However, he will not let us leave until the murder is solved to his satisfaction."

Sir Clyde rested his elbows on the table and cast a disparaging glance at the ceiling. "And who knows when that will be. Hickory Bend's entire investigative force couldn't match wits with the mongrel who eats the garbage out of Scotland Yard's dust bin."

A general moan of disapproval quieted the actor, but didn't erase a grimace of disgust on his face.

Gwen cleared her throat. "In that regard, I would hope that anyone here who has any knowledge or suspicion about the events of March twenty-fourth, the early morning hours of my uncle's death, would come to me or Constable O'Toole with a full and complete disclosure. Even the smallest detail could be significant. It is, of course, in our own best interest to solve this crime soon."

One of the musicians, a red-haired Irishman named Foley who was noted for his temper, thumped his fist on the table. "She's right, ya' know. We can't go on as if living on the dole forever, scratching a penny here and a nickel there. I hired on with Willoughby to make an honest living."

Murmurs of assent filled the room. "I quite agree," Gwen said. "But until the murder is solved, we must tighten our belts, increase our resolve, and . . ."

"Begging your pardon, Miss Barlow." Dickey Squires pushed back his chair and stood.

"Yes, Mr. Squires?"

"If all we're looking to do is start putting on plays and such, why can't we do that right here in Hickory Bend? Leastways until O'Toole gives us the go-ahead? Seems to me that Hickory Bend ticket money is as good as any ticket money upriver."

The room grew eerily quiet. Everyone stared at Dickey and then slowly at each other. Sir Clyde broke the silence with the low rumble of a deep chuckle that soon erupted into a full-blown belly laugh. Anabel answered with a titter that became a most unladylike chortle. And before long, everyone was shaking their heads.

Gwen covered her mouth to suppress her own laughter. "You know, Mr. Squires," she said, "it seems to me that Hickory Bend money is indeed equal to money anywhere. You have quite astounded me, since one logical solution to our temporary financial troubles has been sitting not ten yards away on this very landing." She turned to Jason DeVane. "Mr. DeVane, can we get a license to perform in Hickory Bend?"

"Don't see why not. As long as we can pay."

Gwen smiled. "I'm quite sure my family can afford the cost of a license."

"I'll see to it first thing in the morning," the actor promised.

Gwen's gaze swept all the tables and encompassed every person present. "It's settled then?"

Amazingly, the entire ensemble of the *Jubilee Palace* was in total, and enthusiastic, agreement.

"In that case," Gwen concluded, "I'll see you all in the theater tomorrow morning at ten for rehearsal."

Anabel groaned. "Ten o'clock in the morning?"

"Yes, Miss Whitedove," Gwen said. "After a nutritious breakfast." She tried not to notice the actress's complexion turn green.

The sun had almost set beyond the trees bordering the riverbank when Gwen left the dining room. She was encouraged that a positive step had been taken with regard to the *Jubilee,* and believed that hope was now the prevailing feeling throughout her showboat family. They all had something to look forward to, assuming Jason DeVane would procure the proper licenses tomorrow morning.

She wandered toward the *Jubilee* theater through a short hallway which ended backstage and divided the Johnsons' quarters and the *Jubilee* kitchen. As Gwen parted the curtain to this area and walked in, she thought again about Preston's innocently probing question. Who did have the most to gain from Eli's death? Nearly all the suspects had motives, but many of them did not seem significant enough to provoke someone to murder. Surely one of the suspects stood to benefit more than the others from Eli Willoughby's death. But who? And was the benefit a monetary one or rather the self-satisfaction that accompanies sweet revenge?

A dim light flickered through a backstage curtain and caught Gwen's attention. It had the characteristics of a flame rather than the steady glow of a gas or electric light, prompting her to assume its origin was a lantern or oil lamp. Was someone here with her, someone who was trying not to attract attention? She stopped at the curtain and whispered loudly, "Who's there?"

"Aw, hell's bells, can't a guy get any privacy on this damn boat?"

Gwen's shoulders sagged with relief. There was no mistaking Travis Veazey's croaking baritone, or his choice of words. "Travis, what are you doing back here?"

He parted the curtain enough for her to see inside. A customary frown pulled at his lips. "I live here, if it's all the same to you."

"You live backstage?" She didn't know why the revelation surprised her. Before this, she hadn't given a thought as to where Travis stayed on the *Jubilee*. All she knew for certain was that Peaches had said

Travis had a mat to sleep on. It bothered her to admit she hadn't cared to ask where it was.

He held back one of the drapes and jerked a thumb toward his sleeping area. "Fit for a king, ain't it, Miss Barlow? Or the king's mutt anyway."

She peeked around Travis's lean frame to get a look at his living conditions. Except for the fact that he had to room with crates and assorted props, it wasn't too bad. He had a warm, dry bedroll with a plump, though noticeably stained, pillow. He had the metal lantern to see by. A few ragged clothes were scattered about. The disgusting fish scaling knife with the buck horn handle was on the bed. Perhaps he slept with his prized possession. Gwen wouldn't have doubted it.

"It's all right," she said. *Certainly better than the cold, hard floor of a shanty cabin.*

"Easy to say when you're the grand lady on the Texas deck," he countered. The lantern light illuminated the sneer on Travis's face. "But I suppose everybody on the *Jubilee* figures it's as good as the likes of me deserves."

"It's better than a lot of people have," she said, thinking to remind him that his family occupied much poorer quarters.

He ignored her remark and assumed an offensive attitude. "So what are you doing sneaking around back here? You thinking to catch me stealing some stage makeup?"

"Of course not. And why must you always assume the worst about everyone?"

He snorted. "It's all what a body gets used to."

It wasn't worth arguing with him, so Gwen simply answered his question. "I was just going to the stage to look around since we'll be rehearsing in the morning."

He picked up the lantern and stepped over his bed roll to retrieve his fishing rod, which was leaning against a stack of cartons. "You look all you want, Miss Barlow. It'll be my pleasure to stay outta your way." Handing her the lantern, he added, "You'd be wise to stay away from the electrical panels back here, unless you want to become Peaches's next fried dinner. If it's just a little look you want, use the lantern."

He walked past her, letting the curtain to his private world fall closed. Before disappearing into the hallway, he turned to face her once more. "And don't touch nothing of mine," he warned.

She nodded. Never had she been given an order that was easier to obey.

Truthfully, it was as much morbid curiosity as investigative snooping which led Gwen, lantern swinging from her hand, to the exact spot where her uncle's body had been found. She could just as easily have waited till the morning when she would see every inch of the *Jubilee* theater in bright sunlight. But no, she was drawn here as dusky night shadows settled over the red and gold seats and carpeted aisles and draped the proscenium in a charcoal cloak. In the eerie stillness of a quiet theater, she felt more in tune with the mysterious factors that had combined to steal the life of Eli Willoughby on another still, dark night three weeks previously.

The backdrop which had plummeted to the stage that night hung suspended above her some fifteen feet. She could just make out the muted lines and hues of verdant mountains and dirt pathways painted against a cream canvas background — the *Jubilee*'s version of an Ozark landscape. The drop was impressive in size, spanning the width of the stage. At its bottom, canvas wrapped around a solid object, perhaps a two-by-four section of lumber designed to allow the scene to fall efficiently and rest perfectly level against the stage floor . . . or some other ill-fated object which interrupted its path.

How does it work? Gwen wondered, remembering Marianne's brief description of a system of counterweights. She took the lantern to the wings of the stage, situated just out of sight of the audience behind a curtain. She discovered that the backdrop was supported by a system of three pulleys connected by ropes. The actual process of shifting a weight to lower the scene seemed simple enough. The top of the backdrop was attached by a sturdy line that wound around the first pulley. Three sandbags were attached to a metal ring on that same primary line as it circled down from the second pulley. A secondary line connected to the third pulley was also attached to the ring holding the sandbags. An intricate knot above the ring kept the sandbags from slipping.

Easily enough, when a stagehand loosened the knot connecting the ring to the secondary line, the sandbags raised or lowered, thereby causing the backdrop to do the opposite. As the sandbags went up, the backdrop went down. The entire process, while simple in design and execution, depended entirely on the strength of the metal ring and the reliability of the knot holding it all in place.

Gwen wrapped her hand around the primary line just above the sandbags. It was firm and taut. So was the secondary line. So was the knot. Someone had skillfully put it all back together sometime after the "accident" which claimed Eli. Had the same person just as skillfully created the *appearance* of a safe rigging in the early hours of March twenty-fourth, when actually it masked a deadly fault? And if so, who on the *Jubilee Palace* knew enough about rigging to accomplish such a feat?

All this speculation brought Gwen back to the same questions which had plagued her since arriving in Hickory Bend. How had Eli been drawn so conveniently to this very spot on the stage? Had someone beckoned him to this death mark and then counted on the rigging to fail at precisely the right moment? Or, as it suddenly occurred to her now, had there been more than one person involved in the macabre deed?

She looked up at the pastoral solitude of the Ozark landscape, so peaceful, yet potentially deadly. Once again, she tested the tautness of the lines. Her gaze wandered to the four corners of the stage and the darkened wings, and finally to the back curtain through which she'd stepped just moments before. A cold chill started in her shoulder blades and raced down her spine. The back curtain!

Travis Veazey slept not ten feet away from the spot where Eli had died. Gwen's mind spun with inevitable conclusions. Constable O'Toole had said that everyone who worked on the *Jubilee* was accounted for that dreadful night. They were all in bed, he'd said. Yet Marianne Dresden, whose room was on the second floor at the stern of the boat, was the first to hear Eli's scream. But if Travis was sleeping ten feet away, why hadn't he heard the scream before she had? Why hadn't he been the first to arrive on stage to discover Eli's body?

Was it because he was already there?

Gwen's thoughts darted back to Eli's journal. He'd written that he intended to pay Travis a salary as soon as the young man mastered certain skills in the backstage area. Perhaps he had learned some of those skills — the ones associated with the rigging. But that certainly didn't prove that Travis killed Eli. After all, it was easy to understand the basic operation of backdrops and weights. Even Gwen figured out how they worked right away, and she never considered herself mechanically inclined.

She began pacing, covering the stage from one side to the other and back again. She started talking to herself, her index finger in the air, figuratively emphasizing each salient point. "It's true," she said. "Travis could have lied to O'Toole about being asleep that night. But so could anyone else who occupied private quarters and therefore had no witnesses to refute their stories." *Like Anabel Whitedove. Or Marianne Dresden herself.*

"But still, someone from town could have crept aboard the *Jubilee,* waited for Uncle Eli to return in the early hours, and lured him to the theater. Someone who knows the town well, and knew Eli was at Hattie's Saloon playing poker. Someone like Manfred Kruger, the printer."

Gwen pivoted again and began her precise journey toward the opposite side of the stage. "Or it could have been someone who knows the intricacies of showboats. Solomon Wade or Carson Stockwell. Surely Constable O'Toole didn't question everyone in Hickory Bend!"

Gwen stopped pacing and stared over the backs of the theater seats. "Carson Stockwell!" she whispered in a hoarse voice. "I've forgotten my meeting with him."

At the same moment she realized that one of the double doors at the public entrance to the theater was open. Moonlight speared an amber shaft onto the carpeted aisle. A figure stood just inside, a man, clad in dark trousers and white shirt. Outdoor gas lights illuminated his hair, the color of the spot on a buckeye. He stood facing her, hands on hips, his face shadowed and therefore expressionless.

"Did I hear my name?" he asked in a full, rich voice that reverberated off the paneled walls of the theater.

She whispered it once more as proof that the man was indeed the captain. "Carson Stockwell."

"There it is again." He spread his hands to include the entire *Jubilee* theater. "Excellent acoustics, Miss Barlow. I can hear even your soft, cultured tones."

Her breath caught in her throat. She swallowed to prevent the little sound in the back of her mouth from becoming audible. The door closed behind him, blotting out the moonlight and leaving him in grave shadow. He strode down the aisle purposefully, confidently. And Gwen realized that they were utterly alone in the theater. Eli Willoughby had vowed in his journal to ruin Carson

Stockwell's reputation. If he had succeeded, then in a few seconds, she could very well be standing face to face with her uncle's killer.

Chapter Eight

Carson Stockwell continued down the center aisle of the theater. He stopped at the foot of the stairs leading to the stage, clasped his hands behind his back, and looked up at Gwen with eyes that blended with the gray shadows surrounding him. "Sorry. Did I startle you?" he asked.

She tried to smile, but her lips quivered at the effort. *You rather scared me half to death!* "No, of course not," she lied. "I was expecting you."

He climbed the stairs and walked to within a few feet of her. "The stage becomes you, Miss Barlow. Have you ever thought of acting as a career?"

"I have a career, Mr. Stockwell."

"As a showboat operator?"

"Most assuredly not," she said a little too quickly, and immediately regretted revealing that she might not be qualified for the job. "Before I came here, when I was in Ohio, I was . . ." She paused, not wanting to divulge more of her past to a man she didn't trust. Plus she experienced the fleeting thought that Stockwell might think less of her if he knew she were a simple librarian. Of course, she told herself, it mattered not a fig if he did, since this man's brazen attitude and cocky self-assurance could be hiding the most heinous of crimes. She lifted her chin, hoping it gave her an air of confidence equal to his. And doubting it. "Well, never mind about that. It doesn't matter."

"Whatever your pleasure, ma'am," he said. "I'm aware that discussing your past is not the reason we decided to meet this evening."

Gwen's feeling of unease mounted. Soon she would have to tell Stockwell that she decided not to hire him as captain of the *Jubilee*. She dared not let her thoughts anticipate his reaction or she would lose what little courage she'd mustered.

"No, it's not," she said. Her gaze darted around her immediate surroundings. For safety's sake, she gauged the distance from the stage to the theater door through which Stockwell had just entered. She noted the slit in the back curtain, near Travis's quarters, thinking she could make an escape that way. As a last resort, she judged how long it would take her to flee into the wings and hide among the assorted paraphernalia. Then she fixed

Carson Stockwell with a wary gaze. "Perhaps we should talk somewhere else," she offered.

"Why? I like it here. The theater is the heart of the showboat," he said. "But the pilot house is its brains, and it might be more appropriate."

Appropriate for whom? she wondered. *For someone planning to toss a hapless victim overboard?* "Why the pilot house?" she asked.

"Because it's where I will spend most of my time . . . assuming you decided to hire me. And if you haven't decided yet, then I should take you there to demonstrate on a personal level that I am experienced and capable of operating the various instruments required to guide a boat this size." He spread his legs, assuming a commanding stance and crossed his arms over his chest. A corner of his mouth hiked up in a puzzling grin. "Miss Barlow, are you nervous being here with me?"

She mentally scolded herself for showing weakness. *Stop acting like a twit, Gwendolyn! You're as obvious as a fox skittering from hole to hole in advance of the hunting dogs.* "Of course I'm not nervous. What a ridiculous notion." Summoning an ounce more of courage, she strode past him.

He caught her elbow and turned her to face him. She drew in a sharp breath but locked her gaze on his, determined to meet his boldness with her own pretense of it.

Understanding lit the backs of his eyes. "That's it," he said. "You've decided not to hire me. I didn't think you would succumb to rumor and innuendo, Miss Barlow."

"I did no such thing, Mr. Stockwell. It is true that I decided not to hire you, but only because a better candidate presented himself after you left."

He still held her arm. "Who?"

"That's none of your business." She tugged against his grip, and he released her. Her freedom did nothing to calm the erratic beating of her heart.

His gaze never wavered. "With all due respect, Miss Barlow, you are a liar."

At last she didn't have to feign courage. It had been fueled by an anger that had ignited it into a full-blown head of steam. "How dare you . . ."

"It's a reasonable assumption," he stated calmly. "Hickory Bend is a small town. To my knowledge, there are only two river captains for hire at the present time. You're looking at one of them. The other is Solomon Wade. If you are the clever woman I believe you to be, then you've already discovered the reason Eli Willoughby fired Wade. And I doubt that any amount of persuasion by my competitor would result in your hiring him." He looked over her shoulder toward the backstage area. "You may have the grit to stand here not ten feet from where your uncle lay with his head bashed in, but I doubt you'd be foolish enough to hire a drunken scoundrel like Wade."

She expelled a pent up breath and looked at the ceiling, an overly dramatic heaven-give-me-strength gesture her mother often used and one which Gwen normally abhorred. She then speared Stockwell with a warning look that should have challenged his smug expression. It didn't, but a startling revelation dawned on her. She no longer feared this man. She simply found his brazen behavior distasteful. "There are many types of scoundrels, Mr. Stockwell. One variety has an over-rated opinion of his intelligence."

"It's not intelligence, Miss Barlow. It's common sense. You obviously wouldn't hire Wade, an admitted . . . well, you know what he is. Likewise, you are reluctant to hire a much maligned, and wrongfully accused, fire starter."

So, he'd figured out that she'd discovered the unsavory details of his past. Her best reaction, she decided, was to dodge an attack. She sniffed, an affected and haughty sound, and threaded her hands at her waist. Then she did exactly what he'd just accused her of — she lied. "I don't know what you're talking about."

"Who told you?"

She'd never been very good at deception, and with a sigh of resignation, she gave it up now. "Everyone knows, Mr. Stockwell, that every boat you captain ends up as kindling for river town ovens."

Again that strange sort of grin set Gwen's nerves on edge. But this time it reached his eyes. "Rumors of my exploits have been greatly exaggerated, Miss Barlow," he said. "It was *one* boat that ended up in cinders, the last one I captained. I admit that it did burn to the waterline . . ."

"A-ha!"

The grin widened. ". . . due to the foolhardiness of the boat's owner who decided to accept a racing challenge from an old adversary. You see, Whisky Pete Blaylock, my boss, was a Confederate during the war. Marsh Wainwright was a Yankee. Those two old buzzards refused to admit that the war was over. So when Wain-wright's steam-powered packet met Blaylock's twenty-year-old coal-burning sidewheeler in the middle of the Missis-sippi River one fateful night, a showdown was inevitable."

"A showdown?"

"A race, Miss Barlow. A regular grease-hit-the-fire contest of speed and endur-ance. Whisky Pete called for more steam, and when he wasn't satisfied, he hollered for a lick more. I told him the *Dorothy May* would blow, but he didn't care. Reminding me of my lowly position, he said 'You're the captain, Stockwell. You steer and I'll watch the smoke pipes.' "

Gwen rolled her eyes. "Men."

"It's the damn truth. God never created a bigger bunch of fools. And never was it truer than that night on the river. The *Dorothy May* coughed and sputtered and belched cinders out her stacks till she caught fire and hissed her death into the water. And Wainwright's packet churned ahead and out of sight. Pete and me, and twenty cattle buyers from Moline, swam to shore and watched the sidewheeler turn the night sky orange."

Gwen couldn't say why, but she believed Stockwell's story. "Did you tell the circumstances of this event to my uncle?" she asked.

"I never had a chance. Eli knew Pete from their New Orleans days and he took Pete's word that the upstart Captain Stockwell destroyed his boat. Take it as a back-handed compliment to your uncle, but Eli was loyal to his friends."

Some would question that tribute, Gwen thought.

Stockwell walked to the curtains hanging at the sides of the proscenium and ran his hand down the velvet fabric. "Tell me something, Miss Barlow. How much do you know about this showboat your family has inherited?"

From his tone, he obviously assumed she didn't know much. "I know enough to say that it cost much too much money, that a bankroll to operate it is much greater than common sense and logic would dictate, that at the moment it is an accountant's nightmare . . ."

She stopped as her gaze swept the modern technical details of the stage and the ornate fixtures of the theater. A smile curved her lips. Here she was, spouting her opinions of her uncle's unsound monetary investment when, in reality, she'd come to admire the product of his dreams. When had she begun to think fondly of the *Jubilee Palace*? At what point had she stopped regarding it as a gaudy testimony to a man's folly? Her appraisal surprised her with its intensity.

"But, I'd bet a silver dollar that it is the grandest-looking craft on the Mississippi, Mr. Stockwell," she said. "And no doubt the sturdiest as well."

"That's where you're wrong," he said with that same aggravating confidence.

"What do you mean?"

"The *Jubilee* is grand looking all right. She's got no match that I've seen. But the fact is, she's not built a whit better than the *Dorothy May* or any other vessel on the river."

Gwen inhaled sharply, the resulting gasp indicating both insult and alarm that Stockwell might be right. "You're saying that the *Jubilee* could catch fire and burn?"

"In about five minutes, a risk that becomes even greater if you decide to use the *Jubilee*'s own engines and not a steamer to push her." He chuckled at the look on her face. "River boats are built with some of the thinnest lumber available from the mills. They have to be. If they were made from sturdier beams and planks, along with the iron you find on ocean-going ships, these boats could never navigate the waters they have to travel. They'd hit a snag within a hundred feet of leaving shore and ground themselves in the bat of an eye."

Taking the lantern, Gwen slowly walked down to the interior of the theater. Its grandeur was visible even in the sparse light from Travis's lantern. Was Stockwell right? Was this glorious boat no more than a house of cards? Was all this splendor she'd come to esteem merely a false front for shoddiness and poor construction?

Doubt about her uncle's sanity crept back into her mind as she glanced up at the portrait of Eli Willoughby. *What were you thinking in the last months of your life, Uncle? What made you invest your remaining dollars in so flimsy an extravagance?* She considered the possibility that her uncle had put his money in external trappings while his showboat was actually constructed of weak, frail materials.

Stockwell came to stand beside her. When she looked at him, there was an unexpected tenderness in his eyes, as though he sympathized with her bewilderment.

"Don't get me wrong, Miss Barlow," he said. "I'm not saying Eli cut corners. He didn't. But he had this boat built the way

173

he had to so she'd handle the channels and hidden dangers of the river. The Mississippi is an unforgiving master."

Carson took her arm and walked her to a window facing the expanse of the Mississippi. She looked out onto blackness broken only by a rising moon casting diamond lights onto the dark, even ripples. It was hard to believe that underneath the rhythmic swells and gentle swish of water against the *Jubilee* hull, such hazards waited to destroy anyone who challenged the river's supremacy.

Stockwell spoke in a low voice near her ear. "Did you know, ma'am, that the *Jubilee* draws no more than three feet of water at any time?"

She looked at him, disbelieving.

"Imagine it. All these chairs and that stage and all its equipment. The modern conveniences in the kitchen, the latest instruments in the pilot house — it all nests like a sparrow on about thirty inches of Mississippi. That's the way river boats have to be. A good captain can almost guide one over a prairie on what's left on the grass after a good rain."

A bell sounded on the river, and Gwen turned back to the window, drawn by the resonant, cheerful tones. A steamer, much smaller than the *Jubilee*, chugged past. A few passengers sat on the main deck, their faces illuminated by gas lights and the occasional glow from a cigarette or pipe. Interior lights shone through curtains, making the vessel appear cozy and inviting. That boat, those people's lives, depended on a flimsy skeleton of lumber and the skill of its captain. She heard herself whisper her reaction on a breathy rush of air. "Amazing." There was a lot to be learned outside the covers of a book.

"I'm not a torch, Miss Barlow," Stockwell said in that same low, intimate voice. "I can understand your uncle's reservations about hiring me, or any captain that lost a boat to fire. But I can promise you one thing. If I handle the *Jubilee Palace*, I'll treat her like the grand dame she is. I'll coddle her and pet her, and not demand more of her than she's willing to give . . ."

A tremor ran down Gwen's arms and she wrapped them under her breasts. It was a reaction in direct opposition to the sudden spurt of warmth that pooled inside her. It was almost as if the captain had stopped talking about the boat, and was speaking instead about . . .

Gwen wouldn't allow the thought to take

root. Of course he was talking about the boat.

She continued to stare at the water and the little steamer that was now only a flicker of lights three hundred yards up river. A warning voice inside her hinted that now would not be the appropriate time for Gwendolyn Barlow to look directly into the eyes of Carson Stockwell. She did, however, state clearly and concisely to the window pane, "Mr. Stockwell, I've decided to hire you as captain of the *Jubilee Palace*."

His words reverberated in her ear. "Miss Barlow, you won't be sorry, and I am honored to accept."

She sensed him stepping away from her as he added, "And since I understand there is to be a rehearsal in the morning, I will be here as well to lend my support."

He was nearly to the door before she turned to watch him go. Gwen had just made a decision based almost entirely on that most ambiguous of factors — woman's intuition. God help them if she were wrong.

Chapter Nine

Gwen waited until she was certain Carson Stockwell had had time to leave the *Jubilee*. Then she left the theater by the front entrance and took the less noticeable passageway that led by the water to the stern of the boat. When she neared the back deck, she inhaled the familiar cherry tobacco scent that she remembered from earlier that morning.

Anabel, she thought, and without stopping, she walked quickly to the back stairs so she wouldn't disturb the woman's solitude. Gwen didn't feel like talking to Anabel any more than she assumed the actress wanted to talk to her. Besides, Gwen had another destination in mind. She climbed the stairs to the second floor and went to the room occupied by Lillian and Preston. There were times in a person's life, even a grown woman's, when she simply needed a mother's counsel. This was one of those times, since Gwen still couldn't imagine what had gotten into her to so impulsively change her mind about Stockwell without further investigation.

It wasn't a bit like her to abandon logic in favor of such a frivolous reaction. Perhaps her mother would have some insight.

Light shone through the small window in Lillian's door, and had a calming effect on Gwen's churning emotions. No matter how impatient Gwen became with her mother sometimes, Lillian was still Gwen's safe harbor in the difficult seas of adulthood. It was comforting to realize that the parent/child relationship remained stalwart as time marched on.

Gwen knocked lightly.

"Come in," Lillian called.

Gwen opened the door and stepped inside. She'd seen the room before, of course, and had thought it small and efficiently organized. Tonight, however, it appeared warm and cozy, just what she needed. Both bunks were neatly made. There was no clothing scattered about, a condition Gwen couldn't boast about her own quarters. Her mother sat in a folding rocking chair she'd brought from home. A gas light burned on the wall over her shoulder, and a length of material trailed over her lap and onto the floor.

"Oh, hello, dear," Lillian said. "I'm just working on the new curtains for our window."

"Where's Preston?"

Lillian's skilled fingers didn't miss a stitch. "I wouldn't be surprised if he were in the dark picking posies for that lovely Marianne. I swear, once that single-minded boy gets something in his head . . ."

"I can't imagine where he gets a trait of stubbornness," Gwen said with a gentle grin. She couldn't suppress a chuckle when she realized Lillian was applying a frilly ruffle to her handiwork. Preston's words of warning about such frippery came to her mind. She sincerely hoped he was having fun with Marianne, because he wasn't going to like the curtains at all.

"Sit down, Gwendolyn," Lillian said, motioning toward the lower bunk. "My goodness, you look as if your legs are made of pudding."

Gwen sighed and did just as her mother suggested. Plopping her elbows on her knees and cradling her chin in her hands, she said, "I'm not surprised, Mama. It has been quite a day, and to top it off, I did something very foolish just now. Something quite without forethought."

Lillian smiled and peered at her daughter over the half lenses of her close-work glasses. "I seriously doubt that, dear." She looked back down at her material and took a couple of stitches. "I've never known you to do a foolish thing other than buy that silly bicycle, and perhaps indulge in a lapse in judgment with regard to Latimer in Apple Creek. Frankly I can't imagine you've rushed into anything willy nilly now."

Gwen answered her mother's insult at the beloved bicycle with the same tight-lipped, controlled smirk she always gave her. "Well, you're wrong, Mama, because rushing willy nilly is exactly what I've done."

Lillian stuck her needle through a layer of fabric and set the whole bundle on the floor beside her. She removed her glasses and set them and her clasped hands in her lap. "Talk, Gwendolyn."

It was all the encouragement Gwen needed, and she poured out her troubles. "I probably shouldn't have, Mama, but tonight I hired Carson Stockwell to captain the *Jubilee*."

"Well, of course you did, dear."

"Don't you see? I should have investigated his background, his credentials, his abilities. Instead, I hired him literally on faith."

"Naturally," Lillian said. "I told you this morning that Mr. Stockwell would be perfect for the *Jubilee*. He's charming and more than presentable. And he came just at the right time, guided by fate I would say. What more could you ask?"

Gwen groaned at Lillian's simplistic attitude. "What more, Mama? Why, dozens of things! You can't place your trust in a man just because he's presentable looking!"

"No, of course not. And I didn't."

"You didn't?"

"No. I realized he was the man for the job based on a much more convincing argument."

A sense of relief washed over Gwen, though she knew her mother well enough to fear it was premature. "What convincing argument, Mama?"

"An irrefutable one, Gwendolyn. Woman's intuition. A pity you don't have more of it, dear."

Gwen dropped her forehead into her hands and laughed out loud. For a moment she couldn't stop the flow of nearly hysterical giggles. Hadn't she just admonished herself moments before in the theater for relying on that same female attribute in dealing with Stockwell?

Lillian leaned across the space that separated her from her daughter and patted Gwen's knee. "What's so funny?"

Gwen wiped her eyes and looked up. "Nothing, Mama. I just love you, you know. I really do."

"I know, dear." She slipped her glasses back on her nose and picked up her sewing. "Now don't fret so. Everything will work out for the best." Plying the needle with practiced, efficient strokes once more, she added, "What amazing strides we've made already. And now a rehearsal tomorrow. I'm fairly bursting with excitement."

Gwen nodded her head slowly, realizing that she, too, was somewhat elated about the prospect of fulfilling the showboat's prophecy. "Tell me, Mama, did anything happen after I left the dining room this evening? Was anything else said?"

"Oh, my yes. Everyone was all abuzz about the rehearsal. Preston badgered Marianne into helping him practice his lines. Peaches bustled about the kitchen talking about how Mr. Eli would be so proud that his showboat people were acting again. One of the musicians said he'd have to polish his something-or-other . . . trumpet, I think. Anabel said something I can't repeat about getting up for breakfast . . ."

Getting more than she expected from

her question, Gwen raised her hand to get Lillian to draw a breath. "Mama, I never knew you were so observant."

Lillian looked up from her sewing with a cool, gray gaze. "I try, Gwendolyn. I try."

"Speaking of Uncle Eli," Gwen said, "I think we're going to miss him tomorrow. The others have told me that he was the one *Jubilee* member most qualified to operate the technical equipment backstage. I'm sure he knew how to change scenes, create sound effects, adjust lighting . . ."

Lillian swept Gwen's concerns away with a wave of her hand. "Don't worry about scene changes, dear. Anabel told me that she knows how to do that. Eli taught her all the tricks during the years they spent together." She lowered her glasses again and spoke conspiratorially. "I understand that's not all he taught her, either!"

"Mama!"

"You said yourself, Gwendolyn, I'm observant." She pushed her glasses back to the bridge of her nose. "Anyway, Anabel said she could work the flying scene changes and backdrops with her eyes closed."

Gwen bounded up from the bunk and stared at Lillian. "She said that, Mama?"

"Plain as day. A blessing isn't it, since

that Veazey boy doesn't seem capable of learning to open a bottle cap."

Gwen's mind was already racing toward weightier concerns. "Yes, Mama, a blessing," she said absently. She closed the small distance between her and her mother and then bent and kissed Lillian on her cheek. "I'm going now, Mama. Good night."

Gwen crossed to the door to her mother's cabin, and was just about to open it when Lillian said, "One more thing, Gwendolyn. You didn't say anything when I commented that our captain is quite presentable looking. Don't you think that's so?"

Gwen glanced over her shoulder and gave her mother a half smile. "Mr. Stockwell?"

Lillian nodded, her eyes bright and expectant.

Gwen shrugged, feigning disinterest she didn't feel. "He's well looking, I guess."

"I should say. Think about that remarkable specimen occupying the cabin next to yours in a few days, dear. Can't say as I would sleep a wink under those circumstances."

Unexpected heat flushed Gwen's cheeks. "Mama! What a thing to say."

Lillian's laughter followed Gwen as she stepped onto the second floor passageway and closed the door. Once out of Lillian's perceptive view, she leaned against an outside wall and drew a deep breath. Carson Stockwell living in the very next cabin? She hadn't thought of that before, but it was true. There were two cabins on the third deck of the *Jubilee*, the lavish one which Gwen now occupied, and a slightly smaller, but no doubt well appointed one intended for the *Jubilee* captain.

The implications of such close living conditions between her and Stockwell brought doubt back into Gwen's mind — doubt of a different nature however, and not associated with the captain as a suspect in Eli Willoughby's murder. She'd have to think about that later. Now a much more pressing concern weighed on Gwen's mind. Anabel Whitedove. Lillian's words echoed in Gwen's head. *Anabel can work backdrops with her eyes closed? That means she can also work them in a dark theater in the middle of the night.*

One cast member of *Belle of the Ozarks* was not present in the *Jubilee* dining room the next morning at eight thirty. A half hour earlier, Gwen had given Jason

185

DeVane the three dollars estimated for a performance license, and the actor had left the boat and headed for the Hickory Bend town hall. Now an air of expectancy hung over the rest of the cast members at breakfast as they waited for Jason's return.

Peaches served up the usual fare, consisting of mounds of scrambled eggs, buttery biscuits, and several pounds of fried potatoes. The anticipation of an upcoming performance did not have an adverse effect on most of the actors' appetites. However, Anabel Whitedove, battling drooping eyelids and emitting a string of noisy yawns, ignored her plate in favor of several cups of coffee. Marianne Dresden picked daintily at her food as she usually did.

Gwen sat down next to her mother, surprised to see that Preston, also, was not in the dining room. She was used to seeing him shadowing Marianne, but the chair next to the ingénue's was empty. Gwen spread her napkin on her lap and whispered to Lillian, "Where's Buddy Barlow, our newest star, today, Mama?"

Lillian dripped honey over her biscuit and smacked her lips. "He walked right by the entrance to the kitchen when we came down earlier and said he had to find something backstage."

Gwen stared down at the plate Peaches set in front of her and wondered how any one person could eat even half of it. "Oh, really? What is he looking for?"

"I haven't the foggiest, dear. I didn't ask him. You know how I hate to appear nosy."

Gwen smiled down at her food. Sometimes her mother's assessment of her own personality traits was amazing . . . and far from the truth. "Oh, right. I guess your new creed is to be observant and yet always mind your own business."

Lillian licked a fingertip that glistened with syrupy sweetness. "We'd all do well to follow such advice, Gwendolyn, what with this murder business and all. Not that I think anyone on the *Jubilee* could have wished such a terrible fate on Eli, but I do think it prudent that we all keep our ears perked."

Gwen rested her fork on the side of her plate and leaned in close. "Why, Mama? What have you heard this morning?"

"Nothing, dear. Nothing at all. Still, vigilance . . ."

Whatever Lillian was about to say was lost in the clatter of banging doors and the rumble of wooden wheels. And behind all this commotion, and a rickety wagon loaded with unknown contents, was

Preston. Bent nearly double, hands on one of the wagon slats, he pushed the awkward conveyance into the middle of the dining room and stopped. "Look everyone," he announced. "See what I've found."

Sir Clyde, sitting nearest the wagon, looked over his shoulder at Preston's discovery and shrugged. "Oh, so you've found the posters. They had to be around somewhere. I should think it would be a trifle difficult to hide a hundred and twelve dollars worth of printed material."

Preston beamed, obviously determined not to allow Sir Clyde's diminished reaction to spoil his achievement. "Right. They were in boxes backstage. Tickets, programs, posters — it's all here." He pulled one of the posters from the wagon and held it up for all to see. "Isn't it grand?"

He was right. The eighteen-inch by twenty-four-inch poster was a work of art. Scripted across the top was the title of the play, *Belle of the Ozarks*, with the script writer's name, Eli Willoughby, emblazoned in red letters underneath. In brilliant colors, a lovely young lady, the play's namesake, occupied the center of the poster. She sat on a swing hanging from a tree limb with red and yellow roses twining up the rope handles. She wore a wonderfully simple, yet feminine garment of blue gingham underdress and ruffled pinafore, and she bore a striking resemblance to Marianne Dresden. Close by, a strapping young fellow with a straw hat in his hand leaned against a fence post and stared moony-eyed at the object of his affection. In the background, cows grazed lazily on a green hillside.

Across from Sir Clyde, Anabel Whitedove slurped her coffee noisily. "It's a damn masterpiece all right," she said in a tone that clearly indicated she held the art-work in the lowest regard.

Preston scowled at her before plastering a smile back on his face and approaching Gwen. "See here, Gwennie. I estimate we have nearly a hundred of these. All the actors' names are at the bottom. And there's a little room left over in the lower corner. I thought I'd take these to Hildegard to see if her father could add my name at the bottom . . ."

Gwen placed her hand on her brother's wrist, stopping him from waving the poster in her face. "I don't think so, Buddy. Even if we had money in the budget for more printing, which we don't, I have a hunch Manfred Kruger would toss you out of his print shop and onto the main street of

Hickory Bend before he'd take on more work from the *Jubilee*." Then, as an afterthought, she said, "And don't even think about making any deals that include his daughter."

"Well, we'll see." Preston hid his disappointment behind a doe-eyed expression that clearly said he wasn't about to let the matter drop. For the present, however, he contented himself with returning to the wagon and continuing his exhibition. He produced hundreds of smaller, black and white posters with Marianne Dresden's actual photograph in the center. These were probably intended as hand-outs and pin-ups in towns along the river. There were Anabel's posters as well, proclaiming her a full-blooded Cherokee Indian, and hundreds of programs listing the actors and musicians. The programs also mentioned the accomplishments of the *Jubilee*'s owner and talented script writer, Eli Willoughby.

Uncle Eli was no reluctant bloomer, Gwen thought as she read of Willoughby's exploits, real or imagined. And she now understood where her brother got his propensity to recognize and exaggerate upon opportunities.

"So what do you think, Gwennie?" Preston asked when he finished his show.

"Aren't the posters terrific?"

"Yes, they are. Too bad we don't officially own them." When Preston gave her a quizzical look, she reminded him again. "The bill, brother dear. We haven't yet paid for them. I'm certain Manfred Kruger won't let us forget that little detail."

Preston frowned. "I suppose he'll hound us forever."

"You're absolutely right about that!"

All chatter in the dining room stopped as everyone's attention fixed on the handsome man who'd just entered. Jason DeVane strode to the middle of the room. "I just passed the old coot's shop and he told me to tell you, Miss Barlow, that he expects at least partial payment soon."

Gwen mumbled, "I'm sure he did."

"Oh, pish tosh," Lillian said. "He'll wait. But we can't. What about the license, Mr. DeVane? Did you get it?"

Expectancy hummed in the room like distant thunder. Putting all his acting talents to good use, Jason dragged the moment tortuously. He stared at the floor, shuffled his feet, heaved a great sigh, and then finally produced a legal-looking document from his jacket pocket and proclaimed loudly, "Ladies and Gentlemen and fellow Thespians, prepare to act! Our

191

first performance is in two days."

The announcement was met with a chorus of cheers, some of them even coming from the normally pessimistic Anabel. The only one who didn't seem elated over the prospect of a performance was Travis Veazey. The perpetually sullen lad stood up, scraping his chair along the floor. "Sounds like a lot of damn clap trap to me," he said. "I got till ten o'clock. Think I'll go fishing before all hell breaks loose."

As he left the dining room, he brushed past a whirling cyclone of raspberry crepe and pink eyelet lace. Her golden curls fluttering like buggy springs around her face, Hildegard Kruger waltzed into the room, clapping her hands with delight. "Did I hear you correctly, Mr. DeVane?" she asked. "We really are going to perform?"

Gwen dropped her face into her hands and gulped back the sour taste of eggs and potatoes.

Chapter Ten

At precisely ten o'clock that morning all participants in Eli Willoughby's play, *Belle of the Ozarks*, assembled in the *Jubilee* theater. Within moments, the grandiose room hummed with creativity. Repressed actors finally rehearsed their lines. Preston overflowed with enthusiasm for every word coming from Marianne Dresden's pouting pink lips. Like a plum-colored ostrich, Hildegard Kruger fluttered from one section of the stage to the next, crowing with triumph. And Lillian cheered the actors, pandering to their egos with words of praise and encouragement.

In the orchestra pit, musical notes honked from a quartet of wind instruments, twanged from a pair of banjos, and rumbled and clanged from bass drum and cymbals. And Dickey Squires, a steamboat operator with nowhere to go for the moment, approached Gwen where she stood under a large construction of painted lumber suspended from the ceiling a few feet in front of the now infamous Ozark Mountain backdrop.

He shook his head in amused dismay. "I warned you, Miss Barlow. Those musicians can't hardly play a note."

She smiled wanly. "We still have two days, Mr. Squires, and fortunately our orchestra only has room for improvement." She pointed above her head to the gargantuan prop. "Do you know what this monstrosity is?"

"Sure do. Helped the carpenters build it to Mr. Willoughby's specifications. It's a mountain."

"A mountain?"

"That's right. Mr. Willoughby wanted realism. We lower it at the end of the play when the sheriff confesses his undying love to Belle. Through the first two acts it just hangs there. We called it 'Romance Mountain' when we were building it, because that's where Marianne and Jason fall in love."

From several feet below Romance Mountain, Gwen inspected the details that confirmed Mr. Squires's explanation. Sheets of green fabric intermittently covering brown paint identified grassy areas of the mountain, while artificial tree trunks "grew" from holes in the irregular platform. Using her imagination, Gwen decided that, once the prop was lowered, it probably did resemble a mountain land-scape, complete with rounded peaks. It was indeed a masterful piece of craftsman-ship, yet one dreadful thought surfaced in Gwen's mind. "Did you test the lines sup-porting the mountain, Mr. Squires? I cer-tainly wouldn't want anything unfortunate to happen here today, especially consid-ering what happened before."

Dickey nodded. "I know what you mean, Miss Barlow. I'll double check those ropes right now."

Gwen watched as Dickey began his pre-liminary examination of the rope rigging which held the mountain. After a moment she felt a tap on her shoulder and heard Sir Clyde clear his throat — his customary way of demanding her attention.

"Excuse me, Miss Barlow," he said impa-tiently, "but shall we begin?"

"Of course. Go right ahead."

Sir Clyde arched his thick eyebrows and removed his glasses. "Go right ahead?" he repeated. "And just what exactly do you mean by that?"

Sometimes, despite his demeanor of cul-ture and intelligence, Sir Clyde could make the most obtuse statements. "I mean, go ahead and act."

"And how will we do that without a director?" He drew out the last word as if there were a space between each syllable.

Gwen anticipated the answer to her next question even as she asked it. "Who is the director, Sir Clyde?"

"It *was* Mr. Willoughby." A smile hinting of intellectual superiority curled the actor's lips. "Now it appears we don't have one."

Gwen was beginning to resent Clyde's blatant satisfaction whenever he pointed out a serious lack in the *Jubilee*'s forces. She clasped her hands at her waist and squared off with him. "You are right, Sir Clyde," she said. "It appears we don't. Why don't you assume the duties of director? I'm sure you'll do an admirable job."

Clyde puffed up like a rooster about to crow. "I *act,* Miss Barlow. I don't direct."

It was clear where this conversation was headed, and it was toward a conclusion which only meant more responsibility for Gwen. "Very well, then, I'll do it. How hard can it be?" She realized she would probably regret that flip remark by the end of the day.

Borrowing Preston's copy of the script, Gwen placed the performers for the first act on the stage. Jason DeVane, the love-struck sheriff, whose presence was inconsequential at the opening of the scene, occupied himself with a task upstage. Marianne Dresden stood near the footlights, waiting for her Aunt Winnifred to appear from the wings. Travis Veazey reluctantly admitted that Eli had taught him to operate the sound effects for a locomotive, and he stood in the wings with Anabel waiting for a cue from the director.

"All right, nobody move," Gwen cautioned as she descended the few steps to occupy a seat in the front row. Only partially aware that Hildegard had been bustling about seeing to details of her own choosing, she now realized the girl had taken the seat next to hers.

"What do you want me to do, Miss Barlow?" Hildegard asked. Her wide smile appeared to hold twice the number of teeth needed for an average person.

"Just sit there for now, Hildegard," she said. "I'm sure something will come up."

And thankfully something did. No sooner had the girl slumped in her chair and crossed her arms over her chest in obstinate displeasure when Gwen realized the curtains were all wrong. Hanging straight, as they were, they blocked entirely too much of the scene. "Hildegard," she said, "do you think you could . . ."

The girl bounded out of her chair. "Of course I could. What is it? The lights? The props? I can act, too, you know."

Gwen sighed. "Yes, I know. But what I need you to do is tie back the curtains."

"Oh."

"Travis!" Gwen called his name three times before the young man appeared from the wings.

"Yeah?"

"Would you get two lengths of rope for Hildegard? About three feet long each."

"Can't she get them herself?"

Fortunately for Travis, he correctly interpreted Gwen's mounting impatience when she stood up, threw her script to the chair, and plopped her fists on her hips. He returned shortly with the ropes and stood by as Hildegard attempted to tie back the curtains. In the meantime, Gwen prompted the actors to be ready with their lines and Preston to be ready for his cue. She asked Lillian to sit in the back and judge the acoustics. Everything was actually going rather smoothly at this point, and Gwen's anxiety level dropped to a moderate zone.

"You stupid girl!" Travis's cry rang out through the theater.

"I heard that fine," Lillian called from

the last row of seats.

"You ignorant, sawdust brain!" he continued. "You ain't got a lick of sense anywhere in that useless head of yours."

In the anticipatory stillness of the theater, Hildegard was glaringly dumbstruck at the onslaught of insults. The only movement Gwen detected from the girl was a quivering of her lower lip. However, it was followed in seconds by a hair raising screech. "You horrible, filthy man!" she cried. "Get him away from me, Miss Barlow!"

Gwen ran up the stairs to the stage. "Travis! Your behavior was uncalled for. Apologize to Hildegard now."

"Like hell! She's dumb as possum droppings." He pointed to the rope around the curtain. "Look what the moron did. Tied back that curtain like she was fixing a damn hair ribbon. Any idiot knows you got to use a bowline for this job. It won't slip and you can still untie it easy enough when you have to."

Hildegard swatted at Travis's chest. "You and your stupid knots," she wailed. "You don't know everything."

"Next to you I sure do! I never in all my life seen a dumber, more ignorant . . ."

Gwen stepped between the two. "That's

enough. Travis, go away."

He looked almost hopeful. "You mean it?"

"Yes, go."

After leveling a victorious grin at Hildegard, he slowly sauntered across the stage and through the back curtain, but not before mumbling a series of complaints about how he'd been working like a plow horse and getting no pay. Gwen could picture him gathering up his fishing gear even as the rest of them stood contemplating what had just happened.

Gwen patted Hildegard's shoulder. The girl still sniveled and mewled like a starving kitten. "I'm sorry," Gwen said. "I don't know why Travis acts that way."

Hildegard ran a finger under her nose and raised her chin to its usual lofty level. "Because he's shanty trash, that's why." She turned her tear-smudged face to Gwen's. "The curtains are just fine, aren't they?" she asked.

"Yes, of course." Then addressing the rest of the company, Gwen said, "Now can we all get to work?"

The actors assumed their positions again, but Gwen's attention was drawn to the back curtain through which Travis had just exited. It rippled as if someone were searching for the entrance, and Gwen held her breath. Surely the troublemaker wasn't coming back.

But it was Carson Stockwell who breezed through the opening to the stage. "Anything I can do to help?"

Gwen's shoulders sagged in relief. "Do you know how to use the sound effects board?"

"I can manage it, I think."

"Then yes, you can help. In a moment we'll need a train whistle."

He walked into the wings. After a few seconds, he called out. "Got it. Whenever you're ready. And by the way, what's wrong with the Veazey kid? I just passed him outside and he looked madder than a . . ."

"Never mind that, Mr. Stockwell," Gwen interrupted. "Just be ready with that whistle."

She thought she heard him chuckle before he answered back, "Yes, ma'am."

Except for the initial confusion about a director, the outburst by Travis Veazey, and the mending of Hildegard's wounded feelings, Gwen decided the first rehearsal went as well as could be expected. And since there would be only three more opportunities to prepare, she was grateful.

Carson Stockwell turned out to be a fair sound effects technician, and having no immediate duties as captain during performances, he readily volunteered his services.

At one o'clock Peaches announced that lunch was ready. The others left, but Gwen remained in the theater to go over some details that needed her attention and to utilize some precious moments of solitude to think about Veazey's behavior. The young man's unexplained rage was leading her to draw some most unpleasant conclusions. Carson stayed behind as well to familiarize himself even more with the sound board. Gwen admired his sense of obligation, considering Peaches tempted him with butter beans and smoked sausages, part of the dwindling meat supply in the *Jubilee*'s massive ice box.

"I'll keep it warm for you," Peaches said to Gwen and Carson before she left to serve the others. "And in the meantime, I'll send Danita with some tea."

"That would be lovely," Gwen said.

For the next few minutes, Gwen read the second act over again and made minor changes in the actors' marks on stage. She was taping a red X to the floor to indicate Marianne's mark in Act Two when the door at the front of the theater opened to reveal a visitor to the *Jubilee*. A man's broad form was outlined by brilliant midday sun, rendering his characteristics dark and undefined. Without standing, Gwen spoke loudly, "May I help you?"

A gravely voice rumbled up the aisle toward her. "I 'spect maybe you can. Would you be Gwendolyn Barlow, kin to Eli Willoughby?"

The large figure lumbered toward her, his arms swinging loosely from his elbows, his gait awkward from a noticeable limp. His features gradually sharpened as the door closed behind him, leaving him in the artificial light of the theater. Thin wisps of hair grazed his shoulders. A reddish beard and peppered moustache hid most of his face, but his eyes were alert, almost penetrating, as he stared at Gwen.

She stood slowly and walked near the edge of the stage. "Do you have business with me, sir?"

He opened his mouth to speak, but before the words came, a loud crash reverberated from near the back curtain. Gwen whirled around in response to the commotion. Danita Johnson, her eyes wide, and her mouth open in a silent scream, stood still as a statue. A tray dangled from her hand. Crockery shards littered the floor beside her. A light brown rivulet of tea puddled at her feet.

Gwen rushed to the girl, took the tray and held her cold hand. "Danita, what's wrong?"

She backed up a step and shook her head. Her lips trembled in mute panic.

Gwen looked back at the man in the theater. He'd stopped at the first row of chairs. His lips split in a grin that fell just short of menacing. "Howdy, Miss Johnson," he said.

Squeezing Danita's hand tighter, Gwen asked, "Who is he, Danita? Why are you frightened?"

At that moment, Carson Stockwell walked out of the wings, stood beside the two women, and fixed an unwavering glare on the man below them. "Don't you know who he is, Miss Barlow?"

Suddenly she did. Her heart hammered in her chest. A cold chill nearly choked the breath from her lungs. She let go of Danita's hand and came to the edge of the stage again. "You're Solomon Wade, aren't you?"

"That's right. Solomon Wade's the name." The big man walked to the stage steps and put a booted foot on the first one.

Gwen held up her hand. "Stay where you are, Mr. Wade. Surely you know you're not welcome on the *Jubilee Palace*."

He tugged on his coarse beard and snickered up at her. "Maybe you don't know all the facts, ma'am," he said. "But I was Eli Willoughby's first choice to captain the *Jubilee*."

Gwen crossed her arms at her waist and drew a deep, trembling breath. She was grateful, and surprised, when her words came out strong and confident. "I know that. I'm equally aware that you were fired from that position the next day. At this point, Mr. Wade, I can assure you that I would let the *Jubilee* sink in the Mississippi rather than have you spend one moment in her pilot house."

Wade removed his foot from the step and leveled a flinty glare on Gwen. "Them's cocky words coming from a package that don't look any stronger than a sparrow that fell from its nest."

"Don't let this *package* fool you, Mr. Wade. My contempt for you couldn't be any greater if I were the size and strength of Goliath." Gwen turned away from Solomon long enough to issue a command to Danita who remained frozen at the back of the stage. "Go to your father, Danita. Tell him Solomon Wade is here. Now!"

The frightened girl covered her mouth with her hand and rushed from the theater.

Gwen centered her attention on Solomon Wade once more. She knew she was taking a chance by sending for Phineas Johnson. The *Jubilee*'s reputation certainly couldn't afford any more bloodshed on her decks. But this was a time that called for drastic measures. "I wonder how you will maintain your bravado when Phineas Johnson returns in a moment," she said to her intruder.

Wade had the audacity to laugh at her threat. "Johnson don't cause me more than a blink of concern, Miss Barlow. I just passed the blacksmith's shop in town, and there was old Phineas pumping on those bellows, working up a fine lather in the hot sun. Probably earning a few pennies for this ungrateful bunch on the *Jubilee*. So, you see, Phineas Johnson don't even know I'm paying this call."

The first skittering knots of panic rumbled in Gwen's stomach. "Don't refer to this as a 'call,' Mr. Wade. It is an invasion. I'm ordering you off the *Jubilee Palace* this instant."

He kicked the steps with the toe of his boot. The resounding thud brought a tingle to every inch of Gwen's skin as if lightning had struck the *Jubilee* deck.

"I ain't going nowhere until I had my say," Wade announced. "Willoughby treated me like I was a common cur. Imagine that high-falutin' dandy choosing to believe a Nigra gal over a respected boat captain." He pounded his fist on his chest. "I'm still the best qualified to take this boat up river, and you're gonna listen if I have to . . ."

A strong, steady rhythm pounded on the stage and drew closer. At first Gwen imagined it was the knocking of her knees, but she was infinitely relieved when she realized it was Carson Stockwell's footsteps. He came around her and stopped between her and Wade. "You heard the lady, Solomon. She doesn't want you here, so get out."

Solomon Wade's eyes narrowed and his tongue rolled around inside his cheek, causing the long hairs of his beard to stand out. "I see how it is now," he said. "You've already worked your way into this cozy situation, haven't you, Stockwell? Got the lady wrapped around your little finger. Maybe she don't know all the facts about you. Maybe I ought to be the one to tell her."

Gwen stepped forward to stand beside Carson. "I know all about Mr. Stockwell's background, and yes, I have hired him to captain the *Jubilee*. The position has been filled, so it will do you no good to try and convince me otherwise. There is nothing you could do to change my opinion of you, Mr. Wade. Staying here and arguing will only increase my contempt for you and what you've done."

The man was not easily dissuaded. "I came here this afternoon to save you from making a terrible mistake, Miss Barlow. But I can see now that you ain't a bit smarter than Willoughby was. It's pure foolishness to throw your fate with Stockwell here and a Nigra family that'd as soon slit your throat in your sleep as skin a rabbit. Well, you cut this rope, lady, and you can sure as hell hang by it."

Gwen said nothing, just waited as a menacing stillness hung over the theater. Carson stood beside her. She felt his tension in the squaring of his shoulders and clenching of his fists. She had never been more thankful for anyone's presence in her life. No matter what happened with the captain's position on the *Jubilee* from this point on, she would always remember that he stood beside her now.

When Stockwell finally spoke, his voice was low and commanding. "Miss Barlow," he said, never taking his eyes off Solomon Wade, "it would be my pleasure to show Mr. Wade the door."

Wade rubbed the back of his hand across his mouth. "Never you mind, Carson. This fire-breathing harpy don't need the likes of you to defend her honor. Her and everybody else on this miserable boat is as uppity as Willoughby was. Serve her right if she ended up the same way."

The clearly implied threat snapped what was left of Stockwell's composure. He charged down the steps before Wade had managed to retreat two steps.

Desperation lit Solomon's eyes as he slapped the flat of his hands on Stockwell's chest. "You hold on, now Carson," he spat. "You lay a hand on me, I'll have you arrested and behind bars by nightfall. We'll see how far this monstrosity of Willoughby's floats with her noble captain in the city jail!"

"Let him go," Gwen said. "Mr. Stockwell, please. Don't antagonize him further. I can't very well tolerate another mishap on the *Jubilee*."

Carson did as she asked, but not before shoving Wade half way up the center aisle.

Solomon stumbled, slammed into chairs and cursed the pain to his legs, the man who'd caused it, and the people of the *Jubilee Palace* in general. But thankfully he kept going.

Once Wade had cleared the doorway, Carson came back to Gwen. "Are you all right, Miss Barlow?"

With trembling hands, Gwen did what came most naturally to her in situations of distress, not that she'd ever experienced one of such magnitude as this. She amended her appearance. When her blouse was flawlessly secured in the waistband of her skirt, she answered Stockwell's question. "Yes, Mr. Stockwell, I believe I am."

But it wasn't true. A sudden dizziness washed over her, and he grabbed her elbow. She leaned ever so slightly on his arm, accepting his help. "I think it might be advisable if I sat for a moment however," she said.

He walked her down to a chair and helped her into it. "Wade's a sorry excuse for humanity," Carson said. "Don't judge all river boat captains by the likes of him."

"I certainly shall not," she said. "But I am troubled by the venomous tone in his voice when he spoke of my uncle, and for that matter his attitude toward all the members of the *Jubilee Palace*. He quite hates us all, I believe."

"He expresses a powerful need for vengeance, I'll agree," Stockwell said. "Though his problems are entirely his own doing." Carson paused and sought Gwen's eyes with a steady gaze. "Are you thinking that Solomon Wade killed your uncle, Miss Barlow?"

"I must admit, since I first heard his name, I have considered that possibility. And it is a stronger one now that I've experienced his loathing of nearly everything connected with the *Jubilee Palace*."

Just a short while ago, Travis Veazey had been the target of Gwen's investigative sights. Travis's sudden and irrational outburst with Hildegard, his obvious experience with knots and backstage equipment, and his freely confessed resentment of Eli Willoughby had led her to believe that he was the one most likely to have committed the horrible crime against her uncle.

Now, while Travis was still her main suspect, she wasn't as certain as she had been. Solomon Wade had definitely thrown his hat in the ring of possible guilty persons. It was all so confusing, and Gwen had only her instincts to guide her. She was totally lacking in irrefutable evidence to take to

Constable O'Toole. She wished she could trust Carson Stockwell enough to relate her doubts and theories, but their relationship was simply too fresh and untested to permit such confidences.

Sitting next to her, Carson attempted to soothe her anxiety about Wade with logic. He told her that most men who talk a fierce game do little to back it up. She knew that was true most of the time, but there was something deeply sinister about Solomon Wade. Gwen had no doubt that he had attacked Danita Johnson, and she feared he was capable of much worse.

"I think it's safe to say that Solomon Wade won't trouble you again, Miss Barlow," Carson said. "I want you to concentrate on the performance now and what we can do to get this boat moving. Once these problems are behind us . . ."

He must have seen the concern still in her eyes for he stopped and reverted to his original question. "Miss Barlow, you are convinced that Solomon Wade killed your uncle, aren't you?"

"Actually Mr. Stockwell, I'm not. Two men are equally suspect in my mind at this point. But Solomon is one, yes."

"And the other?"

"If I had a more definitive feeling about

the other, I would tell you, but truthfully, I only strongly suspect . . ."

A piercing scream from the front deck of the *Jubilee* jolted Gwen out of her seat and her thoughts. "That sounds like Peaches!"

More sounds followed — cries and moans as if the black woman had seen a haunting.

Gwen raced for the door. "What in the world?"

Peaches's keening filled the theater. "Sweet Baby Jesus. He's dead!"

Chapter Eleven

By the time Gwen and Carson reached the main deck of the *Jubilee Palace*, Danita Johnson's wails had joined Peaches's. The older woman was on her knees by the ticket booth, rocking back and forth in accompaniment to her long melancholy cries of grief. Her large hands covered her face, but did not block the sounds of anguish that rose and fell with each movement of her body.

Danita stood behind her mother, rocking with that same macabre rhythm of wretchedness. Her hands clutched Peaches's shoulders. Her eyes glistened with tears that spilled over onto her cheeks. "Jesus, save us," she crooned repeatedly.

A few feet from the two women, Lillian leaned against the deck rail, her hand on her chest, her face white as paste. She stared down at the floor until she heard Gwen approach. Then she looked at her daughter, and her features became a distorted mask of horror. "My God, Gwendolyn. It's unthinkable."

"What's happened, Mama? Are you all right?"

Lillian shook her head. "I wonder if anything will ever be right again." She raised her hand and pointed to an area behind the ticket booth.

Gwen took a tentative step forward but stopped when Carson Stockwell's hands circled her arms.

"Miss Barlow," he said, "would you rather I looked first?"

"No. It's all right." He released her, and she stepped around the gaily painted ticket booth. Revulsion churned in her stomach and rose as bitter acid to her mouth. She clutched her abdomen and fell back against the wall of the booth.

Travis Veazey lay awkwardly on the deck. His head, neck, and one shoulder were twisted through two spindles of the ornate railing. A bright red hand print stained a wood post as if that object had been the young man's last grasp of hope in this life. And protruding from Travis's chest was his prized possession, the fish scaling knife with the buck horn handle. A rivulet of blood ran down his shirt and pooled on the polished *Jubilee* deck.

Peaches's endless keening drifted on the still air like the mournful bell of a lost ship. "None of God's children deserves this fate," she cried. And thinking how Travis

Veazey must have suffered in his last moments on earth, Gwen, of course, agreed.

She turned away from the body as Carson stepped around her. Only dimly aware that he knelt by the still form, she was not surprised to hear his pronouncement. "There's no pulse, Miss Barlow. The poor kid is gone."

Dickey Squires ran across the gangway from the embankment as fast as his portly frame allowed. "What the devil's going on here?" he asked, looking at the Johnson women. Their piteous cries had finally abated. Now they whimpered like creatures devoid of all hope. "Don't tell me something's happened to Phineas."

"No, it's not Phineas," Gwen said. She stepped away from the booth, providing a view to the scene.

"Oh, Jesus." Dickey rubbed his eyes and took another look at the body as though the first glance had deceived him. "Damn! The poor mate."

"Please, Mr. Squires," Gwen said, "will you go back to town and fetch Constable O'Toole?"

Dickey left the *Jubilee* and headed in the direction of the constable's office.

"Gwennie, the most wonderful news!" Preston's voice, high-pitched, jubilant, and as inappropriate as a banjo at a funeral, came from the side passageway. He appeared around the corner with Marianne in tow, stood looking at the somber faces, and hesitantly grinned back at everyone. "Why so glum, folks? I've got news that will surely cheer you." He stuck his hand in his bulging pocket and jangled what could only be a profusion of coins. "Just since lunch Marianne and I have sold nearly three dozen tickets, and that's without any real publicity. Our show's going to be a . . ."

Lillian put up her hand. "Not now, Preston."

He stopped jangling. "What's wrong with you people? You act as though you've just lost your best friend."

In unison, all eyes focused on the body at the railing. Preston craned his neck and then gulped back a reflexive gag. "Good God, this is nasty business!" Then he ushered Marianne away from the deck, proclaiming that the details were too gruesome for her tender stomach. Considering that the ingénue burst into a fit of screams upon just hearing the news, Gwen knew he was right.

The others came slowly, one by one, drawn by the unusual commotion at the

Jubilee's bow. Jason DeVane, Sir Clyde, the musicians . . . they returned from their errands or ventured from their quarters and expressed varying degrees of shock, disgust, and thankfully even some compassion. Mostly the same questions circulated among the stunned group in whispers of fear or at least apprehension.

Who could have done such a thing? Could one of us be next? Is the Jubilee *Palace cursed?*

When, after a half hour or so, Constable O'Toole finally crossed the gangway to the *Jubilee* deck, Gwen hoped he could address some of the concerns. She had already formulated her own ideas about the answers to the questions.

O'Toole examined the body for a few minutes, checked the entry of the knife blade, the size of the wound, the condition of Travis's clothing to see if a struggle was indicated. He noted that the position of the body suggested that Travis might have been trying to get to the river, or, simply put, "he just might have fell that way, since the body does some odd twitching in the throes of death."

When he was satisfied with his investigation, O'Toole faced the people of the *Ju-*

bilee. "Can't do much more here, folks," he said. "I'll send the mortician around to collect the body. Then you all can start the clean up." He proceeded to the gangway without another word.

Gwen was incensed. "Excuse me. Mr. O'Toole, can't you at least tell us how you think this terrible tragedy occurred? Surely you have a theory as to what happened."

The constable turned to face her and emitted a long suffering sigh. "I'll have to think on it a while, Miss Barlow, but from what I can see right now, I'd say this is a simple case of accidental death."

She couldn't believe what she was hearing. "Accidental? This young man is lying here with a knife sticking out from his chest — a knife with which he is most familiar and capable of handling, and you call this an accident? You must be joking!"

He crossed his arms over his well-padded waistline and glared at her. "I don't joke, Miss Barlow. I base my conclusions on facts."

"Oh, really? And what facts have you gathered so far that would lead you to this ridiculous conclusion?"

O'Toole waggled a thick finger at her. "You know, Miss Barlow, I don't like your attitude. But despite that, I'll tell you why I think it was an accident." He strode to the body and bent over. "There's a large puddle of water right here by the victim. I think he probably caught something, but the fish, no doubt possessing more intelligence than Veazey did, threw the hook." O'Toole pointed to Travis. "This poor bastard was reaching for his dinner when he lost his footing on a slippery deck and went down on his own knife."

Gwen huffed her opinion of the constable's investigative skills. "Ridiculous. And pure conjecture."

O'Toole took a cigar out of his pocket, bit the end, and spat into the water. "Since you're dying to set me straight, Miss Barlow, let's get it over with. How do you think Veazey met his maker?"

If there was anything Gwen truly hated, it was being talked down to. This irritating officer of the law who'd just scraped a match on his boot sole and now stood puffing away like a steam engine was the most condescending human being she'd ever met. Still, there was a murder to solve, and O'Toole was the only one in town who could officially proclaim a closed case and allow the *Jubilee Palace* to leave the banks of Hickory Bend, hopefully forever! She had to try.

"I think it was murder, Mr. O'Toole."

He blew a ring of smoke into the air. "Oh, so now you think a death on the *Jubilee* is murder? You're singing a different tune this time around, Miss Barlow."

Oh, she wished she could wipe that smug expression off his face. "This time it's obvious, Constable."

He rolled the cigar between his thumb and forefinger and stared at the glowing tip. "And who might the murderer be?" he asked.

She straightened her spine and confidently gave him her answer. "Solomon Wade."

One eyebrow climbed his forehead. At least he'd listened to what she said and was considering her theory. "And why do you think Solomon Wade killed Travis Veazey?"

"Because he was here just minutes before Peaches found Travis's body. And because he hates all of us on the *Jubilee* because Uncle Eli fired him. And because he is known to have committed criminal acts in the past. And because he is an evil man!" She was charging now, and just like a raging bull, she was not about to be stopped. "And I'll tell you something else, Constable. I think Solomon Wade killed my uncle."

A chorus of gasps mingled with murmurs of agreement from the *Jubilee* family behind her. Gwen took courage from the support and plunged ahead. "You arrest Mr. Wade, Constable, and you will have solved both murders associated with the *Jubilee Palace*!"

He stared at her for one long, distressing minute before drawing on the cigar, blowing out the smoke and grinning. "Nope. I don't think so. Solomon Wade didn't kill your uncle."

His statement reflected a swaggering assurance that made her confidence deflate like a day-old balloon. "Why do you say that?"

"Because the night of Eli Willoughby's death, Solomon Wade was drunk out of his head and sitting in my jail. I sat right there watching him all night long." He waved the cigar at Gwen. "Mind you, Miss Barlow, I don't much like Wade. He's a snake, and he's got very few principles. But he's not the snake that killed your uncle."

Solomon Wade in jail the night Eli was killed? And now Travis Veazey dead on the deck of the *Jubilee*? Both of Gwen's major suspects were innocent. Never had she felt so bereft and confused. Plus, she suddenly lacked the faith that the *Jubilee* would ever leave this wretched town.

"Well, someone killed my uncle, Constable," she argued. "You told me so yourself, and now I agree with you. And I'm quite sure someone killed Travis Veazey. You must at least ask questions, interview those who knew Travis . . ."

"I'll just do that, Miss Barlow, if it'll make you happy." O'Toole walked over to Peaches. "Mrs. Johnson. Were you the first one to see Veazey's body?"

"Yes, I 'spose I was."

"Did you notice anything unusual? Besides the body, I mean? Do you remember any details about the scene when you came onto the deck? Did you see anything? Hear anything? Smell anything?"

Peaches's eyes grew round as the biscuits she was famous for. "Smell anything?"

"That's right. Anything at all unusual."

She chewed on her bottom lip, giving the question her full attention. "There was that smell. It was sweet and heavy. I remember 'cause it smelled like cherries. When I first came on deck, I thought someone was cooking. Then I realized it was more like wood smoke. Cherry wood smoke. That's all I remember, 'cause then I saw Travis."

Gwen grew as cold inside as an Apple

Creek winter's eve. *Cherry-scented tobacco.* Without thinking, she said a name out loud. "Anabel."

O'Toole responded immediately to her lack of forethought. His gaze snapped from Peaches to Gwen. "What about Anabel, Miss Barlow? Come to think of it, I haven't seen the Indian woman since I got here." He quickly scanned the faces of the other members of the *Jubilee* family. "Any of you folks seen her?"

No one had, which left Gwen feeling the need to protect Anabel's reputation. "She's obviously not on the *Jubilee,* Constable," Gwen said. "Otherwise I'm sure she'd be here."

O'Toole jerked his thumb toward the embankment where a curious crowd had begun to gather. "Don't see how she could be within a mile of this boat and not notice the commotion. Seems as though most of the town knows something happened here. Why wouldn't she come see for herself like everyone else?"

Yes, why indeed? The question came treacherously to Gwen's mind and demanded an answer. *Not Anabel!* she shouted in a silent plea. "I'm not sure," she said aloud. "But Miss Whitedove is a very private person. She spends most of her time alone. Perhaps she wandered off, away from town."

O'Toole puffed on the cigar. "Why did you mention her name just now, Miss Barlow?"

"Only because I, too, wondered where she was."

Brushing a mat of coarse white hair from his forehead, Sir Clyde stepped away from the deck rail where he'd been observing the scene and came toward Gwen and the constable. "Or perhaps, Miss Barlow, you mentioned Anabel's name because of that foul pipe she's always smoking. And that tobacco . . . what does it smell like?" He rolled his eyes with that air of superiority he seemed always to possess. "Oh, yes . . . cherries, I believe."

"Cherries, is it?" O'Toole speared Gwen with a knowing look. "If you should see Miss Whitedove, you tell her I'd like to have a word with her, Miss Barlow." He started for the gangway, but stopped and turned back before leaving the *Jubilee*. "One more thing. You tell Miss Whitedove not to leave Hickory Bend. You tell her to stay right here."

He continued to stare at Gwen until she responded. "All right! I'll tell her."

But how could Anabel have killed Travis? It

didn't make sense. What did she have against him? Eli Willoughby, maybe. Gwen understood Anabel's motives against Eli. But Travis?

Apparently satisfied with his investigation, O'Toole headed for shore, leaving the people on the *Jubilee Palace* to speculate on their future.

"Constable, wait!" It was Sir Clyde. "I need to ask you one very important question."

O'Toole halted at the end of the gangway. "Yeah?"

"What about our performance? We'd planned to open in two nights here in Hickory Bend. We have the proper license of course. Do you see this . . ." Sir Clyde glanced briefly over his shoulder at the body. ". . . this incident as preventing our plans from going forward?"

"Don't see why it should. Long as you've got that license. Seeing as the victim was only that shanty trash, isn't anybody likely to spend much time grieving over him." He waved a hand in the air as he left. "Sure, you folks go ahead and put on your show. I might even come myself." Then he split the air with a belly laugh and added, "Just don't go having more people die on you!"

★ ★ ★

The Hickory Bend undertaker arrived soon after O'Toole's departure. From him Gwen learned that there were provisions in the town's by-laws for indigents such as Travis Veazey who had the misfortune to die within town boundaries. His remains would be interred in a plain pine box and committed to the hereafter via a narrow cemetery plot in potter's field. Gwen was not to worry about the undertaker's fee, as that would be covered from the mayor's petty cash supply.

Gwen asked about arranging a simple graveside ceremony for Travis, and the undertaker informed her that the Methodist minister, who usually did this sort of thing, was at his brother's in St. Louis. And the Catholic priest probably wouldn't conduct a service since it was obvious the deceased was a heathen, and "you know how priests are about associating themselves with the Godless."

Well, of course Gwen didn't know any such thing, but she resigned herself to the fact that Travis wouldn't be helped into the Kingdom by one of God's own soldiers. She questioned the undertaker about the location of the cemetery and specifically where Travis's final resting place would be. She resolved to visit the grave site and at least leave flowers before the *Jubilee* left Hickory Bend. It was little enough to remember the young man who had been a part of her showboat family, if only for a short time.

As if sensing Gwen's discomfort while the body was carried off, the undertaker assured her that a "hole would be properly dug, and the guest of honor appropriately attired."

So that would be that, Gwen thought, watching as the box holding Travis's body was loaded onto a hearse. She secretly prayed that she wouldn't be without mourners at her own resting place in the future.

Though it seemed somehow insensitive to the memory of the departed, Gwen decided not to cancel the next rehearsal scheduled for seven o'clock that night. After all, the opening performance of *Belle of the Ozarks* was still only two days away. Three hours stretched ahead of her with no specific plans until dinner. Peaches's announcement that she had smelled a cherry aroma at the crime scene continued to bother Gwen, and she needed to satisfy her curiosity as to the whereabouts of Anabel at the time of Travis's death.

Thinking Marianne Dresden might know where Anabel was, she went up to the girl's second deck cabin. Even though a great deal of antagonism existed between the two women, at least on Anabel's part, perhaps the close proximity of their living quarters made them aware of each other's comings and goings.

Gwen knocked on the door, and once Marianne determined who was there, she issued a feeble invitation to enter.

The first detail Gwen noticed was that Marianne was uncharacteristically mussed. She sat up when Gwen came in the room and tried to repair her disheveled appearance, but it was obvious that she was distraught. The lace of her pillow had left a pattern imprint on the side of her face. Her eyes were red from weeping. A book lay ignored on the floor.

"Oh, Miss Barlow," she said, "I must look a sight." Tugging and smoothing her clothes, she added, "Please sit down."

The pleasantry was superfluous since there was no place to sit in the girl's sparse cabin. Besides a domed trunk, a set of bunk beds along one wall, a small washstand, and a narrow bedside table upon which rested a single gas light, there was nothing in Marianne's room to distinguish it from the most Spartan of accommodations. And since the light was not on, it was gloomy. The only window was the small one in the door. Gwen recalled that Anabel had the slightly larger cabin next door, the one with a cheery window facing the river.

Without mentioning the lack of seating, Gwen settled on the floor and tucked her legs underneath her. Her immediate instinct was to reach out to the girl and see if she could offer some comfort in Marianne's time of distress. "I can tell you've been crying, Marianne," she said. "Do you want to tell me what's troubling you?"

The girl sniffled and reached for a hankie on her night stand. "It's this awful business with Travis, I guess," she said. "I must admit I didn't really like him. He reminds me of the men I knew from back home. But no one should end up the way he did. It's just not right."

"No, of course it isn't," Gwen said. "It's very sad. Can you think of someone who should be notified of Travis's death? I haven't found any records of his family in my uncle's papers. Do you know how to contact them?"

Marianne pushed a few strands of lank

hair behind her ear. "Me? No. I'm sure I don't know any more than you do. Travis just showed up here one day on a shanty boat."

"Were you here the day Mr. Willoughby traded . . . I mean, the day Travis arrived?"

"Yes."

"Did you hear any of the transaction that led to Travis being taken aboard the *Jubilee*?"

"I only heard Mr. Willoughby say he'd take Travis on." She paused as if trying to recall other details. "Oh yes, I do remember something Travis's father said."

"What's that?"

"He said his son was trouble. Had been all nineteen years of his life." She blew her nose. "I thought that was a mean thing to say about his own kin. But then I've known men like that, ones that seem to have lost their hearts somewhere along the way."

Gwen patted Marianne's knee. Surely there was a story hidden in Marianne's words. Maybe some day the girl would decide to tell her what it was. "Were you afraid of Travis, Marianne?"

"Afraid? No. He never paid me any mind, so I never worried about him. He mostly just fished . . . and argued with people, especially Mr. Willoughby. I didn't like Travis because of that. Mr. Willoughby was a fine man." It was as if a small flame lit the azure depths of Marianne's eyes when she indulged the fond memory of her benefactor. "But then I don't have to tell you that," she added.

"No, I'm well aware what my uncle was like." *Though my opinion is slightly different from yours.* "Would you mind telling me how you ended up on the *Jubilee Palace*, Marianne? A journal entry of Uncle Eli's indicates that he just sort of found you in a little town down river."

"That's right. I was working with a traveling evangelist's show."

Gwen could certainly picture Marianne in the role of an angel. All she lacked in appearance was a set of feathery wings. "What did you do with the show?" she asked.

Marianne's face flushed with color, making Gwen conclude that perhaps her job with the evangelist wasn't all that angelic. "I'm not proud of what I did, but I needed the money."

Gwen leaned back against a wall and rested her hands in her lap. "I'm not going to judge you, Marianne."

"I talked to people before the show. I found out little things about them that

Brother Reuben could use later. Like if a woman just lost her husband, I'd find out his name and how he died, stuff like that. Then I'd stand behind a screen with holes poked in it so I could see the audience, and when Brother Reuben talked to these people, I'd whisper to him what I'd discovered about them. He was real good at what he did. Got lots of donations."

Gwen tried to keep her opinion of Brother Reuben from showing on her face, but apparently was not successful, because Marianne defended her actions.

"I guess it wasn't an honest thing to do, but it wasn't bad either. Those people liked what Brother Reuben told them about their loved ones. It made them feel good. And they freely gave of their money. And you've got to believe me, Miss Barlow, I never meant to hurt anybody."

"Of course I know that." Gwen understood how Marianne brought out the Sir Galahad in Preston. If ever a person needed to be protected, it was this waif of a girl. "If you ever feel like talking, I'd be glad to listen," she offered. "Sometimes it helps to talk to another woman about things. Lillian would listen too. Remember that, won't you?"

"Sure. Thanks. But I stay pretty much to

myself. Buddy's nice. I talk to him sometimes. It's not that I don't like people. I'm
not like Anabel. I'm just quiet." Her
sudden, unexpected smile dazzled with ap-
peal. "Unless I'm on stage, that is."

Gwen smiled in return and stood up.
"One more thing, Marianne. About
Anabel. Do you dislike her?"

"No. But she doesn't like me."

"Are you afraid of her? Do you think she
would hurt you?"

"I'm not afraid of all of her. Just her eyes
and her tongue."

"What do you mean?"

"She can give you a look that makes you
wish you were invisible. And she can say
hurtful things. I try not to let her words get
to me, but sometimes it's hard."

Gwen had experienced enough of
Anabel's cut-to-the-quick remarks to understand exactly what Marianne was
saying. And she could also understand why
Anabel viewed Marianne as the cause of all
her troubles. But that didn't excuse the
woman's callous behavior toward the
ingénue. Someone was just going to have
to help Marianne develop a backbone!

"Just one question more," Gwen said.
"Do you know where Anabel is now? I'd
like to talk to her."

"No, not for sure. But when she's gone for long times like this, she's usually in the woods north of town. She goes there sometimes with all her bottles and stuff."

"All her bottles?"

"Yes. All sizes and shapes. She puts them in big baskets. I don't know how she carries it all. She must be strong."

Gwen pointed north, toward the stern of the *Jubilee*. "You say she goes this way out of town?"

Marianne nodded.

"Thanks."

It was time for another ride, Gwen decided. She'd already ventured up that way once and discovered her bicycle could navigate the level path with ease. She told Marianne good bye and went down the stairs to fetch the trusty Monarch.

Chapter Twelve

The sun was deliciously warm through the fabric of Gwen's shirt, dispelling some of the terrifying chill of the last hours. Near the riverbank, ring-necked and eider ducks paddled in companionable groups and occasionally ducked their heads into the water to retrieve tempting tidbits. From the highest branches of the hickory trees, swallows and martins chittered and crooned from the shelter of budding leaves.

Most of nature's creatures didn't know that a human being had been murdered on the *Jubilee Palace* just two hours before. Travis Veazey's blood was probably still moist on the showboat's deck while a quarter mile away, life went on as usual. Here in the shade of tall, stately hickory trees, Gwen could almost convince herself that the tragedy hadn't happened. With the wind in her hair and her feet peddling to a rhythm she found soothing and natural, she could almost erase the gruesome image from her mind . . . almost.

But she knew the musicians who'd volunteered to clean the *Jubilee* deck were right now going about their unsavory task. Right now Travis's body was being tended to in the undertaker's office. And right now, she was trying to find the woman who used cherry-scented tobacco and thus had become a prominent suspect in the young man's death.

She heard Anabel's voice coming from the forest before the woman came into view. Gwen stopped, rested her bicycle against a tree, and wandered toward the pleasing sound emanating from a dense section of woods a few hundred yards off the path. Anabel was singing, and while Gwen was moved by the lilting quality of her surprisingly sweet voice, she couldn't make out the words. The inflection sounded French, yet the lyrics were too harsh and clipped to be the melodious ebb and flow of a romance language. Maybe it was Cherokee. Gwen remembered that Anabel had spent time in New Orleans. Perhaps she sang a blended language of the Bayou.

Finally Gwen saw her. Anabel sat in a pool of sunlight amidst a growth of wild ferns, her colorful skirt spread around her. Her long hair trailed down her back in an ebony braid. Baskets of bottles lay within arm's reach. Her head was bent. Whatever lay on the forest floor occupied her full attention. For the moment, she'd even stopped singing.

Gwen waited for some sign that it would be appropriate to request Anabel's attention. She knew her reason for being there was valid, but still she felt like an intruder.

Anabel's dark head slowly raised but she didn't turn around. "I know it's you, Gwen. You'd make a lousy Indian, so you can stop tip-toeing around like a common thief."

The spell was broken. She was the old Anabel again, speaking in a grating tone and using unminced words.

Gwen tromped through the thick underbrush, mindful not to stumble on hidden roots that snaked across the ground. "I was told you might be here, Anabel," she said.

Anabel occupied herself with her project again. "I'm sure I know who told you — that sniveling little spy, Marianne. Someone ought to tell that girl what it means to mind her own business."

"I asked her where you were. It would have been impolite not to tell me."

"Hrumph!"

Gwen skirted around to be able to see Anabel's face. She saw, too, a collection of items whose relationship to each other made no sense at all. There were dark bottles of liquids, clusters of flowers, and bowls filled with floating blossoms. There was even a bottle of brandy. "May I sit down?" Gwen inquired.

Anabel looked up at her with an amused expression. "Do you think I assign seating arrangements in the forest? Even a Cherokee chief doesn't demand that kind of respect." She grinned. "Well, maybe a chief."

Gwen was determined not to allow the woman to make her feel foolish this early in their encounter. She sat, finding the greenery soft and spongy. It would probably stain her camel colored gabardine skirt, but that was a matter for later. "I only asked because I am aware that I'm interrupting your solitude."

"Yes, you are. And for what I wonder." Anabel leveled a narrowed gaze on Gwen. "Something happened at the *Jubilee*, didn't it?"

Gwen was not about to let the innocence of Anabel's question lull her into false security. The suggestion of guilt which shrouded the woman made Gwen anxious enough for her own safety to double her guard where Anabel was concerned. If Anabel did stab Travis, she would be clever enough to create a guise of ignorance of the crime. "Why do you think something happened on the *Jubilee*?" Gwen asked just as evasively.

"I thought I heard a strange sound. Maybe moaning. I have very good hearing."

The scent of wildflowers drifted into Gwen's nostrils. She inhaled deeply, enjoying the respite from the day's tragic events. "It was Peaches," she said.

True concern flitted across Anabel's face, just for an instant. "Not Danita. Not Phineas."

"No. Something happened to Travis Veazey."

Anabel huffed an incredulous breath and pulled a few flower petals from their stems. "Travis? I can't imagine anything happening to make that one's lot worse than it is."

Gwen stared at her, waiting for her hands to quit their task. When they did, she said, "He's dead, Anabel. Stabbed in the chest."

"What? Stabbed?" She crushed some petals in her fists, and they fell, bruised, to her lap. "I can't believe it."

Gwen decided right then, that if Anabel was faking a reaction of concern and shock, she deserved not only the lead role in the *Jubilee Palace* play, but the lead in a major Broadway production. Gwen would have bet her Monarch bicycle that Anabel didn't know that Travis had been killed.

Anabel's copper complexion paled to a sickly yellow. "Why would anyone . . . ? He was such a hard luck case. I guess he didn't have any friends, but I wouldn't have thought he had enemies." She reached across the assortment of plants and bowls and grabbed Gwen's wrist. "That's it," she cried. "You think I did it. You came here to find me because you think I killed that boy."

There was no point denying it. "I had planned to tell you that the reason I came was to remind you of the rehearsal tonight, but that would have been a lie. I'm sorry, Anabel, but I thought there was a chance . . ."

"Why would you think that?" Her voice quivered with panic.

"That tobacco you smoke. Peaches was the one to find Travis, and when O'Toole questioned her, she said she smelled cherries in the air by the body . . . wood-smoked cherries."

Anabel dropped Gwen's hand and reached in her pocket. She pulled out the old birchbark pipe and turned it over in

241

her hand. It was like she was seeing it for the first time, examining every minute detail. Gwen caught the faint whiff of cherry scent even though the pipe was not lit. Certainly it had been smoked recently.

"I was there," Anabel said softly. "I saw Travis before I came here. He was fishing behind the ticket booth, where he usually is. We talked for a minute . . ." The hint of a smile trembled on her lips. "We talked sometimes about the things we didn't like on the *Jubilee*, mostly the people. I guess our disagreeable natures was about all we ever had in common."

"Did he say anything that might shed light on what happened to him?"

"No. Not really. He made a general comment about hating women, but I didn't pay much attention. He hated everyone, plus I knew he'd had that fight with Hildegard." She swirled a bunch of petals around in a bowl. The pleasant aroma from moments before grew stronger. "Wait a minute." She took her dripping finger from the bowl and pointed it at Gwen. "He did say something odd."

"Really? What?"

"He said he could shock a lot of people . . . I guess he meant the people on the showboat . . . if he just told something he knew. He said if he told it, things would change real quick on the *Jubilee*."

A quick rush of adrenalin brought Gwen to full alert. "Did he say what that was?"

"No. And I didn't ask him. I always figure when a person wants to talk, he will. Then I left. When I walked away from Travis Veazey, he was alive, Gwen, I swear it."

Gwen stood up, brushing bits of leaves and twigs from her skirt. "Thanks for telling me what you know, Anabel. I'm not sure what it means, but I'm certain it's important." She started to walk away, but turned back. "By the way, we really do have rehearsal tonight at seven o'clock."

"I know that."

"And one more thing. Would you mind telling me what you're doing with all the flowers?"

"Energizing them, that's all," Anabel said. She chuckled at the confused look on Gwen's face. "Making remedies. My grandmother taught me." She reached into a bowl and pulled out a handful of white blossoms. "These are arrowheads. My ancestors used to eat the roots." She put those back and removed one long, spindly white flower. "This one is lizard's tail. It provides potent juices."

Gwen leaned over and pointed to a burnished blossom in the bowl. "What's that pretty one there?"

"Copper Iris. It smells real strong. So does the one next to it, the marsh marigold."

Gwen was spellbound. Perhaps there was more Cherokee in Anabel than she liked to admit. At least with regard to her knowledge of growing things. "What are you making with the flowers?" she asked.

Anabel hesitated, as if considering whether or not to reveal hidden mysteries to Gwen. In the end, she did. She wrapped her hands around one of the bowls of floating flowers. "See this water? It's from a spring just over the hill. If you float fresh blossoms in spring water and leave it in the sun, the juices from the flowers make the water potent. When it's all blended just right, you add brandy. This preserves the essence. Then you store the mixture in a dark glass bottle."

Gwen had visions of large copper vats and fizzling liquids. She'd never seen a still, but she'd heard they existed in the Ohio backwoods. "Then what do you do with it?"

Anabel laughed. It was a nice sound. "You drink it, of course. It gives you emotional balance."

Now Gwen pictured a whole row of little brown jugs with the corks ready to pop. "Really?" She considered asking Anabel for a quart of the mystery brew just so she could get through the next few days. She might have if she hadn't been scared to the roots of her hair of poisoning herself.

Anabel nodded. "Sometimes I feel a little out of balance with nature, like maybe I'm distressed. I make up a few bottles of this and in a short time, I'm my old self again."

So that's how Anabel viewed her normally complaining, disagreeable self — as being "a little out of balance." Gwen wasn't sure whether the old self Anabel referred to was the one she wanted back, but she didn't say so. She was enjoying these first companionable minutes with the woman. Perhaps Anabel had indulged in a few swigs of "energized" water before Gwen got there, and it was having the desired effect.

"It sounds like your Cherokee grandmother was a wise woman," Gwen said. She headed toward the path where she'd left her bicycle. "I'll see you at rehearsal."

"I'll be there. And, Gwen, I'm real sorry about what happened to Travis, but I hope you believe me that I didn't kill him."

"I do. The Constable wants to talk to you. If he comes around the *Jubilee* again, I'll tell him you were here at the time of Travis's death."

Relief softened Anabel's features. "Thanks. I'll stop by his office later. And Gwen, I didn't kill Eli either, though he deserved it. All the proof you need of my innocence is right there on both men's heads."

Gwen stopped and turned around. "Their heads?"

"Yes. They both still had their scalps, didn't they?"

"They did, yes." Gwen walked the rest of way through the woods thinking about what Anabel had said. Was it possible that Anabel Whitedove had just made a joke?

Gwen rode back to the *Jubilee* and secured her bicycle on the stern deck. Then she walked to the front of the boat, to the ticket booth. No one was there. Steeling herself to face the aftermath of the tragedy, she stepped around the booth. Travis Veazey's body was gone. So were the grisly remains of his death. The musicians who'd volunteered to do the job should be commended, and Gwen made a mental note to thank them again.

Next, she reviewed the details of the crime. She estimated she'd first heard Peaches's screams shortly before two o'clock. It was now a little after five. In just over three hours a man had been brutally murdered, her family on the *Jubilee Palace* had faced a startling reminder of the brevity and frailty of mortal life, and the probability that a twisted and depraved mind lived among them had surfaced once more.

Yet, as she stood staring at the *Jubilee* ticket booth, its borders stenciled with verdant acanthus leaves, the signs detailing prices and show times colorfully painted in elegant script, the cold fact of death seemed somehow surreal. Maybe that described her life in recent days also. Surreal, otherworldly. Maybe that described a performer's life in general. It was the actor's job to transform the mundane existence of the audience into something grand, spectacular, totally and wonderfully imaginative, and therefore . . . unreal.

But guilt was real enough. And someone guilty of terrible crimes was close enough to breathe the same air as Gwen, perhaps even share the same living space. That was reality, grim and undeniable, and she had to find out who the guilty person was before . . .

No, she wouldn't let herself think about the consequences of her failure now. It was enough to handle the reality she knew.

She walked back to the *Jubilee* kitchen. The Johnson family was there. Peaches and Danita sat at the table by the window. Phineas stood at the stove, stirring a pot of something that smelled beefy and delicious. Gwen figured the Negro man was probably responsible for supplying tonight's dinner, and was generous enough to cook it as well.

Phineas looked at Gwen as she entered. His big brown eyes were soft with empathy, as if they'd seen enough of tragedy in his lifetime and easily recognized it in someone else. "Afternoon, Miss Barlow," he said, reaching for a steaming tea kettle. "Sit yourself down there with Peaches, and I'll get you some tea, too."

She smiled at him. "I look that bad, Phineas? That I need you to get my tea?"

"No offense, ma'am, but yes, you do. You ladies have had a hard time today. I wish I'd have been here when it happened." He took a cup and saucer from the pantry, set it on the table, and poured the tea. Shaking his head in sad disbelief, he said, "It's a terrible thing what happened to that boy. Terrible thing. And it wasn't the only bad luck that happened on this boat today."

Gwen almost choked on her first sip of tea. Something else had happened? Panic began a dance in her stomach. She looked at Peaches and Danita.

Danita patted her hand. "Papa's talking about Solomon Wade showing up, Miss Barlow."

Good Heavens. She'd forgotten completely about Solomon Wade. Yes, that was another troubling event of the last few hours.

Phineas sat down at the table. "It's a good thing for Wade I wasn't here. Peaches'll tell you. I don't have a very tight rein when it comes to that man. The good Lord says we got to forgive, but I can't find forgiveness in my soul for that one."

"I know," Gwen said. "I only spent a few minutes with him, and I can honestly say that my feelings toward him are quite close to loathing." She wrapped her hands around her cup to ward off a chill, though it was warm and cozy in the *Jubilee* kitchen. "Phineas, Solomon Wade was here just minutes before Travis died. Do you know if the two of them had ever had a bad relationship in the past?"

"Are you asking if I think Solomon

could have killed Travis?"

She nodded.

"Truly, Miss Barlow, I think Solomon has nothing but vengeance in his black heart. Now whether or not bad blood flowed between those two, I couldn't tell you. But if it did, then yes'm, Solomon could have killed him. I can tell you this, too. Solomon hated Mr. Willoughby, and everybody on the *Jubilee* knew it."

"I know. I thought the same thing you are. But he didn't kill Uncle Eli. Constable O'Toole told me Wade was in jail the night Eli was murdered."

Phineas bowed his head and remained silent for a full minute. When he spoke, Gwen had to strain to hear his words. "Some men'll do most anything to get themselves a good alibi."

"Phineas, are you saying the story of Solomon's incarceration is a lie?"

"I ain't saying nothing for sure, Miss Barlow. It's just something to think on. I just pray there's justice handed down to Mr. Willoughby's murderer. Your uncle was kind to Peaches and me. He done us a good turn by taking us in when hardly no one else would, and he shouldn't have died like he did."

"No, he shouldn't," Gwen agreed.

"Thank you for the tea." She left the dining room and went to her room to change. Perhaps she could rest a few minutes before dinner. But as soon as she sat on Uncle Eli's plush velvet bedcover, the mysteries of the *Jubilee Palace* flooded her mind again.

What had Phineas meant in that implied accusation of Solomon Wade? Was it possible that Constable O'Toole lied about Solomon being in jail? Gwen didn't think so. While O'Toole was opinionated and boorish, he'd shown no signs of dishonesty. But perhaps he was wrong about the timing of events that night. Maybe Wade had killed Eli in a drunken rage and had been incarcerated afterwards.

With regard to Uncle Eli, Wade had definitely had a motive for committing the crime. But according to O'Toole, he lacked the opportunity to accomplish it. Travis Veazey had the opportunity, but no indisputable motive.

Gwen certainly wouldn't dismiss Solomon as a possible suspect, but she had no choice at this point but to focus her attention on other possibilities. She remembered her brother Preston's innocent question. "Who had the most to gain from Uncle Eli's death?" he'd asked.

"Yes, who?" she said now. "And who had anything at all to gain from Travis Veazey's death?" The answer was both elusive and obvious. Uncle Eli's killer, that's who. Anabel told her that Travis Veazey had a secret, and it was big enough to change the status of the *Jubilee*.

"What could it have been?" Gwen said to the empty room. "Did Travis know who killed Uncle Eli?" That was the most probable scenario. And by silencing Veazey for good, the killer definitely had something to gain. Poor Travis. It appeared his secret was of great magnitude — and one that cost him his life.

Chapter Thirteen

The Thursday evening rehearsal went better than Gwen expected. All the actors and musicians showed up eager to get to work. Perhaps preparing for *Belle of the Ozarks* was everyone's way of putting the events of the afternoon out of their minds. One factor made the rehearsal even more successful. Hildegard Kruger wasn't fluttering about insinuating herself into all aspects of the production.

Considering the stressful circumstances under which she'd been living, Gwen slept rather soundly Thursday night, though perhaps having her door double-locked and the chair under the doorknob once again contributed to her sense of well-being. At any rate, she awoke refreshed and ready to see the production of Eli's play into its final stages before Saturday night's opening performance.

Gwen was famished when she entered the *Jubilee* dining room on Friday morning and took a seat between her mother and Preston. She enthusiastically accepted Peaches's platter of eggs, potatoes, and sourdough bread and took generous portions for herself. She had consumed about half her meal in the time it took for Preston to finish his. He pushed back his chair and went to the window to look upon the sunbathed riverbank and the awakening town of Hickory Bend.

"Looks like it's going to be a nice day," he said. "I should be able to go into town for a few minutes to sell more tickets and put up posters."

"That would be encouraging," Gwen said.

"If it's like this tomorrow, the parade should be quite a success and draw a lot of attention."

He was referring to the opening day pageantry of marching into town with the actors in full costume and the musicians in their band uniforms. It was, Gwen had learned, showboat tradition that river town people looked forward to. The *Jubilee* troupe would not disappoint them.

Preston turned from the window and caught Gwen's eye with a mischievous wink. "Don't shoot the messenger, Gwennie, but bad news. Here comes your least favorite Hickory Bend resident."

She dropped her fork onto her plate. "Oh, no. Not Constable O'Toole. I don't think I can face him this early in the morning."

"Forgive me, Gwennie. It's actually your *second* least favorite resident. No, make that your second and third. I just noticed Hildegard bringing up the rear behind her amiable father."

Gwen slid her plate into the center of the table. She wouldn't be eating any more now. "Oh, wonderful." She stood beside Preston at the window. Indeed, Manfred Kruger was marching like a militiaman toward the *Jubilee Palace*. "He wants money, Preston. I can tell by the determination in his step and the snarl on his face."

She called to Peaches. "Is there anything left of the five dollars I gave you yesterday for food?"

Peaches shook her head. "I used that up at Davenport's and traded him a cleaver for tonight's roast."

Lillian clapped her hands. "Peaches, your cleverness always amazes me. Eli purchased a fine assortment of knives, so we don't need a cleaver anyway."

Exasperation simmered toward an outburst, which Gwen managed to control. "Mama," she said, "that's hardly the point. Have you got any money on you?"

"Me? Why, no."

"Preston?"

He pulled his pockets inside out. All that fell to the floor was a lint covered stick to what once had been a piece of rock candy.

Gwen quickly scanned the faces of the actors and musicians who all suspiciously avoided eye contact. Their attentions were glued to their plates as if fried eggs had never seemed so fascinating.

"Don't fret, Gwennie," Preston said. "Maybe he just wants to talk."

Gwen leaned on the window sill and stared at the door to the dining room. The heavy clomp of boots told her she didn't have long to wait.

Manfred Kruger burst in the door, speared her with a purposeful glower, and said, "Miss Barlow, we need to talk."

Gwen caught Preston's smug expression out of the corner of her eye.

Hildegard swept into the room in a cloud of pink satin and white lace ruffles. Even her bloomers were fringed with several layers of rippling white lace. She elbowed her way past her father, which was no easy task since Hildegard was a large girl and Kruger's robust form occupied most of the center of the room.

She shot an irate glare over her shoulder at Kruger. "Don't be mad at me, Miss

Barlow," Hildegard said. "I told Papa not to come. I said he'd only make trouble for me if he interfered and made you angry."

Kruger scowled at the back of his daughter's head and bit his lips in an obvious effort to control his temper.

Gwen drew a fortifying deep breath and walked toward her visitors. The last thing she needed this morning was to be thrust into the middle of a Kruger family quarrel. "What can I do for you, Mr. Kruger?"

He crossed his arms over his chest. "What you can do, is tell me what the blazes is happening on this . . . this floating catastrophe of yours."

A few days ago, Gwen might have agreed with Kruger's description of the *Jubilee*. Suddenly his choice of words only fueled her fury. Stunned once again by this reversal in attitude, she realized that though it had crept up on her slowly, it now enveloped her totally. "Eli's Folly" had definitely become the "Barlows' Treasure," lock, stock, and problems. Now she felt almost maternal in her loyalty to the *Jubilee*'s velvet curtains, garish upholstery, and oddball assortment of dwellers. She would have to think about this . . . when she had time.

She faced Manfred Kruger with fire in

her heart. "There's no need to be rude, Mr. Kruger."

"Rude? You're the mistress of a den of murderers, and you have the nerve to call me rude?"

Hildegard clasped her hands in desperate supplication. "Papa! You're ruining everything for me just like always! Go home!"

"Be quiet, Hildegard!"

Gwen's toes tapped like a timpani drum. One Kruger was bad enough, but two of them could test the patience of Job. "If you find the *Jubilee* so distasteful, why in Heaven's name are you here?" she said, feeling infinitely proud of the question.

"Only to escort my daughter. Hildegard insisted on coming here today despite the despicable goings-on yesterday. Mind you, I didn't like that Veazey one whit. He was distasteful and crude and probably ignorant as a toad. When he came sniffing after Hildegard, I warned her to stay away from him. I threatened him with a shotgun . . ."

Gwen couldn't help it. She emitted a most unladylike snort. "Hildegard and Travis? Why, from everything I've observed, they hated each other."

"Of course my Hildy despised him, but that doesn't stop Veazey's kind. They see a

258

young lady of quality and they come after her with no regard to the difference in background and breeding. Uppity. That's what that boy was."

Hildegard shook her head, her curls fluttering like golden corkscrews. "I almost never agree with Papa, Miss Barlow, but that part's true. Travis was uppity."

Kruger stared down his nose at his daughter. "Be quiet, Hildegard." Then he turned his attention back to Gwen. "I'm not sorry Veazey's dead, but I am sickened to the core about the idea of a murder . . . no, two murders, in Hickory Bend in a short period of time. And both on this glittering, gaudy graveyard you call a showboat!"

Normally Gwen hated repeating herself. This time was the exception. "Then why are you here, Mr. Kruger?"

"Because a man can only take so much, and I couldn't take any more carrying-on from Hildegard about the rehearsal this morning. This girl could whine a starving man into giving her his false teeth." At a scathing look from his persuasive little angel, Manfred softened his tone. "Look, I know you folks depend on Hildy. I know how important she is to this production."

So many ways to refute that statement

came to Gwen's mind. Unfortunately she couldn't utter any of them. A girl's sensitive nature was at stake, and just the day before Gwen had seen how Hildegard reacted to criticism.

"I just had to let her come back, even considering the danger. But I told her she could only come if I personally escorted her. And, Miss Barlow, you have to guarantee her safety while she's on board the *Jubilee*."

"I will certainly do my best, Mr. Kruger."

"I don't much care for you show people, Miss Barlow," he said. "You know that. But Hildy has her mind set on this acting business." A pained expression crossed his face when he glanced at the smug set of Hildegard's tight lips. "And when Hildy gets her mind set . . . well, you know how it is."

Did she ever!

Kruger squeezed his eyes tightly shut, apparently choosing his words with caution for the first time. "I don't have to like you, Miss Barlow, to trust you. And I guess I trust you to see my girl home once this rehearsal is over."

An oh, so sweet grin plastered itself on Gwen's face. "Your flattery has positively turned my head, Mr. Kruger. I will walk Hildegard home myself when we finish."

"All right then." He patted his daughter's shoulder awkwardly. "You folks are getting a right fine assistant in the bargain. And she can act, too. Hildy'd be a real asset to this playacting of yours . . . if you can clean up this mess around here."

"Yes, indeed," Gwen managed to respond.

The printer nodded, concluding his point, and strode to the door.

"Excuse me, Mr. Kruger?" Gwen said.

He turned around.

"Something you said before has me a bit puzzled."

He waited, his hand on the doorknob.

"You said you once took a shotgun to Travis Veazey."

He half snorted, half chuckled. "Oh, no you don't, Miss Barlow. You can't pin Veazey's death on me. I aimed a shotgun at him all right, and I'd have taken a whip to him if he hadn't stopped coming around Hildegard. But I didn't kill him." He held his hands palms up so everyone in the dining room could view them. "It's ink you see on my fingers. Not blood."

When he left, Gwen found herself wondering . . . Kruger hadn't asked for any money. She should be relieved, but when she saw the look of triumph in Hildegard's eyes as her gaze followed her father from the room, Gwen didn't know if she'd come out ahead.

Gwen left the *Jubilee* dining room and went directly to the theater, hoping to steal a few minutes alone before the others arrived for rehearsal. She walked onto the stage and peered over the audience seating designed to accommodate three hundred people. To hear Preston talk, it wasn't going to be difficult to get that many Hickory Bend residents to come to the *Jubilee Palace* opening night. If nothing else, her brother had been blessed with irrepressible optimism. In that respect, he was his mother's offspring.

Gwen, the practical one, knew that it didn't matter if three hundred people showed up, or only thirty. The *Jubilee* troupe was committed to perform now. At seven thirty the next night, the band would play for a half hour, and then the premier showing of Eli Willoughby's *Belle of the Ozarks* would light up the *Jubilee* stage. An hour and a half later, the actors would take their bows amidst a chorus of cheers or boos, and the showboat's career would be officially launched. And as director, it was Gwen's job to see that everything progressed as smoothly as possible.

She walked to the middle of the stage and looked up at Romance Mountain. Once she'd seen the elaborate prop lowered to the stage, she realized what an engineering feat it had been to create it. It was the perfect backdrop for the lovely Belle to accept her handsome sheriff's declaration of love. Gwen could picture every young woman in the audience with their hands over their pattering hearts when Jason DeVane pledged his undying devotion to Marianne Dresden. And she laughed to herself when she thought of Preston, playing the hapless but honest umbrella salesman, gritting his teeth in the wings.

Deciding she would quickly scan the actors' marks taped for the performance, Gwen moved to a spot in the middle of the stage. Each actor corresponded to a different taped symbol, with Marianne's being an X, Jason's a triangle, and so on. Gwen had personally taped most of the locations herself, using different colors for each of the three acts. She'd been careful to take into account sound projection, curtain frames, lighting . . .

She had just checked the first marks when she suddenly found herself in the middle of a golden pool of light. A brilliant beam speared down upon her from the guide wires. She glanced toward the wings where the electric board was located, but couldn't see anyone because of the light in her eyes. "Who's there?" she called.

The light dimmed to a soft glow and Carson Stockwell stepped out of the wings. "I hope I didn't startle you," he said. "But I just couldn't resist."

Of course he'd startled her. Almost as much as his unexpected appearance unnerved her now. He was a striking man in his wheat colored cambric shirt with the sleeves rolled up for comfort. His hair, slightly darker than the shirt, fell in tousled waves over his forehead. Carson Stockwell managed to look refreshingly casual while the rest of the world merely appeared mussed.

Gwen pulled herself together with her usual tucking and primping exercises. She wished a few curly strands of her hair had actually escaped the prim knot at her crown so it didn't look like she was futilely searching for something gone amiss. "Of course you didn't startle me," she lied. "But now is hardly the time for playing games, Mr. Stockwell."

"I disagree, Miss Barlow. After what's been happening on the *Jubilee Palace*, I think a bit of levity is precisely what's needed. Besides I couldn't help myself. When I saw you standing there I just had to complete the picture and see what you'd look like as an actress on center stage."

Her hands wafted about aimlessly. She'd primped all that was logical, and now it was all she could do not to stuff her hands in her pockets. "How silly, Mr. Stockwell. I'm not an actress. I much prefer working behind the scenes."

He crossed his arms over his chest and grinned. "Then perhaps you are denying your true talents."

"Such talent in my family is entirely Buddy Barlow's," she said. "And that suits me just fine. Now turn off that light, please. We don't want to waste electricity."

"Of course not." He went into the wings and did as she requested, leaving the *Jubilee* theater washed in only the natural light of a sun-soaked morning. When he returned to the stage, his grin was replaced by a more serious expression. "So how are you really this morning, Miss Barlow? It must have been impossible to put the events of yesterday out of your mind and concentrate on opening night."

"Indeed. But we have a formidable task ahead of us, Captain, and we must look forward as well as back."

"Are you any closer to discovering the identity of the killer or killers?"

How she wished she could answer his question in the affirmative, but that would be completely inaccurate. "No, I'm afraid not. But I feel each day will bring me a little closer to that goal." She walked forward a few paces and back again, thinking. "I'm missing something, Mr. Stockwell. I feel as though the answer to this mystery is clearly in front of my nose, but I'm not seeing it. I will keep searching however. It's only a matter of time until the clues fall into place or the guilty party commits a misstep."

He nodded. "Your determination is admirable. I know you once must have seriously suspected me of doing away with your uncle, and I'm relieved that I'm not on your list of suspects in the Veazey case."

She stopped pacing and considered his seemingly offhand statement. He didn't know it, of course, but he'd just forced her to consider a most unpleasant scenario. She truly hadn't thought of Carson Stockwell in relation to Travis's murder, but now she found herself doing exactly that. She easily recalled where the captain was just before Peaches's screams. He had been boldly tossing that scoundrel Solomon Wade from the *Jubilee* theater.

But before that . . . before Danita came in the back of the theater with the tray of tea items, his whereabouts were not clear. Gwen had been working on the stage, and she assumed Carson had been in the wings familiarizing himself with the *Jubilee*'s technical equipment. At least that was the reason he gave her for not going to lunch with the rest of the *Jubilee* troupe.

But had Gwen actually seen him in the wings during the time lapse between Peaches's announcement of lunch and the appearance of Solomon Wade? She realized now that she hadn't. It had only been a few minutes, but that was enough time for Carson to leave the back of the theater, locate Travis behind the ticket booth, and accomplish the deed.

But why? What did Carson Stockwell have to gain by killing Travis Veazey? Did Travis's secret have something to do with Stockwell? Was Carson the one responsible for her uncle's death? Was Travis threatening to expose him?

She glanced at Carson now and realized

he was staring intently at her. Uncomfortable, she quickly averted her eyes and pretended to concentrate on the floor marks once again, though she wasn't really seeing them.

He took a step toward her, forcing her to confront him. Concern was etched in his features. "What is it, Gwen?" he asked. "What are you thinking? Have you had a revelation about the murders?"

Even though she was experiencing a good deal of anxiety over the prospect of Stockwell being a suspect, she couldn't help but realize he'd just called her by her first name. The easy familiarity lent his questions the legitimacy of sympathy, even caring. But perhaps Carson Stockwell was every bit as good an actor as the *Jubilee* players. She couldn't afford to let her guard down about anyone. Not now.

An involuntary flinch rippled through her as the *Jubilee* captain came closer, and she prayed he hadn't noticed it. She also couldn't afford to appear vulnerable. "What did you know about Travis, Mr. Stockwell?" she asked, assuming an offensive demeanor.

He stared at her a moment longer before answering. She supposed he, too, was weighing his options and deciding upon the best course of action.

"Not much," he said. "I didn't know him well. I've only seen him around town a few times. He's not the type of chap I'd like to see with my daughter, though . . . if I had one, that is."

His statement, made so casually, brought Gwen to an acute awareness. "Isn't that odd," she said. "That's exactly what Manfred Kruger just told me in the dining room."

The captain's eyes widened and remained focused on Gwen. "Really? But the difference of course is that Kruger actually *has* a daughter."

"What are you saying, Mr. Stockwell?"

"You're suggesting I'm being purposefully evasive, Gwen, when in reality I wish I could help you with this dilemma. Truly I do, but I'm afraid I don't know any more than you do. Probably less."

Voices came from the rear of the stage. The actors were arriving for rehearsal. As difficult as it was, Gwen had to relegate the *Jubilee* murders to the back of her mind. She looked at Carson. "You have convinced me of one thing this morning, Mr. Stockwell," she said.

"What's that?"

"You appear to have become quite

skillful at operating the light board."

He smiled at her, a smile much too quick and unrehearsed to be associated with a cold-blooded murderer. But then, how did a cold-blooded murderer smile?

"Thank you, Gwen," he said. "And while I'm thinking of it, please call me Carson. I think we know each other well enough."

I'm not sure I know anyone well enough any more!

Chapter Fourteen

"Can I prompt the actors, Miss Barlow?"

Gwen whirled around, nearly colliding with a swishing concoction of silvery pink and starched white. "What? Oh, Hildegard, I didn't know you were right behind me."

"I've been behind you for the last ten minutes. Haven't you heard anything I've said?"

The truth was, Gwen had heard numerous sounds that could only have come from Hildegard's mouth, but she hadn't really been listening. There was so much to do and time was running out for the *Jubilee* actors, so she hadn't concentrated on where her "assistant" was or what she'd been saying. She stopped now and gave the girl at least half of her attention. "You want to cue the actors' lines?"

"Oh, yes. You'll be impressed with the job I do."

Gwen called Preston to obtain a script and when he tossed it out to her from the wings, she handed it to Hildegard. "Very well, then. You may prompt."

Hildegard reluctantly took the script. "I don't really need this. I know all the lines anyway."

"You know all the actors' lines?"

"Of course. I've read the play dozens of times. Did you forget? My daddy printed all the scripts for Mr. Willoughby."

Gwen rolled her eyes. "Yes, of course your father would have printed the scripts." *The charge for that service was no doubt included in Uncle Eli's debt!*

She directed Hildegard to take a position in the orchestra pit and then clapped her hands loudly, commanding the attention of the actors and musicians milling around the stage. "Places everyone for Act One."

The musicians scrambled to their chairs. Anabel went into the right wings. Marianne waited downstage for her aunt to arrive on the train. Sir Clyde stood to the side, preparing to eye Marianne lecherously. Jason DeVane appeared occupied upstage. And Carson Stockwell went into the left wings with Preston to sound the train whistle.

"All right everyone," Gwen said. "That looks good. Before we begin, I want to announce that tonight at seven o'clock we will conduct a full dress rehearsal. But right now we will attempt to test our sound effects and lighting techniques so that any problems can be worked out before the rehearsal tonight. Mr. Stockwell," she called, "are you ready?"

"Yes, ma'am. Prepared to toot."

"And Preston . . . er, Buddy, you understand that you are to assist Mr. Stockwell until it's time for you to appear on stage?"

"Got it, Gwennie."

"Very well, ladies and gentlemen. Let us begin Act One of *Belle of the Ozarks*."

Gwen sat in the first row with her mother and watched the production. She only interrupted the actors or technicians when a mistake was so glaring that it called for her immediate attention. Otherwise she jotted down notes to go over later. She did not enjoy the same restraint from Lillian, however, who apparently thought it was her job to interrupt at regular intervals. Lillian repeatedly grabbed Gwen's arm or whispered exuberant praises in her ear about their talented troupe of actors.

"Mama, please," Gwen said at one point. "I can barely hear the lines and I'm only sitting a few yards from the actors."

"Sorry, dear, but it's all so exciting. Just think, tomorrow night we'll be the talk of Hickory Bend. Now aren't you glad we came, Gwendolyn? Can't you just feel the pulse of creativity pumping furiously in your bloodstream? I know I can. It's all I can do to sit still."

Gwen smiled to herself. "Mama, you *aren't* sitting still." Then an unsettling thought occurred to her and she whispered in Lillian's ear. "Mama, did Anabel Whitedove give you anything to drink today out of a dark blue bottle?" The last thing Lillian Barlow needed was a libation intended to relieve distress. The woman hardly knew what the word meant.

"Just a taste. It was after I saw Miss Whitedove take a swig or two after breakfast. You can't blame me for being curious, and Anabel was quite willing to share. I don't know what the substance is, but Anabel does seem quite content of late. It must have a calming effect."

Gwen stared straight ahead at the stage and spoke too softly for her mother to hear. "Calming?" *Not for you, Mama.* "Apparently it affects different people in different ways."

Belle of the Ozarks ended with the sheriff administering a chaste kiss on the lips to his lady love. At precisely that moment, Carson Stockwell lowered the curtain. Gwen and Lillian applauded vigorously until the curtain was raised again.

"That was actually quite good," Gwen said. "With a few modifications which we'll go over before tonight's rehearsal, I'd say we're ready for opening night."

Among the actors, emotions ran from relief to exhilaration. Gwen dismissed everyone but Preston, Jason, and Marianne. She asked them to stay behind to run through a scene in Act Two. Once Jason and Marianne had taken their positions on stage, Gwen sat down with Preston. "Something was just not right about this scene, Preston. See if you can tell what it is."

"I know what it is," Preston grumbled. "DeVane will end up holding Belle's hand, not me."

"Be serious, Preston."

"Oh, Miss Barlow!" Hildegard called from the last row of audience seating.

Gwen rubbed the back of her neck. It didn't relieve the tension created from merely the sound of the girl's voice. She turned around. "What now, Hildegard?"

Her protégé's face drooped like melting wax, and Gwen immediately regretted her sharp tone.

"I guess I should go home now," Hildegard said.

Gwen made an effort to sweeten her

tone. "Yes, that's a good idea, Hildegard. Thank you for your help. You may go home now."

Hildegard shuffled out the door just as Gwen realized her mistake. She jumped up from her chair. "No, Hildegard, wait! You can't go home!"

The girl poked a much happier face through an opening in the door. "Why not? Do you need me?"

"Well, not at the moment. But I promised your father I'd walk you back to the shop. Please wait outside until I'm finished here and then I'll take you."

"Oh, all right."

Gwen recognized that tone of reluctant capitulation from when a much younger Preston finally sauntered off to wash his hands after the third request from Lillian. But satisfied the girl would wait, Gwen sat down again and turned her attention back to the stage. "So Preston, do you notice anything unusual?"

"Sure don't, Gwennie, but start the dialogue. Then maybe you'll see something."

Jason and Marianne began talking, and Gwen listened intently. In the actual performance, Marianne would be standing in the center of her Ozark Mountain town. The sheriff would have approached from

276

several feet away, leaving appropriate space for an unchaperoned couple. Just the sheriff and Belle were in this scene, and she was expressing her concerns over the hotel's financial crisis and the banker's threats to foreclose. It was supposed to be an intimate scene, one in which the audience's sympathies would grow toward Belle. However, as the scene progressed, that intimacy was not evident. The two future lovers could have been conversing as strangers about the pleasantries of the climate.

"That's it!" Gwen shouted. She marched up on the stage with Preston following behind. "Your placement is all wrong," she said. "This scene is supposed to take place downstage, nearer the audience."

Marianne's face crinkled delicately with confusion. "But we're on our marks, Miss Barlow. See? My X in red tape is right here, and Jason's sign is close to mine."

"That can't be," Gwen said, walking toward the back of the stage where the actors were. She bent down to examine the tape. "I set those marks myself yesterday. I remember taking into account the purpose of the scene . . ." She walked downstage a few paces. "I distinctly remember putting the marks here."

No one said anything for a minute, and Gwen realized that she was the object of curious stares from her three companions. "Stop that," she said. "I *know* I put the marks here."

"Look, Gwennie," Preston said. "Don't take it so personally. Everyone makes mistakes. Why, with opening night only twenty-four hours away, I can understand . . ."

"But I didn't make a mistake!" Gwen protested. She pointed down at the floor. "I *know* where I put those marks."

"It doesn't do any good to fret over it now. If you want the marks there, then move them. I'll help."

Preston walked upstage. Marianne and Jason moved to the side to let the director do her job. But when Gwen joined Preston at the site of the inappropriate marks, she froze in place. Her consternation was replaced by immobilizing shock. "Preston, don't touch that tape," she whispered hoarsely.

"What now?"

"Look where Marianne's mark is."

At Preston's befuddled look, Gwen pointed to the ceiling. "It's right under Romance Mountain."

"So?"

"So? Where's the most dangerous place

for an actor to be in this theater?"

A light of understanding dawned in Preston's eyes. "Under Romance Mountain."

"Of course. If anything happened . . . if the rigging slipped like it did the night Uncle Eli was killed . . ." Gwen could have sworn her blood turned to ice water and she grabbed Preston's arm. "Marianne could have been killed."

Preston wrapped his hands around Gwen's upper arms and stared hard into her eyes. "But nothing did happen, Gwennie. Get a hold of yourself. Sure, you made a mistake, but you caught it before there were any consequences."

Gwen shook her head vigorously. "But I swear I didn't put these marks here. I would have noticed the mountain."

"But who else would have done it? And why? Who else had access to the rolls of tape?"

"I don't know the answers to the first two questions, Preston, but as for who had access to the tape, it could have been anyone. I leave all three rolls on the table in the left wings. Anyone could have picked them up."

Preston dropped his hands and looked over his shoulder at Marianne. She and

Jason were watching with wary expressions, though they probably hadn't heard what was said.

"Look, Gwennie, let's not make any more of this. We're making our lead actors nervous. Maybe you did it . . ." He paused at the scathing look she gave him. "Okay, maybe you didn't. Maybe someone else pulled the tape marks up accidentally and put them back down in the wrong place. It could have been an honest mistake. Anyway, what are the chances that mountain would have come down on top of Marianne? I checked the lines and the sandbags myself. You could hold an elephant over this stage with our rigging."

She answered him with a tight-lipped frown. "The best rigging in the world is only as good as the humans operating it."

"The important thing is," he continued, "we found the error and we'll correct it. No harm done." He patted her shoulder. "Now come on, let's get some lunch. I'm starving. I'll move the marks later when we won't alarm our actors."

Gwen agreed, although the thought of eating was not the least appealing. Besides she still had to walk Hildegard back to the print shop before her responsibilities were over.

★ ★ ★

"I know this is silly, Miss Barlow," Hildegard said when they'd cleared the landing and were approaching Main Street. "My father is quite overprotective of me. I'm sure you have much more important things to do than walk me home like a bodyguard or something."

"It's all right, Hildegard. I don't mind." In truth, Gwen didn't object to the short walk. It helped clear her mind of the potential catastrophe in the theater. And once they were in the Hickory Bend business district, she had a chance to see the colorful *Belle of the Ozarks* posters nailed to posts and trees around town.

In a short time it had become apparent that the *Jubilee Palace* was preparing for a spectacular opening night. In fact, the posters seemed to be drawing a great deal of attention from the people in town. Perhaps the *Jubilee* production might even lure some of the residents from Hickory Bend gambling parlors and saloons. Gwen stopped in the middle of a small gathering to admire one of the larger posters. "Preston did a nice job with our publicity," she said to Hildegard.

"Oh, yes," Hildegard agreed. "Buddy is simply amazing. Of course it was my father

. . ." she dipped into a little curtsy, ". . . and *I* who made the posters in the first place according to Mr. Willoughby's instructions."

"You're absolutely right, Hildegard," Gwen said. "And you did a fine job. In fact, when I take you to the shop, I'm going inside to tell your father how much I appreciate his work."

"That would be nice," Hildegard said, "though Papa isn't likely to be very polite in return. After all, you do still owe us money."

Gwen's nerves sang with impatience. Did she have to hear about Uncle Eli's debts from both Krugers? "Yes, I know," she said. "And I will start eliminating that obligation as soon as possible. Maybe even the day after tomorrow if opening night goes well."

Hildegard grinned with confidence. "I just know opening night will go perfectly."

They entered the shop, and Gwen approached Manfred Kruger at his desk in the little fenced-in office. He looked up, and before he realized who was there, he almost smiled. Seeing Gwen, he immediately took control of his facial muscles and scowled. "It's you," he said. "You've brought my Hildy back safe and sound?"

Gwen forced her own lips to curl pleasantly. "Yes. And I came in to tell you how nice the posters and flyers look around town. I know they will go a long way in bringing an enthusiastic crowd to tomorrow night's opening."

For a moment he seemed almost pleased. "It wasn't easy printing those big posters, you know. Had to keep changing ink colors and running the same paper through the press. Made a few mistakes that I never even told Willoughby about. Covered the cost of those myself."

"Well I appreciate your skill and time, Mr. Kruger."

"No more than I'd appreciate a little payment, Miss Barlow . . ."

Hildegard burst through the swinging gate before Gwen could come back with an appropriate retort. "Hi, Papa. Did Miss Barlow tell you? We're having a full dress rehearsal tonight. You're not going to be all grumpy and not let me go, are you?"

Kruger sighed. "No, Hildy, but I suppose I'll have to go with you. I can't have you wandering around town by yourself with a killer on the loose."

Hildegard's lips curled with the same catlike satisfaction they always did when she got her way. "There, Miss Barlow, you won't have to try and get along without me."

"My, Hildegard, that is a relief," Gwen said, although it was all she could do not to respond with a more honest answer. She had to content herself with the edge of sarcasm that went unnoticed by Hildegard and her father.

"We'll leave from the café after supper, Hildy," Manfred Kruger said. "I'll stay with you for the duration of the rehearsal and see you safely home again."

"Just don't get in the way of my work, Papa. I have responsibilities, you know."

Finding the dialogue between the Krugers tiresome, Gwen backed out of the office. "If you'll excuse me, I have things to do . . ."

Neither Manfred nor Hildegard acknowledged her, so she walked quietly to the door. When she opened it, a crumpled piece of paper caught a breeze and skittered a few feet to a baseboard under a window. Gwen recognized the ivy border on the lower left hand corner which was visible to her. It was the decoration used on *Jubilee Palace* flyers.

Thinking it wasteful to throw away a piece of *Jubilee* advertising, Gwen picked it up. Might as well take it with me, she thought. I can always tack it up in the dining room. She left the shop, closing the door softly behind her.

Gwen was half way up Main Street when she smoothed the flyer against her hip so she could read it. She held it up in the sunlight. At first it looked like several of the other *Belle of the Ozarks* promotional flyers except for a smudge at the bottom — probably the reason it was being discarded. But on closer scrutiny this flyer was astoundingly different. Gwen's eyes widened as if they were having difficulty interpreting what was plainly in front of them.

In the space where Marianne Dresden's photo was supposed to be, there was a photo of Hildegard Kruger. Where Marianne's name should have appeared as lead actress for the *Jubilee* troupe, Hildegard's name was scripted in bold black letters.

At first Gwen smiled at what she interpreted as a manifestation of Hildegard's fantasy. Such imagination was perfectly normal for a seventeen-year-old girl. Why, hadn't Gwen herself, when she was a young girl, indulged in her dreams by scribbling her desired married name on a piece of paper? Hadn't she sketched pencil drawings of herself and some gallant young fellow walking arm in arm? Hadn't she envisioned herself a writer of gothic novels and written her pen name over and over? Of course. Every girl did things like this. And it was certainly easy enough for Hildegard to switch her photograph with Marianne's. She worked in a print shop, after all.

Gwen folded the flyer neatly and put it in her pocket. "Poor Hildegard," she said as she reached the end of Main Street. "Her dreams are not likely to come true on the *Jubilee Palace*. Even if Marianne deserts us or dies . . ."

Dies? Gwen halted at the top of the sloping embankment to the *Jubilee*. All at once her feet were incapable of taking one more step. Her lungs were unable to draw in a breath. Only her heart worked furiously, pumping blood to every tense nerve ending. "If Marianne dies . . ." she whispered again. "The tape marks under Romance Mountain!"

Shaking herself free of her immobility, Gwen ran down the riverbank to the showboat. The dire implications of the flyer, now clear, blocked out everything in her brain but the gruesome possibilities. She didn't even see her brother Preston coming around a corner of the promenade until she collided with him at full speed on the bow of the boat.

"Whoa, Gwennie," he said, taking her arms and forcing her to remain still. "Where's the fire?"

She gulped a quick breath of air. "It's no fire, Preston, but it could be something much worse."

"What now, for Heaven's sake?" he asked. "I'm beginning to realize that life in Apple Creek was amazingly dull!"

"No, it can't be," she said, ignoring his quip. She urged a sense of logic to quell her escalating fear. "Hildegard is persistent to the point of annoying, but she's not a murderer. She wouldn't methodically plan to kill another human being in cold blood."

Preston let go of her arms. "I quite agree," he said, "though I'm not at all sure with what . . . except that Hildegard is definitely annoying."

Gwen began pacing the circumference of the *Jubilee* deck. "And though she's a big girl, she certainly couldn't or wouldn't have run a knife into Travis Veazey's chest. Not over a minor argument."

Preston, all at once alert to his sister's words, pivoted in a circle to track her erratic strides. "Are you really saying that Hildegard killed Veazey?"

Gwen stopped and stared at Preston as if seeing him for the first time. The accusation sounded ridiculous coming from his lips. "No. No, of course not," she said and then resumed her circuitous path. "But what about the flyer?" She chewed her bottom lip. "I know I'm on to something here."

Only dimly aware of Preston's incessant babbling, Gwen let her mind rehash all the events of the last few minutes. Like receiving a flash from an electric light, her brain suddenly illuminated another theory, one which followed logically from her first, impetuous notion and made infinitely more sense. She stopped pacing and looked at Preston, though her focus was on the elaboration of her hypothesis.

"Hildegard's father," she said. "Manfred Kruger certainly has the strength to kill Travis. And he made his contempt of Travis blatantly obvious. He practically admitted this morning in the dining room that he would have done most anything to eliminate him from his daughter's life. Maybe the secret that cost Travis his life was about Manfred Kruger."

"Secret? What secret?" Preston asked.

Anxiety forced Gwen to march again. "But why would Kruger have announced his feelings about Travis publicly if he really had killed him?" she asked, ignoring Preston's question. "It doesn't make sense."

"Finally you've said something I can relate to, Gwennie," Preston said. "None of this is making any sense. Would you mind telling me . . ."

". . . unless . . ." Preston's words trailed off to insignificance as Gwen paced. "Perhaps he thought his outspokenness on the subject ultimately made him less of a suspect. In the same manner, his forthrightness in discussing the presence of a killer on the *Jubilee* and his concern for Hildegard's safety made him appear truly fearful of becoming a victim. It was a clever psychological ruse to divert suspicion away from himself."

"So you're saying Kruger killed Travis?" Preston said.

Gwen raised a finger, indicating he shouldn't interrupt. "Manfred harbored enough hatred toward Eli to have watched a heavy backdrop fall on him with near glee."

"So you're saying Kruger killed Uncle Eli?"

"But what did Manfred have to gain by Eli's death — besides the personal satisfaction of seeing a broken promise and bad debt avenged?" Gwen paused and glanced at her brother as if he might provide some insight.

Preston's features screwed up in confusion. "Am I supposed to answer that?"

"Of course!" Gwen said, experiencing something close to an epiphany. "Perhaps deep down, Manfred wants his daughter to be a star of the stage as much as Hildegard herself does. When Eli refused to take Hildegard on as a member of the *Jubilee* troupe, that might have driven Manfred over the edge. And now he sees the possibility of Hildegard getting a second chance if he eliminates Marianne in another stage accident."

Spurred to action at Gwen's last statement, Preston lunged at her and grabbed her arms again. "Marianne? Kruger is going to eliminate Marianne?" He shook Gwen until she pierced him with a warning glare.

"Let me finish, Preston. Manfred could have printed the bogus flyers himself in anticipation of Hildegard claiming Marianne's role."

"Flyers? What flyers?"

Theories and hypotheses swirled in Gwen's brain like a whirlwind. And they all led to the same conclusion about the *Jubilee* killer. She backed away from Preston and placed both hands against her flushed cheeks. "The tape marks, Preston. I understand now. Kruger brought Hildegard to the *Jubilee* this morning. He could easily have entered the theater when no one else was there and changed the marks. A poster in the wings clearly indicates which symbols correspond to which actors."

Gwen placed a hand on her forehead, fighting a sudden, overpowering dizziness. She grasped the railing to steady herself. Preston came to her side and placed a trembling hand on her shoulder.

"You've done it now, Gwennie. If you're trying to scare me, I'm right out of my wits."

"It is scary, Preston. Much of what I suspect about the *Jubilee* murders is still speculation, but three nearly irrefutable facts about the deeds have emerged today with near crystal clarity."

She enumerated the points on three fingers. "One . . . whoever killed Eli and Travis had access to *our* theater and very possibly has a plan to commit a third murder there sometime soon. Two . . . the killer most probably has a connection to the Kruger Print Shop. And third . . . I fear

291

Marianne Dresden's life is definitely in danger."

Preston balled his hands into fists. "We've got to find her, Gwen."

"Find her?" The idea that Preston, who had become Marianne's shadow, was in the dark about the girl's whereabouts was a complication Gwen hadn't considered. "Don't you know where she is?"

Preston shook his head. "I was going to ask you if you'd seen her when you started on about all this macabre business."

She took his sweating hand in hers. "Don't worry, Preston. We'll find her, but I suggest we start looking now!" As soon as a sketchy search plan could be formulated, Gwen and Preston raced to find Marianne and prevent another tragedy on the *Jubilee*.

Chapter Fifteen

Marianne Dresden dabbed at her eyes with one of Gwen's lace-trimmed handkerchiefs. "I can't believe this, Miss Barlow." She looked up at Gwen with luminous blue eyes. "Why would anyone want to hurt me?"

Preston bestowed upon her his most sympathetic countenance. "It's absolutely incredible, Gwennie. I doubt Marianne has so much as swatted a fly in all her nineteen years. Certainly she's never done anything that would make anyone in Hickory Bend want to see her harmed."

Gwen had been so relieved when she'd finally seen Preston and Marianne coming from the woods north of town. What a time for the young ingénue to decide she wanted to commune with nature! When Gwen asked her what possessed her to go off by herself after the horrible events on the *Jubilee*, Marianne answered that she felt safer away from the showboat, not on it. Perhaps she had a point.

Gwen had searched the *Jubilee* and the shops in Hickory Bend for the young woman, all the while her anxiety increasing by the minute. By the time she saw Preston and Marianne emerge from the trees, several hours had passed. She left the showboat to intercept them and quickly brought them back to her quarters on the top deck. Now Gwen sat beside Marianne on the bed while Preston occupied the desk chair close by.

"I realize it's hard to accept, Preston," Gwen said. "I wanted to deny it myself, but I think I've uncovered enough evidence to be concerned for Marianne's welfare."

"I know you're right," Preston agreed. "I suppose it's a comfort of sorts to know the killer isn't anyone on the *Jubilee* at least."

Gwen nodded. "I've never really believed that any of us could have killed Uncle Eli and Travis, but I always operated under the principle that it's best to err on the side of caution."

Marianne stopped sniffling long enough to give Gwen her full attention. "Preston said you have a good idea who the killer is, Miss Barlow."

"You understand I'm not one hundred percent sure. Much less really. At this point I'm drawing on some evidence and a great deal of intuition." She drew a deep breath and came out with it. "I think the killer is Manfred Kruger."

Marianne gasped, and Preston reached over from his chair and took her hand. "It sounds far-fetched, I know," he said, "but Gwennie has come up with some very logical observations." He gave his sister a warning look. "Observations which I believe she is going to explain in more detail now."

Gwen stood and began to theorize about the danger to Marianne. She told the girl and Preston her hunches about the tape marks and the possible plot to kill the ingénue with Romance Mountain in much the same way Eli Willoughby had been killed. Then she showed them the flyer from the print shop and explained her theory about Hildegard taking over the lead part in *Belle of the Ozarks*.

She concluded with her suspicion of Kruger's motive. "Preston, you once told me that the murderer would be someone who has something significant to gain by committing the crime. Well, I think Kruger is that person. I believe he is obsessed about procuring a spot in the play for Hildegard. I know he wouldn't admit it, but it's very possible he wants his disrespectful, demanding daughter out of his life for a while, and seeing her float away on the *Jubilee* would be just the answer."

Preston inched his chair closer to Marianne. "It's something to consider, Marianne. Maybe Kruger *would* kill to get his daughter a part in a play and bring some peace into his own life. I've noticed myself how Hildegard tries his patience."

"People have killed for less," Gwen said. "And when you think about it, this is the perfect scenario for Kruger. Eventually someone would be convicted of the murders, or the constable would close the case. When that happened, all the evidence, and quite possibly Kruger's whining daughter, would sail out of Hickory Bend, never to be seen for months."

"That's a fine kettle, isn't it, Gwennie?" Preston grumbled. "Kruger rants on about how he doesn't like or trust us, but it's all right to stage a few accidents on our boat and use us to relieve him of his daughter."

Marianne rubbed a delicate finger under her nose. "I agree that Hildegard can be quite difficult," she said. "Why do you think Mr. Kruger killed Mr. Willoughby, Miss Barlow?"

"He may have killed Eli for basically the same motive — to eliminate the obstacle to Hildegard's dream of joining the acting troupe. Plus he hated Eli for backing out of

296

their deal and not paying his debts. We all can attest to the fact that he's expressed his contempt for Eli often enough. Perhaps that contempt ran even deeper than we realized."

"And Travis?" Preston asked. "Why did he kill Travis?"

"To protect Hildegard from his influence," she said. "Kruger complained that Travis had been making advances to Hildegard. I'm quite sure he was not happy with the unlikely but possible outcome of Travis becoming part of the family. Not only would that mean that Hildegard would have married beneath her in Kruger's eyes, but she would have brought another burden into his household."

Gwen stopped and walked to the window. There was, of course, another reason Kruger may have killed Travis, but Gwen was not ready yet to reveal the purely speculative clue she'd recently gotten from Anabel. Gwen didn't understand it herself at this point. She believed that Travis had boasted to Anabel about having a secret. Did the secret concern Manfred Kruger? Did Kruger kill him to bury the secret with the younger man's remains? Those were questions that needed to be answered, but now Gwen kept her explanations to Preston and Marianne simple and reasonably logical.

"I really believe that Kruger wanted to fulfill his daughter's ambitions that much," she said, "and rid himself of her at the same time. But he had to eliminate Travis. You must admit, Preston, that Kruger has expressed a violent nature on several occasions."

"I think you could be right, Miss Barlow," Marianne said. "I've known all along that Hildegard resented me. I didn't like it when you allowed her to stay on the *Jubilee* every day."

"I'm sorry, Marianne," Gwen said. "You should have told me."

"No, it's all right. It wouldn't have been my place to say anything. But I could just imagine her going home to tell her father how she wanted to be lead actress in *Belle of the Ozarks*. Maybe she talked about it so much that his patience just sort of, I don't know, snapped."

Gwen and Preston were silent for a moment until Preston finally cleared his throat and spoke. "All right. Let's assume for the sake of argument that Kruger is the killer. What are we going to do about it? Are you going to the constable with this theory, Gwen?"

She shook her head. "No. I'm sure O'Toole wouldn't believe me. You're my brother, and you think I might be a few pages short of a book. O'Toole already has a low opinion of us. I don't want to add to that image. Besides, why should he believe a newcomer to Hickory Bend, especially one whose credentials are suspect because of Eli Willoughby's reputation? No, I'm sure O'Toole would laugh at this idea, right before he called the sanatorium to take me away."

"Then what's next? If you're right, Kruger could strike at any time."

A small squeal, as if from a wounded animal, came from Marianne's throat. Guilt flashed in Preston's eyes and he came to sit next to her. "Sorry to scare you," he said.

"I'm going to try and get more evidence," Gwen said. "I heard Manfred say that he and Hildegard are going to the café before tonight's dress rehearsal. That's the perfect time for me to go into the print shop and look around. Maybe I'll find enough evidence to take to O'Toole."

"You're certainly not going alone," Preston protested. "What if Kruger catches you?"

"I'll be careful."

"Absolutely not, Gwennie. It's too dangerous and you don't know anything about snooping." He held up a finger as a solution occurred to him. "Take Stockwell with you."

"No, Preston. I want as few people as possible involved in this right now. Snooping isn't an activity I would have imagined for myself, either. But it will be fine. I'll be fine. And perhaps we'll get some answers."

Preston heaved a great sigh of portending doom. "All right. You're forcing me into this. I'll just have to go with you."

Gwen couldn't help smiling at her brother's belated and unconvincing attempt at bravery. "I'm going alone," she said. "No arguments. Besides, you need to stay here with Marianne. I don't want you to let our star out of your sight."

Obviously relieved, Preston put his arm around Marianne's shoulder. She calmed at his attention, convincing Gwen that something definitely was happening between the two of them.

"We can trust Gwennie," Preston said to her.

"Yes, you can," Gwen said. "In the meantime, Preston, I think I've given you an assignment you will enjoy."

Marianne blushed in that charming way she had.

"You two stay together," Gwen warned. "I doubt that Kruger is bold enough to attempt anything in front of witnesses."

Preston nodded his agreement with both the plan and Gwen's assessment of Kruger. "Do you think he might try something tonight?"

"I don't know," Gwen said. "He's definitely coming to the *Jubilee* with Hildegard. He said he didn't want her walking around town alone with a killer on the loose."

Preston snorted. "But it's perfectly all right if she walks *with* one!"

"Don't tell anyone about this, Preston," Gwen said. "I'm sure rumors fly around Hickory Bend every bit as fast as they do in Apple Creek. If Kruger turns out to be innocent after all, and it leaks out that we suspected one of the town's sterling citizens, we would only end up damaging our reputations even more. And I don't think I would relish being tarred and feathered!"

"Okay, Gwennie. No one will hear this from me."

Gwen looked at the clock on her bureau. "I've got to go. The Krugers should be leaving for the café any time now. If anyone asks where I am, say I'm resting before the rehearsal." She raised a finger to Preston to emphasize her last point. "Act normally, Preston. Leave Buddy Barlow in the background. Don't draw attention to yourself or Marianne. I'll be back in time for rehearsal. And hopefully with enough evidence to prove either Kruger is the killer, or I didn't know what I was talking about."

"Deep down, what do you hope happens, Gwennie?"

She stopped at the door to her cabin and turned around. "At this point, I just want to free the *Jubilee* from the bonds that hold us to Hickory Bend. I don't think sitting at this riverbank for months was the vision Uncle Eli had for his masterpiece when he built it."

Gwen checked the promenade outside her quarters, and finding it empty, she slipped outside. As she closed the door, Preston called out, "Be careful, Sis."

In the last minutes a soaking drizzle had begun to fall. Gwen found the gloomy twilight somehow fitting to the job that lay ahead. She turned up her collar and ran from the *Jubilee* toward Main Street and the print shop. It was a good night for hiding in shadows.

★ ★ ★

Between Davenport's General Store and the Hickory Bend Barber Shop there was a narrow alley which provided at least minimal protection from the rain. It had begun to fall more steadily when Gwen reached Main Street. She stood under a sloping eave with her back against a wall and watched the print shop across the street. Light glowed through the window, indicating two things.

First, cloud cover had forced Manfred to light a lamp in the gloomy interior of the shop. That was a piece of discouraging news. Gwen certainly couldn't use a lamp when she was inside and risk being discovered. Second, a light meant the Krugers hadn't left yet for the Hickory Bend Café. That was good news. Gwen would have sufficient time to snoop thoroughly.

She didn't have long to wait. Within minutes, the lamp was extinguished in the shop, and Hildegard and her father came out the front door. Hildegard held a large umbrella over their heads while Manfred locked the door. Gwen wasn't concerned. She hadn't planned to enter through such an obvious portal anyway. She'd find another way inside.

Once she saw the Krugers enter the café,

Gwen darted across the street. The downpour had kept pedestrians inside businesses and shops, and Gwen assumed she'd skirted the buildings which bordered the print shop without being noticed. The service road behind the shop was already slick with mud. Gwen raised her skirt and slogged her way to a window next to the back door. It slid open easily. She climbed inside and shook rivulets of rain from her clothing and hair.

As she anticipated, light was barely adequate inside the back room of the print shop. Rain clouds had reduced everything to shades of dismal charcoal gray. Boxes and cabinets blended together in rows and stacks of muted shadows and shapes. While her eyes slowly adjusted to the gloom, Gwen went right to work searching for clues.

Most of the cartons contained what one would expect of a printing concern — bottles of ink and lubricants, letters and symbols to be inserted in the inking trays, extra cranks and handles to keep the machines running.

A large trunk against one wall caught Gwen's eye. She tested the lid, found it unlocked, and looked inside. There was enough light for her to recognize the surprising contents, and she couldn't contain her excitement.

"My stars!" she cried in a hoarse whisper. Concealed under a blanket were hundreds of the flyers with Hildegard's picture replacing Marianne's. Still reeking with the scent of fresh ink, they provided verification of Gwen's theory. She took one of them and folded it into her pocket.

Encouraged by the discovery of the flyers, Gwen's hope for more clues escalated. She investigated a tall cabinet lined with shelves of paper and cardboard. At the bottom of the cabinet, under a mound of printer's aprons, she found three canvas bags, exactly like the ones used on the scenery rigging of the *Jubilee Palace*. Each of the bags was filled with sand, further replicating the ones in the theater. But there was one distinct and incriminating difference. Even in the poor light, Gwen could see that these bags were poorly sewn along the bottom seams with wide basting stitches. The sandbags used on the *Jubilee* were held securely with tiny button-hole stitches to prevent any leakage of sand and thereby reduce the risk of an accident such as the one that supposedly killed Eli Willoughby.

The purpose of the sandbags was obvious in light of the misplaced tape marks under Romance Mountain. Someone intended to switch the bags securing the mountain and replace them with the faulty ones whose stitches could be cut with a simple pair of household shears. And that someone was the same person who'd moved the tape marks on the *Jubilee* stage. The outcome would be disastrous for the *Jubilee*'s lead actress.

But it was in a tape-sealed box marked "Records, 1890–1895" that Gwen found the significant clue that filled in the gaps in her theory and clearly pointed to Manfred Kruger as the *Jubilee* killer. She probably wouldn't have looked inside the box, assuming that it contained paperwork related to print shop operation in years past, except she noticed that the tape had recently been loosened and reapplied rather sloppily.

She opened the box and scanned the contents, which consisted of filled ledgers and old correspondence. One envelope, however, stood out from the others because of its larger size and recent postmark. This package had been mailed over three weeks previously from Caruthersville, Missouri, a small community Gwen knew was located further south on the river. The return address indicated it was sent by the sheriff of the town.

Gwen lifted the flap and withdrew the contents. A piece of paper had been folded to fit the envelope, and when Gwen opened it she realized that she was looking at a wanted poster, the kind that appeared in post offices and was even nailed to trees around the country, but which hardly ever appeared in quiet Apple Creek, Ohio.

She took the poster to the window to have the best possible light with which to view the image. The likeness was shocking and unmistakable. Even though the picture had obviously been hand drawn she recognized the person who was wanted by the sheriff of Caruthersville. He had long, unkempt hair, sharp, almost gaunt facial features, and several days' growth of scraggly beard. The narrow eyes looking up at Gwen from the picture were definitely Travis Veazey's, and the young man was wanted for murder.

Gwen sank to the window sill and stared at the picture. Murder! She remembered the times she'd actually defended Travis to her brother and to Constable O'Toole. And all that time the disagreeable man had been hiding from his recent unsavory past on the *Jubilee Palace*. Preston had been right. When Eli Willoughby traded Travis from his family for a sack of potatoes, the Veazey family had come out ahead.

She read the details of the crime which occurred in March. Supposedly, Travis had become drunk and belligerent after participating in a target shooting match. He'd waited for the man who'd won the contest, stabbed him, and robbed him of the prize money. The alleged murder weapon was also drawn on the poster and it was gruesomely familiar. It was the buck horn fishing knife Travis constantly had in his possession.

Gwen's stomach lurched as she recalled the image of Travis on the deck of the *Jubilee*, that same knife protruding from his chest. She remembered seeing the knife in Travis's hand and later, laying on his sleeping mat. His frantic, almost obsessive attachment to it had puzzled her at the time. But now she understood that the fondness he felt for the knife went far beyond mere pride of possession. To Travis it was a symbol of power.

"Oh, my God," she whispered. "To think Uncle Eli hired this man to work on the *Jubilee*. Didn't he ask any questions? Didn't he investigate the man's background?"

Another piece of paper was in the envelope. It was a letter from the sheriff of Caruthersville, and it was intended for Manfred Kruger's attention. The letter asked Kruger to print copies of the poster, give one to the law enforcement officer of Hickory Bend, and post the others around town in conspicuous places. Obviously the sheriff was counting on the civic-minded cooperation of other river town citizens to help him catch his suspect.

The implication of the sheriff's request was obvious at once. Since Gwen had never seen the posters in town, and since Travis was clearly in no imminent danger of being arrested when the Barlows arrived in Hickory Bend, the posters had never been printed and O'Toole had never been notified of Travis's crime. Manfred Kruger had simply ignored the sheriff's request.

Questions came to Gwen's mind and she spoke them aloud. "Why didn't Kruger comply with the sheriff's request? Kruger obviously hated Travis. Why didn't he turn him in immediately?"

It didn't make any sense. If Kruger had simply followed the sheriff's instructions, he would have eliminated the man he saw as a threat to Hildegard's existence. So why hadn't he? A possible explanation struggled to take shape in Gwen's mind. She suddenly knew she was on the verge of piecing together the puzzle parts of the *Jubilee* murders. "Yes, Kruger would have freed Hildegard from Travis's influence," she said, "but he still would have had the problem of Eli Willoughby's betrayal."

She tapped the poster and letter against her palm as she paced the narrow confines of the storeroom. And then it came to her, rushing forth from the muddled recesses of her mind on the low dulcet tones of Anabel Whitedove's voice. "That's it!" Gwen practically shouted to the empty room. "That's what the secret is about."

All at once Gwen understood the magnitude of the secret Travis bragged about to Anabel. It concerned Manfred Kruger's involvement in her uncle's death as she had suspected, and it was linked to another crime — blackmail!

"Of course," Gwen said. "Kruger used the information about Travis's crime in Caruthersville to further his own agenda." Perhaps her original suspicion about her uncle's death had been correct — with one exception. Threatened with blackmail, Travis had killed Eli Willoughby and made it look like an accident. He certainly had the knowledge of knots needed to rig the ropes that held the backdrop. His argument with Hildegard in the theater proved that. And it explained why he hadn't admitted to hearing Eli's cry at the time of the murder, even though Travis's mat was only a few yards from the crime. This was a fact that had puzzled Gwen from the beginning.

Now it made sense. Naturally, Travis had heard Eli's cry. He had been the cause of it. Somehow he had slipped the knot that resulted in her uncle's death. But it truly had been Manfred Kruger who pulled the strings — until he feared his puppet would divulge the truth and he did away with Travis and his knowledge of the crime.

There were still holes in the theory that had to be filled in, but Gwen knew what she had to do. She would leave the print shop and immediately return to the *Jubilee Palace* to tell Preston and Marianne what she'd learned. When she was convinced that those involved had been alerted to the danger threatening that night, she would send for O'Toole. It was still possible that the constable wouldn't find the evidence convincing enough to arrest Manfred Kruger. But if he saw Kruger in the act of committing another crime, then he would have to arrest him. And that necessitated a trap to catch Kruger in the act of attempting to kill Marianne. A plan to accomplish this had already begun to form in Gwen's mind. She just hoped that Marianne would agree to execute it.

Gwen tucked the two papers back into the envelope and secured the whole package into her skirt pocket with the flyer. Then she replaced the lid on the box of records and reached around it for the loose tape to reseal it in the same manner she'd found it. She fumbled with the tape. Her fingers shook almost beyond the point of controlling their movement.

It was no wonder. She suddenly realized that she'd experienced two significant occurrences in the past minutes. She'd discovered that her hunch about the murders now appeared to be correct. And she'd realized that she was acquainted, for the first time in her life, with a murderer — two murderers if she counted her short relationship with Travis. What girl's fingers wouldn't tremble under the onslaught of such life-altering revelations? Especially a librarian's from Apple Creek, Ohio.

She calmed herself enough to concentrate on leaving the storeroom in the exact same condition as when she entered. That probably explained why she didn't hear the front door open or why she was ignorant of footsteps approaching the back of the shop. In fact, the first indication that she wasn't alone occurred when she heard the subtle click of someone's hand on the doorknob.

Gwen's heart leapt to her throat. Kruger and Hildegard were supposed to go to the *Jubilee* after supper, not back to the print shop! Her frantic gaze darted to the window, her only means of escape, and she realized with mounting terror that she didn't have time to open the window and step over the sill to the safety of the out-side. The knob turned. Gwen panicked.

The trunk. She'd left the lid open on the trunk filled with flyers. It was her only chance of avoiding discovery. She shoved the box of records back with the others. With no seconds to spare, she climbed in-side the trunk and pulled the lid down. Despite fear pounding like galloping horses in her head, and her own breath coming in short, desperate gasps, she heard the door open and then rattle softly into the jamb as it closed again. Next, she heard muffled footsteps on the storeroom floor.

Chapter Sixteen

Gwen's heart pounded a rhythm of panic in her ears. She drew a long, though shallow breath, the most immediate antidote she could think of to keep the scream building in her lungs from escaping. "Stay calm, Gwen," she told herself. "Concentrate on what is happening outside, where the sounds you hear could be coming from a killer."

For one horrifying second, she feared she hadn't closed the lid on the trunk in time and whoever entered the room had seen her. But apparently that wasn't so, because no one lifted the lid to investigate. That realization quelled the panic so at least she could think.

She focused her attention on the footsteps. They made soft thuds across the floor and caused small vibrations in the bottom of the trunk and in the small of Gwen's back. The steps were steady and constant, leading Gwen to believe that only one person had entered.

She listened intently. Whoever was out there stopped near the window. The next sound Gwen detected was the click of a latch. It was followed by the squeak of hinges. The cabinet door had been opened. She remembered opening that same door moments ago, hearing the same noise, and thinking that it needed oiling.

For the next few seconds there was only silence. It was followed by a grunting sound as if her unknown companion were lifting a heavy object. Gwen doubted the person was removing stacks of paper. This was certainly not ordinary operating hours for the print shop. She could recall only three other items of any consequence in the cabinet. The trio of sandbags. They were filled to near bursting and weighed several pounds each. That would explain the labored breathing moments before.

Dread swept over Gwen like a cold water wave even though her rain-soaked clothing and the stifling humidity had already combined to make the trunk uncomfortably warm. She shivered at the consequences of the sandbags being removed from the shop. If Manfred Kruger were in the storeroom as Gwen believed, and he had removed the bags from the cabinet, then he was intending to carry out his plan to end Marianne's life under Romance Mountain tonight.

But there were still almost two hours

until the dress rehearsal. That was plenty of time for Gwen to return to the *Jubilee*, find Marianne and Preston, and inform them that her original suspicions were accurate. But time was precious, and she prayed for Manfred to leave the print shop quickly.

She heard the footsteps again and assumed they were approaching the door to the main shop. They didn't. Whoever was in the storeroom grumbled in a low, hoarse voice, though Gwen couldn't make out the words. Then the footsteps came toward the trunk. Gwen clenched her hands until her nails bit her palms. Her mouth went dry as cotton. *Don't open the trunk!* She mouthed the words over and over in silent desperation. She gritted her teeth when the lock rattled at the intruder's touch. This was it. She was about to be discovered. The trunk of Hildegard Kruger's flyers was about to become Gwen's coffin.

But the lid remained closed. Something hit the side of the trunk. Once, then twice, and Gwen stifled a terrified gasp. It felt as though the person outside were kicking it. Again she heard that muffled, unintelligible syllable of intense displeasure. It was followed by a harsh rasp of metal on the lip of the lid.

Realization broke through the muddle of Gwen's brain, and with it came increasing terror. Gwen was not being discovered. She was being locked in. She tamped her escalating fear and forced herself to view this latest development as a positive thing. At least she wasn't facing the last minute of her life — yet. Obviously Kruger had no knowledge that she was inside the trunk. The grumbling and kicking she'd heard had been directed at his own failure to lock the trunk in the first place.

In a situation such as this, however, relief is short-lived. Gwen found it difficult to maintain even a modicum of optimism. She was about to become a prisoner.

The smooth mechanical clink of metal teeth convinced her the lock had taken hold. How would she warn Marianne and the others about the danger from Manfred Kruger now? She couldn't tell them about the sandbags, couldn't explain about the poster of Travis Veazey and her theory about his death.

These thoughts sent Gwen's anxiety spiraling to dangerous heights. Again, she forced herself to remain calm. She had lived her life very successfully up to this point by drawing on reserves of logic and common sense, and she would do so again.

She lay very still and listened. By concentrating on her physical surroundings, perhaps she wouldn't succumb to her mental apprehensions.

She heard the footsteps of her captor retreat from the trunk and soon after she recognized the sound of the door settling into the jamb. She was alone. Never before had she been so utterly in that state. But for now it was a blessing.

"Think, Gwen," she said. "You can get yourself out of this mess." She pushed at the lid of the trunk, hoping the lock was old and unreliable. It didn't budge. The length of the trunk was no more than five feet at most, but she managed to roll onto her stomach and work herself half way to her knees. She used the strength in her back to try and loosen boards in the lid. They held fast.

Gasping with unaccustomed exertion, she tried the sides of the box, pushing with her feet, knees and hips. "You're strong, Gwen," she encouraged herself. "All you need to do is locate one weak board and you'll be free." Unfortunately the trunk was made of stuff as sturdy as the lock, and she soon collapsed on top of Hildegard's flyers, the heavy woolen blanket wadded into a ball at her feet.

When she'd caught her breath, Gwen tried to alert someone in Hickory Bend to her distress. She hollered. She screamed. She pounded the sides of the trunk and kicked at the bottom. When she remembered the window was closed, she cursed her bad luck. The rumbling harbingers of a storm building outside nearly drowned out her efforts even to her own ears.

Minutes passed that seemed like hours. Never before prone to claustrophobia, Gwen imagined the rough, black walls of her narrow prison closing in on her. Maybe it was the near total darkness, as oppressive and confining as the wood barriers. Minimal light seeped through paper thin joints between the slats, but the late afternoon was so dreary and gray, that it made little difference. Gwen held her hand in front of her face. She could barely detect the space between her fingers.

Her damp clothing stuck to her skin like fly paper. The temperature in the trunk became increasingly uncomfortable. Gwen told herself to think about anything other than the miserable circumstances of her current situation. She began to imagine Manfred Kruger at the *Jubilee* theater and a plan that would trap him in a few short hours. She closed her eyes, shutting out her hot, narrow prison, and plotted, step by step, the path to Kruger's ruin.

She would first alert Preston and Marianne to the danger Kruger presented. Somehow she would convince Marianne to participate in her scheme by standing on her mark under Romance Mountain as Kruger anticipated. Preston would never be more than a few feet away from Marianne in case something went wrong. Gwen would enlist the aid of Carson Stockwell. She would send for Constable O'Toole, and he and Carson would hide and watch Gwen's drama unfold.

"Yes, this can work," she said. "Manfred Kruger will be duped into believing he can accomplish his goal to kill Marianne and put Hildegard in *Belle of the Ozarks*." Gwen smiled in spite of her predicament. "But he will be wrong. Manfred Kruger will spend the night in the Hickory Bend jail — as soon as I get out of this damnable trunk!"

She tried to keep the vision of Kruger's capture in her mind. But an overpowering dizziness clouded her senses. She attributed it at first to an increasing panic of confinement. But she soon realized that the pungent vapor of fresh ink coming from the posters was making her lightheaded. She covered her nose with her hand, but that was only a slight improvement.

She needed to get the posters as far from her face as possible. Since she was unable to turn her body around so her head was in the opposite position, she began moving the flyers away from her nose. By handfuls, she slid the flyers down her torso toward her feet. The task left her weak and nauseated, so that when she finished, she had to lie still and get her wits about her. She pulled the tail of her blouse from her waistband and breathed through the soft cotton fabric. It smelled of bleach and helped mask the ink fumes, at least momentarily.

Her thoughts wandered to the *Jubilee Palace*. Not knowing what was happening on the showboat increased her distress. She had to assume that Manfred and Hildegard went to the *Jubilee* from the print shop. And she also figured Manfred had the weakly stitched sandbags with him. Sometime, perhaps when everyone was busy preparing for the dress rehearsal, he would switch the sturdy bags with the faulty ones. "And the only one who knows his plan is me," she said, futilely kicking the side of the trunk again.

Tears sprang to her eyes at her utter

helplessness. This was certainly not the way her investigative visit to the print shop was supposed to have turned out. She was supposed to have found clues that pointed to the killer and rushed back to the showboat to warn the actors about the danger. She had indeed found clues, irrefutable ones, she now believed, but she was definitely not able to warn the others.

At least she had told Preston and Marianne of her theory and made Preston promise to watch out for Marianne. Because of her uselessness now, she was grateful for her foresight then. But what would happen when she didn't return to the *Jubilee* for rehearsal? Would Preston become alarmed and come to find her? "Please, no, Preston," she cried out now. "Don't come here. Stay with Marianne."

Logically Gwen knew that she could stay alive for several hours, possibly a day or more, in the trunk, if she conserved her air and remained calm. Of course that would change if Manfred Kruger returned and found her there. In that event, Gwen was quite certain her time on earth would be cut much shorter. Still, her chances were better than Marianne's. If Manfred's plan progressed as Gwen hypothesized, the ingénue would die in the middle of the second act of *Belle of the Ozarks.*

Tears that had burned the backs of Gwen's eyes slid over her lids and down the sides of her face. "Oh, how did I end up in this hopeless predicament," she lamented, while hating herself for giving in to unproductive emotion.

Thunder growled outside. Somewhere lightning found purchase, perhaps in a tree top in the woods that bordered Hickory Bend. Its loud crack resounded in the print shop and rumbled beneath the trunk. Gwen took out her frustration by stomping on the flyers, and scattered them around her feet. The smell of ink swirled up once more. She gagged on the fumes and, with precious minutes ticking away, felt her world ebb into total blackness.

Gwen awoke dizzy and confused. Her head pounded as her brain searched to explain her dark, narrow world. But it was her stomach that reminded her of her predicament. It threatened a revolution that would definitely make her situation worse. She choked back the sour taste of bile that rose in her throat and fought the return of panic. How much time had passed? If only she knew. There was no thunder, so the storm had passed. Questions rose one after another. Was she doomed to die in this trunk? Had Preston come to find her? Had Marianne met her horrible fate?

Suddenly these questions dispersed to the corners of her mind. Footsteps sounded on the wood floor. Someone was in the print shop!

If it was Manfred Kruger, then her last memories of life would be of ink fumes and nausea. She weighed her options quickly before the person on the other side of her prison decided to leave. It was better to face the future she didn't know than to slowly suffocate in the one she did. She called out, "Hello! Who's there?" She pounded the side of the trunk with her fists.

"Gwen? Is that you?"

She recognized the voice and rejoiced. It was low and coarse, hardly above a whisper, but it was familiar. "Help! Get me out of here!"

There was a light tapping on the lid of the trunk. The voice hissed. "Shhh . . . Gwen, be quiet."

"Carson?"

"Yes, it's me. Keep your voice down. Someone will hear you."

Relief flooded her at the same time indignation forced her to snap back, "Well, pardon me for saying so, Carson, but at this point, that is precisely what I'm trying to accomplish."

He chuckled! He actually had the audacity to laugh at her situation. The last traces of dizziness fled with her urgency to breathe fresh air again. "Carson, get me out of here!"

"I'm going to," he said. She could tell his face was right next to the lid. "But you must be quiet. Kruger will hear trespassers in his shop and come back to do us both in."

She had to admit that made sense, so she lowered her voice. "Well, hurry up."

He fumbled with the mechanism. "Damn, this is a good lock."

As if she didn't already know that!

His footsteps retreated across the room. "Carson, what are you doing?"

They came back. "I've found a press crank. I think this will do the trick."

He inserted his makeshift tool between the lock and the top of the trunk and twisted. Gwen prayed the crank proved stronger than the cast iron of the ages-old lock. It did. Wood splintered, the lid rose, a soft glow spilled upon the contents of the trunk . . . and Gwen.

Carson reached for her. "Damn, Gwen,

are you all right?"

"I've been better, but yes, I think so."

Carson backed up a step and waved his hand in front of his face. "What's that smell?"

"Which one? Ink? Damp clothes? Musty blanket?" Thank goodness she didn't have to add the contents of her stomach to the list. "Ink, I think. But never mind about that. What time is it?"

"Seven thirty. Preston was worried when you weren't back and it was almost time for rehearsal. He was reluctant to tell me what's been going on, but I wheedled until he did. He filled me in and told me to come find you."

"Thank goodness for Preston's fore-sight." Gwen rose to her elbows and drew a deep breath. Obviously nothing dire had happened yet, or Carson wouldn't be re-acting in such a calm manner. Still there was no time to lose. "Rehearsal's starting," she cried. "Get me out of here."

He settled his hands under her arms and lifted her to a standing position. "Did you find anything out?"

"I did." She stepped over the side of the trunk. "Manfred Kruger is the *Jubilee* killer. At least it appears that way to me."

Carson was suitably impressed at her

findings. His low whistle hinted at admiration. "No kidding?"

She glanced down her length, taking in the damp disheveled appearance of her clothing. "Do I look like I'm in the mood for jokes?"

"No, ma'am, you do not."

She stepped toward the storeroom door, wobbled, and gratefully accepted Carson's help. "I must get back to the showboat right away. Unless I'm mistaken, Kruger has despicable plans for some faulty sandbags and our own Romance Mountain."

Carson guided her to the front exit. "Let's go."

Once they were outside, Gwen felt better. She breathed in a long gulp of air as rejuvenating as the first day of spring. "I'm fine," she said in response to the concern still in Carson's eyes. "I'm going to the *Jubilee*. You get Constable O'Toole and meet me there as soon as possible. As I recall, Act One only lasts a half hour."

Carson didn't argue. He headed down Main Street at full speed.

Chapter Seventeen

Gwen crossed the gangway to the *Jubilee Palace* and paused at the main entrance to the theater long enough to peek inside the double doors. The rehearsal had just started. Good. Preston had decided to go ahead with Act One rather than raise suspicion about Gwen's absence. It was a smart idea. Belle was center stage, her attention on the wings where the unseen train bringing her aunt was soon to arrive.

The musicians were in the pit along with Hildegard Kruger. Gwen saw the top of the girl's golden head and assumed she was waiting to cue the actors their lines. Gwen also assumed either Preston or Dickey Squires was in the wings operating the sound board since Carson was in town. Two people were in the front row of audience seats. Gwen recognized her mother's tidily coiffed bun, and she knew at once the gentleman sitting two chairs away from her was Manfred Kruger. His uncommon height and bald pate were easily identifiable.

Relieved to see Manfred in full view of

the actors, at least for the moment, Gwen ran around to the kitchen entrance of the *Jubilee*. She passed by the Johnsons' quarters and swept through the curtains covering the backstage entry. The train whistle sounded, and Anabel, as Aunt Winnifred, walked on stage.

Gwen immediately rushed toward the wings to check the rigging of Romance Mountain. Before she got there, Preston saw her and cut across the rear of the stage from the sound effects panel. "Gwennie! Where have you been?" he asked breathlessly. She thought for a second that he was going to demonstrate his relief at seeing her by grasping her in some sort of embrace. "I've been in a near panic," he said.

"That's nothing, Preston," she said, continuing toward the ropes and pulleys, "I've been in *total* panic."

His gaze skidded downward from her wild hair to the damp hemline of her skirt. And he apparently decided to abandon the hugging idea. "What in the world happened to you? You look positively dreadful."

"Never mind that," she snapped. "What's happened here?" A glance at the sandbags holding the mountain answered her question and brought a strangled curse to her lips. "Damnation!" The faulty bags were there, suspended from the pulley that would ultimately drop Romance Mountain to the stage floor. And no one had caught Kruger in the act of switching them.

Gwen studied the sandbags. Canvas fabric between the thin threads bulged with the weight of sand almost to the point of bursting. She glared at her brother. "My God, Preston, didn't you watch the rigging of Romance Mountain?"

His face was a mask of confusion. "What's wrong?"

Gwen regretted her accusatory tone. She'd warned Preston about the mountain, but he didn't know about her discovery of the sandbags in the print shop. More calmly she said, "Look at these weights, Preston. Look closely. What do you see?"

He examined the bag nearest him with intense scrutiny. His complexion turned a sickly gray. "Criminy, Gwennie, these aren't our bags. These things are lethal! When did that happen? I kept one eye on that rigging and the other on Marianne until just before rehearsal was to start. By then I was so worried about you, I must confess I let my guard down. I sent Stockwell to find you. And then I had to man the sound board myself . . ." His voice rose to an excited pitch. "Criminy, there was so much going on at once!"

Gwen patted his arm. "It's all right, Preston. You did your best."

He nodded vigorously. "I really did. That devil, Kruger, must have done this. He's here, Gwen." He jerked his thumb toward the audience seats. "See for yourself."

"I already did. Obviously he's planning to proceed with his deadly plan tonight."

Preston groaned. Gwen had never seen him so shaken. His gaze darted wildly around the backstage area, fixed on the sandbags again, and then speared downward to the platform. He pointed a shaking finger at the floor. "The marks, Gwen! I never moved them!"

"It's all right," she said. "In fact, I'm glad you didn't move them. I have a plan."

He pressed a trembling hand to his forehead. "It had better be a good one." His voice raw with panic, he said, "Where the devil is Stockwell? Did you see him in town? I had to tell him a little about your theory, so he would understand how important it was to find you. Now I don't know where he is, and we need every able-bodied man on the *Jubilee*. We can't very well depend on Sir Clyde to defend us, and

I doubt DeVane would risk getting a hair out of place."

"Carson rescued me," she said. "And thank goodness. I've sent him to fetch O'Toole."

Preston let out a pent-up breath. "That's a bit of good news anyway." His relief was fleeting, however, and his eyes grew wide with renewed panic. "Rescue you? Whatever from?"

"You won't believe where I've been . . ." she started to tell a short version of her escapade.

"Gwendolyn Irene Barlow!" Lillian's use of all three names had its usual effect, and Gwen clamped her mouth shut.

Lillian shook her finger, a sure sign that someone was going to pay hell. "Look at you. Disgraceful. Where have you been — out playing in mud puddles? And late for rehearsal." She began swatting and picking at Gwen's clothing as though she were trying to brush cockles from a dog's fur. But a sound that strongly resembled a chuckle rumbled from her throat, and she said, "Old Latimer should see you now — his eyes would pop out of his proper head."

Gwen gently thrust her mother's hand aside. "Not now, Mama. I promise I'll clean to a squeak when all this is over."

Sir Clyde's husky voice boomed from center stage. "Now see here, Miss Bradley, the bank cannot operate solely on a young woman's good intentions . . ."

Gwen pictured the actor's eyebrows waggling lecherously.

". . . no matter how lovely that woman may be." He paused for effect. His voice dropped to a menacing level. "Now, if that woman's intentions were suddenly to turn a bit naughty . . ."

"Mr. Crenshaw, please!" Belle squawked innocently.

Preston sighed. "Isn't she wonderful? Tomorrow night Sir Clyde will be booed from the stage."

Lillian beamed. "I can hardly wait."

"Let's hope there *is* a tomorrow night," Gwen said and then grabbed Lillian's arm. "Mama, I need to ask you a question."

"Of course, dear."

"Has Mr. Kruger been sitting next to you since Act One started?"

Lillian narrowed her eyes in concentration. "I'm not certain. Most of Act One, I would say. Why do you ask?"

"I can't tell you now, and for Heaven's sake, don't say I asked about him. Can you do that, Mama? Can you be discreet and not say anything at all?"

Lillian feigned a hurt expression. "Really, Gwendolyn, I've been the model of discretion for the last several days. I haven't said a word about how you've been looking at Stockwell."

Gwen bit back a curse. What a time for her mother to bring up something so ridiculous. "Mama, how you get such notions in your head I'll never know. Now please just go back to your seat."

Lillian ambled away. "All right, dear, but I'd really like to stay and prove my point." She flashed a quick glance at the rear curtain. Carson Stockwell, careful to stay hidden from the view of musicians and actors, had just entered with Constable O'Toole. He saw Gwen and gave her a thumbs-up sign.

Gwen glowered at her mother until Lillian, somewhat subdued, headed back to her seat in the audience. Then Gwen rushed to intercept Carson and O'Toole.

"What's the meaning of this, Miss Barlow?" the constable asked. "I was in the middle of the most delicious beef pie my sister brought from LaGrange."

"I'm sorry about your pie, Mr. O'Toole, but surely you agree that capturing a killer is worthy of your skipping a meal."

Apparently some of the pie had found its way to the constable's stomach, because he belched up a reminder of its spicy flavoring. "Yes, if this is truly about catching a killer."

"It is," she said. "I'm positive the person responsible for the *Jubilee* murders will be revealed tonight." She looked at Carson and gestured toward the backstage curtain. "Mr. Stockwell, if you'll just take the constable behind that curtain. Keep a close watch on the left wings, gentlemen, and listen for a sign from me. This mystery will soon be solved."

"Just what exactly are we watching for, Miss Barlow?" O'Toole asked.

"You'll know, Constable. I guarantee it. I don't have time to explain everything now, but I doubt you'll be disappointed." And to the *Jubilee* captain, Gwen whispered, "Be ready to react, Carson. I'm counting on you."

Carson led a grumbling constable to their hiding place.

Silence fell over the stage until Sir Clyde called to the wings. "Could we have curtain here, if it's not too much trouble? In case anyone's interested, the bloody act just ended."

Preston darted to the ropes that controlled the heavy drape. "Coming right up, Sir Clyde. Keep your bloody British braces on!"

While Dickey Squires and a couple of the musicians set the stage for Act Two, Gwen took Marianne and Preston into the dining room and shut the door. In the shortest possible time she needed to inform them of the incriminating clues she'd discovered at the print shop, and enlist their help in carrying out her plan to trap Kruger.

It seemed safe for the moment to assume that conditions in the *Jubilee* theater would remain status quo. Just a handful of people knew about Gwen's plan, and those few hadn't told the others. The sandbags had already been switched. Constable O'Toole was hidden behind a curtain under Carson's watchful eye. Now all that remained was for Manfred to reveal his hand near the end of the scene when Marianne was positioned under Romance Mountain.

Gwen sat across from Preston and Marianne at a dining room table. The young actress couldn't sit still. She fidgeted constantly, as if she didn't have the foggiest notion what to do with her hands. Her leg, crossed over the opposite knee, rocked back and forth to a metronome of fear. "I'm really scared, Miss Barlow," she said. "Preston says you're sure that Manfred Kruger is going to drop the mountain on me tonight."

Gwen might have been angry with Preston for getting the girl in such a frenzied state, but that wouldn't have been fair. Marianne should know the danger she faced and be given every opportunity to make the decision as to how she wanted to deal with it.

"That's right, Marianne," Gwen said. "I'm even more certain that Manfred committed the murders of Eli and Travis. And it is also very likely that he plans to add you to his list of victims tonight."

Marianne buried her face in her hands. She didn't succumb to tears, though the high pitched sounds that came muffled through her fingers were quite close to sobs. "What are we going to do?"

Preston moved his chair closer to Marianne's and slipped his arm around her shoulder. "Yes, Gwennie, what have you got planned? And I hope it's something pretty damn clever."

"I think it is," Gwen assured him. "But it's not without risk, I'm sorry to say." She explained in detail about the clues she discovered and how she expected Kruger's plot to unfold. "So you see, the poorly stitched sandbags have already been switched with the sturdy ones. Kruger is in the audience, presumably to wait for Hildegard to finish her responsibilities. But I think he's here to take advantage of the perfect opportunity to snip the basted stitches of the unsafe bags."

Marianne shivered. "And that will be when I'm under Romance Mountain."

"Unfortunately, yes." Gwen tried to show her sympathy with Marianne's plight with a gentle touch. "But Preston will stay near you every minute. We can hide him behind a piece of scenery so Kruger won't know he's there. And of course we're going to do everything we can to assure that nothing bad happens to you. Carson and O'Toole are watching from behind a curtain. I, too, will be nearby. I promise you that at the first inkling that Kruger is about to cut those threads, we'll have all the evidence we need and we'll stop him before he cuts the first one."

Preston did a poor job of trying to mask a troubled frown before he spoke. "I've always heard that timing is everything in the theater, Gwennie. But until now I never realized just how true it is." He leveled a serious gaze on Marianne. "What do you think, Marianne? You don't have to go through with this, you know."

"That's true," Gwen agreed. "You can say no, I'll call off the rehearsal right now, send everyone home, and try to convince the constable of Kruger's guilt with the evidence I have."

Marianne's delicate features showed signs of extreme distress. Faint lines appeared around her eyes and mouth. After a few moments she raised a troubled gaze to Gwen. "But that might not be enough for the constable to arrest him. And it doesn't mean that Mr. Kruger won't try again."

Gwen shook her head. "No, it doesn't."

"Or that someone else might get hurt, like Anabel. He might decide that Hildegard could have Anabel's part."

Gwen hadn't even considered that aspect. "Yes, I suppose he could."

"And if we call off the rehearsal, that means we are no closer to solving the two murders."

"We're certainly no closer to apprehending the guilty party," Gwen said.

"Or to getting Constable O'Toole to let the *Jubilee* move from Hickory Bend."

Gwen nodded. Marianne's thought processes were clearly following a logical path.

All at once, Marianne's frailty seemed to disappear from her countenance and was replaced with a hard edge of determination. "I'll do it," she said. "For the *Jubilee* and for you, Miss Barlow. But mostly for Mr. Willoughby. He was the kindest man I've ever known."

The muscles in Gwen's body relaxed with relief while at the same time every nerve tensed with awareness of what lay ahead. Regardless of Marianne's reasons, she had reached the morally correct, courageous conclusion. And now it was up to Gwen to insure that she wouldn't regret it.

Gwen, Preston, and Marianne returned to the theater only to be accosted by Sir Clyde complaining about their absence. "Really, Miss Barlow, can't you take care of personal business on your own time? First your brother tells us you're resting . . ." the word dropped with contempt from the actor's lips. "Next, you arrive after the first act has begun, and now you run off to who knows where between acts. I really must protest . . ."

Gwen's hands curled into fists which she could picture connecting with Sir Clyde's aristocratically long nose. "I am only too aware of your penchant toward protestation, Sir Clyde. And I will definitely keep it in mind at the end of this season when it's time to rehire the *Jubilee* troupe!"

Her implied threat was met with a gasp of surprise from the other actors. Bright pink infused Sir Clyde's cheeks. "Now, see here . . ."

Gwen clapped her hands, smothering Clyde's argument. "Places for Act Two, everyone," she called, and watched with satisfaction as the actors and musicians scurried to comply. A pleasant tingle of power straightened her spine, and she hoped her confidence would carry over to the task that lay ahead.

The first scene of Act Two, set in the hotel lobby, progressed without incident. Belle discussed solutions to the hotel's financial problems with her Aunt Winnifred. Preston, the amiable umbrella salesman, offered to contribute a portion of his profits for a small corner of the hotel lobby in which he could set up a display of his wares.

When Preston's few lines were finished, he darted into the wings to wait with Gwen for the scene when Marianne would take her mark under Romance Mountain. "I must admit, Gwennie," he said, "I've never been so scared in all my life. What if something goes wrong?"

"It's up to us to see that it doesn't." Gwen refrained from confessing that every possible tragic conclusion to her plan had crossed her mind in the last minutes. She glanced toward the back curtain where Carson Stockwell remained hidden with the constable. As if reading her thoughts, Carson stuck his head out to flash her a wink and a gesture of crossed fingers. He was ready.

The scene in the hotel lobby concluded. Two of the musicians scrambled to push the flat of a registration counter into the wings and replace it with a rolling backdrop of trees. Gwen peeked around the proscenium curtain. Manfred Kruger was still seated close to Lillian. He would make his move at any moment.

Soon Marianne walked to her mark under the mountain to begin the scene in front of the trees. Gwen smiled at her, hoping to instill confidence. The poor girl's lips trembled a tentative response. Preston was hidden on stage behind the backdrop of trees. He pretended to check the wheels of the backdrop in case someone noticed his presence. He was ready.

Gwen darted behind the registration

counter and crouched down. The *Jubilee* troupe had assumed their positions for this crucial moment in Act Two. From all appearances, there was no one in the wings to observe Kruger when he proceeded with his diabolical plan. Gwen's heart thundered until she feared it would leap from her chest. She drew a deep, quivering breath. Her decision to involve Marianne suddenly felt like leaden weights on her shoulders. What if Kruger succeeded? What if Preston leaped to save Marianne and he were killed as well? She thought of her mother and hot tears welled in her eyes. So many lives would be ruined.

The scene began with Marianne contemplating the dire circumstances of her life. Thinking she was alone with her musings, she spoke eloquently about the hotel's problems, her personal dislike of the lecherous banker, and her hopes and dreams regarding the sheriff. She stayed on her mark, though Gwen imagined how difficult it must have been to do that. She would not let the girl's trust in her go unrewarded.

Seconds dragged by with agonizing slowness while all of Gwen's senses remained alert to every sight, sound, and sudden change in her surroundings. Where was

Kruger? Now was his perfect opportunity to accomplish his mission. In just moments, DeVane would enter the scene, and Gwen doubted that Kruger would risk being seen by another actor on the stage. Her gaze darted from the dangerous sandbags to the compact space around them. She couldn't believe that Kruger hadn't appeared.

A ripple of movement caught her eye. The side curtain rustled, receded, and fell back. Someone was coming! Only it wasn't Manfred Kruger. Dressed in uncharacteristically drab colors, Hildegard crept silently toward the sandbags.

Gwen's mind struggled with confusion. Damnation! What was the bothersome girl doing backstage now? Why wasn't she in the orchestra pit doing her job? Hildegard was spoiling everything. Of course Kruger wouldn't take the chance of being observed by his daughter. Gwen's first instinct was to hiss a warning and wave Hildegard away. But that would only alert her to a set of unusual circumstances that she would no doubt tell her father. Disappointment, cold and bitter as day-old tea, washed over Gwen. All this preparation was going to amount to nothing.

And then she saw it. Hildegard's hand

withdrew from a deep pocket in her dress, and a glimmer of steel flashed in the soft glow of the backstage gas light. She turned her head quickly, glancing in all directions. Then she raised her free hand and grasped the lowest sandbag. In her other hand was a pair of long shears. In a split second, she snipped the line of stitches in the first sandbag. Sand poured onto the floor while Hildegard reached for the second bag.

The mountain hitched above Marianne. A pulley whined at added pressure. Gwen screamed.

Preston darted from around the backdrop. He barreled headlong into Marianne, wrapped his arms around her waist, and rolled with her out of harm's way.

Carson Stockwell ran from behind the back curtain with Constable O'Toole following closely behind.

Sand from the second and third bags made pyramids on the floor. Romance Mountain dropped like a falling redwood to the stage, landed with a resounding crash, rocked the *Jubilee Palace* like flotsam, and sent plumes of dust into the air.

And Hildegard, staring wildly at all the commotion, dropped the scissors and burst into hysterical wails.

Chapter Eighteen

Total chaos described what happened next in the *Jubilee* theater. Within seconds everyone associated with the showboat rushed to the stage and wings. Some shouted. Some cursed. Some were simply struck dumb. The platform was nearly filled with Romance Mountain, which had surprisingly arrived center stage without suffering too much damage. The same could not be said, however, of the principal players in Gwen's dramatically orchestrated performance.

Preston took Marianne away from the excitement and sat with her in the audience seats. He supplied her with a handkerchief donated by Lillian and let her weep softly with her head on his shoulder. Preston had never looked happier or more heroic.

Lillian bustled around on stage making certain each member of her *Jubilee* family was safe and unharmed. Once satisfied on that account, she began gathering each person's translation of the drama that had just ensued. Gwen knew her mother would not hear the same version twice.

Constable O'Toole was more methodical about his investigation. He led a weeping, raving Hildegard to a chair in front of Romance Mountain and forced her into it. He told three of the *Jubilee* musicians to guard her since Manfred Kruger hovering over his daughter did not constitute sufficient security. Manfred objected to his daughter being treated this way and swore Hildy was being railroaded by the "despicable people of the *Jubilee Palace*."

Hildegard's piercing sobs were punctuated by repeated declarations of innocence. "I didn't do anything, Papa! Make them believe me."

Gwen longed for cotton in her ears.

Ignoring Manfred's protests, O'Toole announced he wanted to question the nearest observers about the events which had brought *Belle of the Ozarks* to a crashing halt. It was agreed unanimously that Gwen should speak first since it was her suspicions that had led to the outcome.

Still numb with shock at the surprising revelation of the guilty party, Gwen nevertheless had managed to piece together a set of circumstances which made sense to her and led logically to the new, startling conclusion of Hildegard's role in the near fatal fall of the mountain. After all was said and done, Gwen had cast all the right actors in this drama of life and death. She'd simply been mistaken about the lead player.

As she related events to the constable, her revised theory about the murders became even more plausible. She recalled the details leading to Travis's death and realized that the clues actually pointed to Hildegard as much as or more than they did Manfred. She told O'Toole about finding the inappropriate tape marks on the *Jubilee* stage and about the altered flyer on the floor of the print shop — the one with Hildegard's photograph in place of Marianne's. She pointed out that both of these circumstances could easily be attributed to Hildegard.

Her voice lost some of its confidence when she described her experience in the Kruger storeroom. The horror of confinement in the trunk was still excruciatingly vivid in her mind. Though she couldn't positively identify the person who'd come into the storeroom and locked her in the trunk, she told the constable that she now believed that person had been Hildegard.

Naturally O'Toole asked her why she hadn't come to him immediately with her preliminary findings before she took it upon herself to snoop inside the print shop. Hadn't he told her to report any un-usual circumstances?

Yes, of course he had, she calmly ex-plained, but she originally suspected Manfred of committing the murders. In light of O'Toole's attitude toward her and the *Jubilee* family, she rather doubted that he would have seriously considered the Hickory Bend printer to be guilty of murder. To his credit, O'Toole did not argue that point.

O'Toole listened intently when Gwen told him about the sandbags in the print shop cabinet and about the large number of flyers in the trunk. When Gwen reached in her pocket and produced the letter and wanted poster of Travis Veazey sent by the Caruthersville sheriff, the last vestiges of doubt vanished from O'Toole's eyes. "Kruger, get over here!" he hollered.

A humble Manfred shuffled toward the constable. He'd listened to Gwen's expla-nation, and it was obvious that the last minutes had shaken the over-proud printer to his core.

O'Toole held up the poster of Travis Veazey. "Have you ever seen this?"

Kruger shook his head. "No, I have not." He bestowed a pitiable glance upon his daughter.

O'Toole approached a still defiant Hildegard and held up the poster. "What about you, young lady? Have you seen this poster?"

Her answer was nearly obscured by another bout of hysterical bawling, but she did express her disbelief that anyone could care a fig about a no-account, murdering shanty man.

"Hildegard!" Manfred shouted, succeeding in reducing his daughter's screeching to a few miserable sobs. "Answer the question and tell the truth!"

"All right! I've seen it. So what?" Her eyes blazed fire at Manfred.

O'Toole placed his hands on the arms of Hildegard's chair, holding her captive to his stern glare. "Did you kill Travis Veazey?" he asked point blank.

Obstinance flashed in Hildegard's eyes. She pursed her lips before she shouted, "He was dreadful, that awful boy! I hated him and so did everyone else."

Standing a few feet away with her husband, Peaches Johnson snapped back, "I didn't hate him. I just felt sorry for him."

"Then you're a stupid woman," Hildegard said. "Because Travis was a foul murderer. I did everyone a favor when I stuck him with that horrible old knife of his."

Manfred squeezed his eyes shut, apparently trying to block out the vision of reality he could no longer ignore. "Oh, Hildegard . . ."

Her lips turned down in a tight frown before she blurted out, "You shouldn't talk, Papa. You hated him as much as I did. You wanted him dead. You said so often enough."

O'Toole cleared his throat, clasped his hands behind his back, and stared at her. "Hildegard, did you kill Eli Willoughby?"

"No!"

O'Toole belched, his beef pie obviously moving through his intestines with the force of attacking infantry. "Well, then, who the hell did?"

Hildegard clamped her mouth shut.

Gwen held up her index finger. "Excuse me, Constable. You might consider Travis Veazey as a suspect in that murder."

"Veazey?"

Gwen explained her theory about Travis's involvement in Eli's murder. She first told the constable about being puzzled when Travis said he hadn't heard Eli's screams the night of the murder, despite his sleeping mat being so close to the stage. And she further revealed that Travis had had some kind of relationship with

Hildegard. This was a fact that angered Manfred and even prompted him to threaten to kill the young man.

"I'm not sure," Gwen said. "After all, Constable, you are the trained investigator, and I can only speculate, but I have a hunch that Hildegard's relationship with Travis involved blackmail. I think Hildegard used the information about Travis's past in Caruthersville to coerce him into assisting her in Eli's murder."

Hildegard's eyes darted spears of venom at Gwen.

O'Toole nodded reflectively. "And just how do you speculate Hildegard did that, Miss Barlow?"

In the last minutes, as Gwen had revised her original theory about Manfred being the killer to include Hildegard as the guilty person, the facts had fallen into place surprisingly easily. In fact, she was surprised she hadn't thought of it before. She admonished herself for jumping to a conclusion about Manfred which precluded other suspects. That was something she would never do again, if, heaven forbid, she was ever placed in these unpleasant circumstances.

"Travis was extremely knowledgeable about knots, Mr. O'Toole. In the short time I knew him, I witnessed him bragging about his expertise. In fact, he and Hildegard argued about this once in the theater. Assuming that Hildegard knew this as well . . ."

Gwen glanced at the girl and witnessed the hatred in Hildegard's eyes.

". . . assuming she knew, then she probably enlisted his help in altering the rigging of the backdrop that killed Eli. She no doubt threatened to reveal Travis's past to you, Constable, if he didn't help her kill my uncle."

O'Toole rubbed his chin. "Why did Hildegard want to kill Eli, Miss Barlow?"

Gwen allowed herself a smug grin. "You once told me that you are the motive expert, Constable. Can't you figure that out?"

O'Toole grumbled at her impertinence but he did stop to think. When he had it figured out, he faced Manfred. "Of course. You and Willoughby had a deal to put Hildegard on the stage. That fell through, as you told everyone in town."

"That's right!" Hildegard shouted, much more animated now that she sensed the chance to drag an accomplice into her mire of guilt. "Papa hated Mr. Willoughby as much as I did. Mr. Willoughby was awful and mean. After Papa and I did all his printing, and Papa took me to this stupid showboat to put me on the stage, Mr. Willoughby just laughed. He said he'd never put such a big, clumsy, silly girl in his play."

Hildegard raised wide eyes to her father. "Remember, Papa? Remember when he called me big and clumsy? Everyone in town knew he said those awful things. I'm not clumsy or silly at all." She fingered the curls at her temples and smiled with a smugness Gwen couldn't fathom. "Mr. Willoughby was a liar and a hateful person," she added. "And besides, he owed us lots of money."

Manfred groaned. "Oh, Hildy . . ."

O'Toole leaned over Hildegard's chair again. "But your papa didn't kill Mr. Willoughby, did he?"

Hildegard scowled at the constable and squirmed against the wood slats at her back.

"So, I figure it happened this way," O'Toole said to Gwen. "Your uncle came home soused as a seaman that night. Hildegard somehow lured him to the stage. Veazey waited in the wings to slip the knots and drop the scenery so it would look like an accident, which it did for a while until I started sorting things out and that little lady . . ." He pointed to Marianne Dresden. ". . . told me her suspicions."

"I hate her!" Hildegard blurted out. "She can't act!"

"I can believe you hated her, all right," O'Toole said. "I stood right here and watched you try to crush her under about five hundred pounds of lumber."

Manfred Kruger leaned against Romance Mountain and covered his face with his hands. "Oh, Hildegard . . ."

"What I can't figure out," O'Toole said to Hildegard, "is why you killed Travis."

"He was stupid," she said. "He told everyone on the *Jubilee* that I was stupid, but he was the stupid one. He actually started liking Miss Barlow. He said he was going to tell her I talked him into killing her lying uncle so the *Jubilee Palace* could finally leave Hickory Bend." Her voice rose several notches in another desperate bawl. "I couldn't let the showboat leave. Not without me!"

A purely unexpected pang of remorse wrapped its claws around Gwen's heart. So poor Travis had a semblance of a conscience after all, and he was going to reveal the secret that would have freed the *Jubilee* from Hickory Bend. She made a promise to herself to visit his plain marker in potter's field the next day and lay some wild flowers.

Constable O'Toole folded the notebook he'd been scribbling in and tucked it in his pocket along with the poster and letter about Travis. "I guess that's all we need to know for tonight," he said. "Manfred, you go on home. I'll be taking Hildegard with me."

"Papa, no!" she hollered at him. "You said you'd walk me back. You can't leave me alone."

Looking like he'd aged thirty years in the last half hour, Manfred Kruger stumbled by his daughter and down the stage stairs. Without a word or a glance in anyone's direction, he walked slowly up the center aisle and out the double doors. No doubt he heard his daughter scream that she hated him as he left.

Chapter Nineteen

At eight thirty the next morning, Gwen left the *Jubilee* dining hall and went into the theater. She sat in the middle of the first row of seats and looked at the stage. The bottom edge of Romance Mountain was just visible below the proscenium curtain. It probably would not be noticeable to anyone who did not know it was there. Of course that's the way scenery should be — unobtrusive until it was needed to enhance the play. However the night before, Romance Mountain had been anything but unobtrusive to Gwen.

The musicians had done an admirable job of returning the mountain to its lofty position and securing the rigging once more. The original, safe sandbags had been reattached to the pulley, and now Gwen trusted the monolith of lumber to properly rise and fall above the *Jubilee* stage for years. Still, everyone in show business would be grateful when someone developed ways of moving scenery that were less susceptible to tampering.

Gwen settled back against the cushioned squabs of her chair and looked higher, above the framework of velvet drapery, to the portrait of Eli Willoughby. "Well, Uncle, this is it," she said. "I hope you would be pleased today with the progress that has finally occurred on your palace. Opening night for your play is just a few hours away. The actors and musicians are right now getting into their costumes for the parade."

She smiled when she thought of her brother and the suit he'd found in a trunk of Eli's belongings. She'd never before imagined Preston as a showman, but that's just what he would become once he donned the fantastic garb of the *Jubilee*'s creator.

"I think you would be proud of your nephew and the interest he has taken in this enterprise of yours," she said to the portrait. "And I know you would have been proud of your daring ingénue, Marianne, last night. And I guess you knew your sister far better than I know her now."

Gwen recalled the day Mr. Cavanaugh came to Apple Creek, Ohio. It wasn't so long ago in time, but seemed years in experience. From the first moment Lillian shouted enthusiastically to her children, "My dears we're going into show business," Gwen never would have believed that this outlandish scheme could have proven beneficial for the stoically traditional Barlows.

"But you were right, Uncle Eli," she said. "Mama seems born to this life of endless possibilities and constant fluctuation. Except for that bit of lightheadedness she experiences on the third deck of the *Jubilee*," Gwen added with a smile. "I'm still not so sure about me, though. I'm not convinced you'll make a river-going entrepreneur of Gwendolyn Barlow."

She tilted her head, scrutinizing the portrait from another angle. Funny. The visage in the portrait had changed since the Barlows arrived on the *Jubilee Palace*. The painted face of Eli Willoughby did not seem nearly as stern or threatening as it had the first night the family viewed his portrait, despite Gwen's knowledge of his sometimes abrupt and almost heartless ways of dealing with people.

In fact, if she used her imagination, that part of her that she was becoming more familiar with, and enchanted by, every day, she could almost convince herself there was a cunning twinkle in the old man's eyes. Which is why she giggled now and told him, "But I must admit I'm having something of a good time trying."

"Gwennie!" Preston's holler from outside the theater startled Gwen from her one-sided conversation. "Where are you, Gwen? I'm having a devil of a time fixing this bow tie."

She stood up. "Got to go, Uncle. But one more thing. I'm glad you didn't turn out to be the fearful ghost that Preston hinted you would. You might have had your faults in mortal life, but I much prefer to think of you this way, almost as a friend in your afterlife."

She marched up the center aisle to the double doors of the theater. But before going out she turned back to the stage and did something extremely out of character for a serious-minded librarian. She waved at a portrait of a dead man on the wall and called cheerfully, "See you tonight."

The parade was to officially begin at ten o'clock in the morning. At nine forty-five, Gwen, Lillian, Peaches, and Danita stood in front of Davenport's General Store, a prime location for viewing the proceedings. As townspeople came to talk to her, Gwen quickly learned that rumors did indeed travel as fast in Hickory Bend as they did in Apple Creek, or probably any small town in America.

Mr. Davenport himself, one of the town residents who, until recently, had shunned the *Jubilee* family for the horrendous crime of being associated with Eli Willoughby, came out on his sidewalk to hold a civil conversation with Gwen. He expressed his surprise in learning that the Kruger girl had been responsible for the killings, though he'd often considered her "a little touched in the head for all her extravagances."

"She won't hang, though," he told Gwen with almost judicial assurance. "Her being a woman and all. But she'll turn gray in the state penitentiary all right."

The shopkeeper looked up and down Main Street and whistled his surprise at the turn-out of citizens for the *Jubilee* parade. "I've heard that tickets for this performance have been selling like day-old bread," he said to Gwen.

She had to think about his simile for a moment, since old bread was not her particular choice for consumption. "Yes, we've sold nearly all our tickets for both nights," she responded.

Sensing that the *Jubilee* production might actually be a success, he then offered the business hand of friendship to

Gwen. "It might be wise for you folks to stock your larders at my store before going up river."

. . . and before stocking them at the next river town in someone else's store, you mean. But Gwen kept her thought to herself and merely smiled at the man before promising to send Peaches that afternoon to make her selections, and to pay cash of course.

Commotion at the end of the street drew Gwen's attention away from Mr. Davenport. The parade was about to begin. Preston, as the leader, would soon advance down the street. As soon as he got his horse under control, that is. Gwen had not voiced her opinions when he'd told her his plan to rent a horse from the livery. Now he was facing the problems she had anticipated when he announced that he'd managed to acquire a quite spirited animal. Apparently this noble beast did not appreciate being festooned with a feathered headdress, bridle bells, and a sequined blanket.

Murmurs of anticipation rippled along Main Street and with them Gwen's excitement built as well. Which is why she jumped with surprise when someone said her name. The voice originated from behind her, and it definitely did not belong to her mother or Peaches.

She whirled around, coming nose to neck with Carson Stockwell whose off-kilter smile had the strange effect of wobbling the sidewalk beneath her feet. Gwen squealed, a silly breathless sound that brought a flush of mortification to her cheeks. She always prided herself for remaining immune from female affectations. "For Heaven's sake, Carson, are you trying to scare me to death?"

His eyes caught the sun and seemed to grin with the rest of his face. "A bit skittish this morning are we, Gwen?" He removed his hat and nodded toward Gwen's other female companions. "Ladies."

Gwen found it impossible to ignore her mother's pointed look of I-told-you-so. She stared at the road and mumbled, "The parade, Mama. It's starting."

"Of course, dear. I wouldn't want to miss anything." She moved a few feet to allow Carson room between her and Gwen.

"So how are you this morning, Gwen?" he asked. "Have you recovered from your ordeal?"

His concern seemed genuine so she answered honestly. "I must admit that it was quite late before my emotions stopped playing havoc with my mind. I suppose it didn't help that we all stayed up late discussing the near tragedy to Marianne and the events of the past weeks. When I finally retired to my cabin, I doubt I slept before the wee hours of the morning."

"I should have suggested a brandy to calm you before I left. It would have helped, I believe." He looked around her to glimpse the beginning of the parade and said with aggravating casualness, "I'm moving into my quarters on the *Jubilee* today. If you ever need anything, I'll be right next door, you know."

Oh, yes. She knew.

"Is there any news this morning?" he asked. "Have you seen Kruger?"

At the mention of the printer, Gwen experienced a burst of sympathy. "The poor man. He came out of his shop this morning and ventured up the sidewalk just far enough to talk to me. He actually apologized for Hildegard's actions, though it was unnecessary for him to do so. He said he especially regretted not looking into the valise Hildegard had him carry from the print shop to the *Jubilee* last night. Hildegard told him it contained props for the performance, when in truth, he was transporting the sandbags which Hildegard

364

used to try and kill Marianne."

"Of course if he had looked inside the valise," Carson pointed out, "we probably never would have caught Hildegard in the act of committing the crime."

"That's true," Gwen agreed. "Still, I hope he doesn't assume Hildegard's shame and take her guilt upon his own shoulders." She found herself staring fully at Carson's face. His steady jade gaze was quite unsettling, though not unpleasantly so. After a moment she focused her attention once more on Main Street. "Also, I received a visit this morning from Constable O'Toole," she said.

"And?"

"And, he confirmed what we all suspected last night. Hildegard confessed to everything, including moving the tape marks on the *Jubilee* stage."

"That's good," Carson said. "But there's something about Hildegard's tampering with the sandbags that still bothers me."

Gwen turned back to him, her curiosity far outweighing her previous measure of discomfort. "What is it, Carson?"

"I can't understand why Hildegard went to all the trouble of sewing new sandbags when she simply could have cut the ropes on the original ones and brought the mountain down." He shrugged his shoulders. "She had the scissors with her anyway."

Gwen smiled. The *Jubilee* captain was astute as well as competent. She had wondered about this herself and had come up with a theory which was confirmed by O'Toole that morning.

"Hildegard is a big, strong girl, Carson," she said. "Strong enough to overcome Travis when she had the element of surprise on her side. But she wasn't strong enough to cut the *Jubilee* ropes in the same brief seconds it took to cut the threads on the bags."

Stockwell was listening intently, so Gwen told him about the experiment she'd performed the night before. "I tried cutting a section of rope myself last night with my mother's shears. It required a great deal of time and effort to sever the fibers — too much time if one hopes to accomplish a goal without being detected." A vision of Eli's portrait flashed in Gwen's mind. "As everyone knows, my uncle spared no expense when it came to outfitting the *Jubilee Palace* with the best possible materials. That demand for excellence extended to scenery rigging as well."

"And too," Carson said spontaneously, "a cleanly cut rope would have eliminated the accident theory Hildegard hoped to establish by using faulty bags."

Gwen bestowed an admiring glance upon her captain. "Absolutely, Mr. Stockwell." She shook her head slowly, struck once again with melancholy at the surprising outcome of the young woman's life. "It's amazing to me how ambition can lead to such terrible consequences," she said. "Manfred told O'Toole again that he never saw the letter from the sheriff of Caruthersville or the posters Hildegard printed up with her picture as lead of *Belle of the Ozarks*. Poor Hildegard had such unrealistic dreams, and she lacked the ability to cope with disappointment. Ironically, the one scene where she played the lead role, the one with herself cast as murderess, led to her downfall. O'Toole said she will spend the rest of her life either in prison or a sanatorium."

"But it's still true that it was Travis who actually killed your uncle?"

"Yes. Hildegard blackmailed him into helping her by threatening to reveal the information on the wanted poster. She convinced Travis to wait in the wings until she had lured my inebriated uncle to the stage underneath the backdrop. Travis had rigged the rope with a knot that he slipped when Eli was in position. The whole incident looked like an accident, an unfortunate mistake."

"Hmmm. What a shame that Veazey didn't use his skill for a noble reason," Carson said.

Gwen nodded. "Travis was going to tell me about his role in Eli's death, which is why Hildegard killed him when she did."

Carson frowned. "Travis's admission at that point, while it would have benefited the *Jubilee*, would have been too little, too late, don't you think?"

"Yes, but I can't help believing that Travis wasn't all bad. Unfortunately we'll never know if he really did murder that man in Caruthersville. Only two men know the answer to that mystery, and now both of them are dead."

"I wouldn't waste much sympathy on Veazey," Carson said. "He didn't have to participate in Eli's murder."

"I know."

Taking her elbow, Carson shifted Gwen's attention to the street. "On to less morbid topics. Look at Preston. He's downright dashing."

He was indeed. The horse had settled

into a respectably calm gait and Preston rode him with assurance, though Gwen couldn't say whether it was real or pretended. He wore a red and white striped jacket, white pants, and a top hat with a red ostrich feather that fluttered in the breeze. As he progressed down Main Street, he called to the crowd. "Come one, come all, to a night of thrills and chills. Unforgettable heroics and dastardly deeds."

Gwen smiled up at him as he passed by, thinking his pitch could have described the actual events of the previous night. And hoping such phrases would only relate to the *Jubilee*'s *performances* from now on.

Anabel followed Preston in all her Cherokee glory. She wore a leather dress that dripped with strings of colorful beads and silver medallions. Beaded leather moccasins adorned her feet. Her ebony hair was threaded into two long braids, each decorated with blue and orange feathers. She handed out the posters proclaiming her heritage, apparently willing to display her Indian background for the good of the troupe. She smiled at Gwen as she walked by on silent feet. Gwen wondered if perhaps the woman hadn't been sipping a bit of her energized mixture.

Marianne came next, outfitted in a blue and yellow gingham dress with a white pinafore. Her spun gold hair, covered by a ruffled bonnet, trailed down her back in waves. She was the essence of country purity. And Sir Clyde was her total opposite. He pounced like a cat behind her, his black cape covering his lower face suggestively. The people lining Hickory Bend's Main Street hissed the villain with enthusiasm.

And they cheered the sheriff with equal gusto. Jason DeVane, in starched shirt and thigh-hugging trousers, was enough to melt even the coldest spinster's heart as he marched down the street with chin high and back straight. His gleaming white hat rivaled his sheriff's badge in reflecting the sun's rays.

Last came the *Jubilee Palace* band, a wonderfully entertaining blend of showmanship and discord. Wearing gray trousers and gold jackets with silver epaulets, the musicians tooted and bleeped and pounded with fervor. The entire ensemble consisted of two trumpets, an alto horn, a trombone, two banjos, and a bass drum. Bringing up the rear, the *Jubilee*'s legitimately talented piano and calliope player beat a tambourine above his head. By concentrating especially hard, Gwen was able to pick out the notes of "Oh, Dem Golden Slippers."

It was all artfully delightful. And when it was over, Hickory Bend residents who hadn't yet purchased their tickets to one of the two performances, and who suddenly feared they might actually be missing an event of some import, lined up in front of Preston with coins jingling in their hands.

Gwen caught a glimpse of her mother's profile. Lillian's countenance seemed lit from within with motherly pride.

Two days later, the morning of April 17, 1898, after two sell-out performances of *Belle of the Ozarks*, the cast and crew of the *Jubilee Palace* prepared to leave Hickory Bend, Missouri. Townspeople gathered at the riverbank to see the showboat off. Two of these illustrious citizens came on board.

"Just want to say again that I'm sorry for all the trouble you folks have been through." Manfred Kruger, who had attended the last night's performance after all, stuck his large hand out to Gwen.

"We're not the only ones in Hickory Bend who have been through a hard time, Mr. Kruger," she said. She had an envelope in her free hand, and she held it out to Manfred.

"What's this?"

"Thirty dollars. First payment of Eli Willoughby's debt to the print shop."

Reluctantly, Kruger accepted the money. "I almost feel guilty about taking this," he said.

"Nonsense," Gwen corrected. "You have every right . . ."

He held up a finger to stop Gwen and a hint of humor brightened his eyes. "I said 'almost', Miss Barlow."

Gwen smiled at him. "I'll send more on a regular basis," she promised.

"I'll be looking for it."

Constable O'Toole stepped between them. "All righty, little lady. Looks like you got your wish and you're finally moving this bucket up river."

"That's right, Constable. In spite of my uncle's other mistakes, I'm told he built a river-worthy craft, and it's time we tested that hypothesis."

"You did a good job, Miss Barlow, keeping your eyes and ears open. We make a good team, you and me."

Gwen arched a skeptical brow at the constable and stared for a long moment, considering her next words. Deciding his comment wasn't worth an argument, she merely said, "Indeed, Mr. O'Toole."

Phineas Johnson announced the gangway would be stowed on the boat in the next few minutes, and the constable ambled toward it. "The *Jubilee Palace* is welcome here any time," he called to Gwen over his shoulder.

Gwen tilted her head and gave him a tight-lipped grin. "We'll keep it in mind."

Phineas and three musicians pulled in the gangway. Others coiled the massive mooring ropes onto the *Jubilee* deck. For the first time since the Barlows arrived in Hickory Bend, the showboat was free of the riverbank, like an infant separated from its mother's grasp for its first exciting, fledgling moments of independence.

A steady hand wrapped around Gwen's arm. "Will you come with me, Gwen?"

She faced Carson Stockwell. "Where are we going, Captain?"

"To the pilot house."

A tingle of exotic pleasure coursed through her. "Me? You want me in the pilot house?"

He grinned at her. "I'm told your mother won't go. This is a celebration, isn't it? And because of that, a Barlow should definitely be a part of it. Don't you want to see your uncle's masterpiece and your mother's inheritance take its premier watery step to the future in the middle of the great Mississippi?"

Oh, yes, she most certainly did. "Lead the way, Captain."

Standing beside Stockwell in the glass enclosed perch of Eli Willoughby's exquisite floating palace, Gwen felt as free as an eagle who scorned all things earthbound. Yet as much a part of the mighty river as a graceful otter who frolicked in the water, his silken back glistening in the sun. She was part of something moving and unending. Something eternal and limitless, whose wandering path fed into miles of boundless ocean.

The cares of the past gave way to the challenges of the future, but Gwen took the lessons of Hickory Bend with her, embedded forever in her mind and heart.

Carson Stockwell lifted the speaker in the pilot house and spoke in a clear, commanding voice to the musician who waited for instructions at the stern of the *Jubilee* with a similar instrument to his ear. "Bring her about, Mr. Grimm," he said. "And steady on."

The helper would relay the captain's instructions by hollering to Dickey Squires at the controls of the *Dixie Damsel.*

"We should hire a proper first mate as soon as possible, Miss Barlow," Carson said. "Though Grimm is doing an admirable job for a banjo player."

"We most certainly will, Carson."

There was a slight bump from the bow of the *Dixie Damsel,* and the *Jubilee* began a graceful one-hundred-and-eighty-degree turn in the middle of the river. Dickey Squires whooped a phrase that might have been more appropriate at a rodeo. Smoke poured from the steamer's stacks, and at Stockwell's order, the two boats moved in tandem north, up the river.

Colorful banners fluttered from the promenades and the calliope played. The people of Hickory Bend waved goodbye to the people of the *Jubilee Palace.* And Carson Stockwell, his narrowed gaze on the gently flowing river, took "Eli's Folly" toward her destiny. Squinting with concentration, Carson said, "I'm a happy man right now, Gwen. So happy I could kiss you, I think."

Gwen's heart hitched uncharacteristically, and an altogether strange but pleasant warmth spread like apple butter through her limbs. "I'm experiencing a certain contentment myself, Captain," she said. "So much so that I could almost let you."

She kept her eyes on the river, except for that brief second when she stole a glimpse of Carson's profile and saw him smile.

About the Author

Cynthia Thomason's publishing career includes both historical and contemporary romance novels and a historical cozy mystery set on a fictional Mississippi showboat. At the 2000 Romance Writers of America national conference, she received the National Readers' Choice Award for best long historical romance for *Homespun Hearts*. She and her husband own an auction company in Davie, Florida, where she is a licensed auctioneer and estate furniture buyer. She enjoys antiques, traveling the U.S., her Jack Russell terrier, and hearing of her son's escapades in college. Please visit Cynthia's Web site at www.cynthiathomason.com.